SECRETS
UNDER THE
JUNIPERS

Praise for Suzie Clarke

Enigma

"Clarke does a masterful job of telling this story. She utilizes the elements of mystery and suspense to their fullest. She understands the strong allure of espionage and the realm a female spy must inhabit, capitalizing on it in ways that fill the lungs of this story...There's a lot of heart-thumping moments, but Clarke is ever mindful to keep the storytelling balanced, blending the tension and release nicely. The formula is appealing, especially for those that crave a rousing, engaging plot...The romance is nicely done, too...Clarke delivers a captivating tale that explores the complexities of human nature, moral dilemmas, and the enduring power of love amidst chaos."—*Women Using Words*

Western Blue

"*Western Blue* by Suzie Clarke is a slow burn, gun slinging historical set in the Old West. If there's one thing I really enjoy it's a good heist, especially the getting the gang together part. Getting this gang of desperate, tough and hardworking women together is a real high point for me. All of the characters are great, even the very bad guys who make the women miserable, because they're unique and have good motivations...The laughs and romantic scenes are well spaced out because most of the book is about the struggle to not just thrive but simply survive. While not overly dramatic, there are a lot of tense and thrilling moments that are a lot of fun."—*The Lesbian Review*

By the Author

Shadow Series

Moon Shadow

Shadows of Steel

Shadow Dancers

Enigma

Western Blue

Secrets Under the Junipers

Visit us at www.boldstrokesbooks.com

SECRETS
UNDER THE
JUNIPERS

by

Suzie Clarke

2026

SECRETS UNDER THE JUNIPERS

ISBN 13: 978-1-63679-845-5

This Trade Paperback Original Is Published By
Bold Strokes Books, Inc.
P.O. Box 249
Valley Falls, NY 12185

First Edition: January 2026

CREDITS
Editor: Shelley Thrasher
Production Design: Stacia Seaman
Cover Design by Tammy Seidick

Acknowledgments

I'm deeply grateful to those who helped this book reach fruition, to Bold Strokes Books publishing personnel, my editor Shelley Thrasher, and my fellow authors who gave their support and expertise. Above all, thank you to my readers. You make my efforts to create a story worthwhile and rewarding.

I'd like to give a special thank you and acknowledgment to Douglas Bohon, Chief of Police, Tallmadge, OH, and John Desmett, Police Detective, Retired, for their willingness to answer what must have seemed like endless questions, and for taking the time to share their experience and knowledge regarding cold case investigation. I couldn't have written this book without them. My thanks will never be enough for what you do.

Data varies, but thousands of children are abducted by strangers every year in the United States. In most cases, the perpetrator makes first contact within a quarter mile of the victim's home. I was almost one of those children, and it happened within eyesight of my house. No one knows why some children escape and others do not. May we all do everything we can to prevent these hellish crimes from happening.

To all those who must bear the unspeakable pain
of losing a child through crime

CHAPTER ONE

B itsy Hanover stiffened when the warm Georgia breeze brushed against her, bringing her back from her stupor. How long had she been at the crime scene? She glanced at her wristwatch, eyeing the numbers. Three hours and forty-seven minutes. It felt more like all day. A week. Maybe even a year that she'd stood there, watching, taking it in, wishing it wasn't real.

She wasn't as near to the dig site as she wanted to be. She could see only a portion of what they were doing. A marmoset of a man with *Medical Examiner Staff* in red letters on the front and back of his jumpsuit had warned her twice already to stay back, but she kept easing closer, as if unable to restrain herself, compelled to be as near as she could.

He straightened, then brushed his white-gloved hand across his sweaty little forehead, pointed at her, and scowled. "Ma'am, do not cross the yellow tape again, or I'll have the police remove you from the scene." He went on with his work.

The hell he will. Bitsy hesitated, then realized he really would do it, and being forced to leave would only cause more anxiety and add more turmoil to an already unspeakable day. She slid her foot back and reluctantly retreated the required distance, continuing to study the dig site in all its hideous commotion. Workers scurried about, dressed in white plastic suits. White booties over their shoes. White gloves. White, billowy clouds. White. White. White. Yet a dark foreboding hung all around her. She could feel it, sense it, almost touch it. It was an odd sensation in the sunlight. Shouldn't it be warm and bright here? But how could it be?

Coroner's staff scoured the dirt with their trowels, screens, and small picks, stopping every now and again, placing a gathered treasure into a clear plastic bag with the word EVIDENCE marked in red. *EVIDENCE.* Pieces of the crime scene. But it wasn't just a crime scene. It was where her childhood friend, Hallie Lynn Peeples, had lain for thirty years, since she was ten years old. The earth had cradled her and held her all this time.

"A crime scene." Bitsy whispered the phrase under her breath, easing into the words, trying them on to see how they fit. She was too exhausted and overwhelmed to say them with any force. "Crime scene." This time they came out as a moan, a lamentation. Someone had put Hallie Lynn there. Murdered her, then threw her in, like she was trash. A stuttered breath brought bitter pain mixed with anger and bone-aching sadness. The disbelief lingered, draping over her, clinging to her, making it hard to breathe. "Hallie." Her name slipped from Bitsy's lips, mixing with tears, sliding down her cheeks. She didn't wipe them away this time. What was the point? Besides, she had no energy left to do it. Hallie's body wasn't there anymore. They'd shipped her remains to the state lab.

Bitsy startled when a familiar soft voice spoke in her ear and a firm hand patted her back.

"There's nothing you can do for her here." Lilly Ashburn, Bitsy's longtime assistant at the art dealership, squeezed her shoulder. "Why don't you go home to your momma's? I know she'll want to see you."

Bitsy recoiled at the thought of leaving. She folded her arms across her chest, pressing tightly, trying to hold back the pain. "I can't." Her cell chimed for the seventh time. *Momma.* She shut it off, slipped it into the pocket of her pink-flowered sundress, and focused on the workers who were shoveling near the empty grave.

Lilly rubbed Bitsy's arm. "It's okay to leave. And before you ask, no! No one is saying anything. I did hear a cold case investigator from up north has been assigned to the case, but I don't know when they'll get here. If you won't go home, then come on back to the office. You need some water and rest. You're going to make yourself sick."

The thought of Hallie Lynn in that crude grave for thirty years crashed into Bitsy, slamming against the reality that if she'd remembered anything from the night Hallie Lynn had been abducted, it might have helped find her.

She took a deep breath, then let it out, as if breathing for Hallie Lynn. "She's been dead all this time. Not just missing or taken by someone. Murdered." The words trailed off, but their meaning permeated the air like the stench of something unbearable.

Lilly rested her head against Bitsy and wrapped her arm around her waist. "She's not been positively identified yet. It could be someone else."

Bitsy grazed the grass with her sandal, focusing on the mound of dirt next to the dig site. "It's her. Grace, from the county sheriff's department, told me she had a pendant around her neck. She loved that damned thing so much she never took it off. I asked her once why she wore it. She said her mother gave it to her."

Lilly tightened her grip around her waist, as if to reassure her.

Bitsy appreciated the gesture, but the bitterness and pain were all she could feel, grasping her, tearing at her, encircling her like the yellow tape marking the crime scene.

Lilly positioned herself directly in front of her, blocking her view of the workers and the site. "Let's go, darlin'. She's at peace now."

Bitsy rejected the thought. "Peace? Not hardly!" The words came out sharp, like they'd been ground on a whetstone. She repeated them, softer, to let Lilly know she was sure of what she was saying. "She's not at peace, and neither am I. There'll be no peace until we find out who did this and they're rotting in hell." She turned away. "Come on. You're right. She's not here anymore. I need to leave."

She'd already heard three different people give their version of how Hallie Lynn's remains had been discovered, but they were basically the same. Henley Development had hired Mr. Crenshaw, owner of the local excavation business and brother to Bitsy's psychiatrist, to take down the unsightly cluster of juniper and shrub trees northwest of Savannah in preparation for the county's summer project of expanding the park. He hadn't been more than thirty minutes into the job when Harold, the lead surveyor, started waving his hands with a horrified look on his face. Mr. Crenshaw immediately shut off the excavator and jumped down from the cab to see what all the commotion was about, and it took only a half step to realize why Harold was so upset. There, among the dug-up debris, was what looked like a decomposed body part sticking out of the dirt. Both the men staggered back like they'd been sucker-punched in the gut.

Everyone knew it was Hallie Lynn Peeples. Had to be. Why? For one thing, it was a child—anyone could see that, and there was the dark, faded but still curly long hair, and the necklace.

Bitsy wasn't sure if it was harder knowing or not knowing that Hallie Lynn was dead. All this time she'd imagined her somewhere, alive, living her life the best she could. Now she couldn't avoid the cold, harsh reality of her death.

She'd been the last person to see her on that fateful evening in October 1995, and now Bitsy's life would be torn open again, shredded into tiny pieces by the investigation. They wouldn't leave her alone. They'd keep probing, hounding her to remember, like they did when Hallie Lynn was first taken. The trauma of the event had caused her to block out the critical details. At least that's what all the professionals had said.

A tension headache crept up her neck, settling at the back of her head, then slithered into her temples. She massaged with her fingertips, telling herself she'd get past it. Tomorrow she'd wake up and not blame herself like she'd done every day for the past thirty years. Sure she would.

She'd wanted to help the police that night. Wanted to give them as much information as possible so they could find her friend, but everything blurred and faded when she attempted to recall it. Over the years it'd gotten worse. Now all she felt was nausea and panic when she tried to think about it. She wanted to remember. Didn't anyone understand?

CHAPTER TWO

F BI Special Agent Cecilia McConnel parked the rental car in the lot next to the river and got out, surveying her surroundings, trying to get her bearings. She tugged at the front of her sweat-soaked cream-colored silk blouse, hoping to keep it from sticking to her skin in the sweltering, humid Savannah heat. "God! How do these people survive down here?" Summer was just getting a good start. She wasn't used to being without her suitcoat or carrying a purse, but she had to either wear her gun and holster and draw attention to it or stuff it in her handbag.

She looked left, then right, making sure no one was in earshot of her grumbling. After she crossed the trolley tracks and walked one block down the cobblestone street of the historic River Street District, she managed to find the address she was looking for. She'd started to enter the cluster of shops when a long, deep horn blasted. Startled, she turned toward the sound and saw a magnificent paddleboat, the *Georgia Queen*, pulling away from her dock.

McConnel made her way along the wide hallway toward the fourth door on the right. Outside, the sun had beat down so brutally her brain had felt like an over-easy fried egg. But in here there was just heat, thick and stifling. It hung in the air and refused to yield, even though the huge ceiling fans demanded it. She passed the open doors to the multiple shops. This wasn't what she'd expected. No spit-shined buffed floors, no bustle of people scurrying on their way to find the best deals or browsing so as not to miss a single alleged Southern treasure marked down fifty percent. Sets of old china from the 1800s, Christmas ornaments, antique furniture, and on and on. No one stopped to say hello in that slow Southern drawl that rolled off their tongues like butter dripping from a fresh ear of steamed corn. The building was surprisingly empty for nine in the morning, and quiet.

The tile on the floor had intermittent cracks and looked clean enough, but it didn't have a glossy shine, just a dull, worn haze. The hallway smelled like a mixture of newly laundered clothes and a day-old pastrami sandwich, with a hint of lingering furniture polish.

She wiped the sweat from the side of her face, aware she'd smeared what little makeup remained. She made a mental note. *No more foundation in the South.* Positioning herself in front of the door marked *Hanover Agency, LLC* in thick, black block letters, she squared her shoulders and knocked. Why she chose to bang on the thick Plexiglas window right in the center of the name, she'd never know. Maybe because the wooden frame looked splintered? Whatever the reason, she immediately regretted her choice. The *A* stuck to her knuckle.

"Damn."

She quickly peeled it off her skin and tried to place it back on the door's window.

It dropped and fluttered to the floor.

She picked it up from a crack in the tile, spat on it, and pressed it back into place. A little off the mark, but a valiant effort nonetheless. Or so she thought. She watched it fall again. "Damn it." Before it floated past her knees on its return journey, she grabbed it. Now what? She could try again to put it back where it'd escaped from or throw it on the floor and pretend it'd been there all along. From the looks of the empty, stark hallway, no one would notice anyway. But her conscience wouldn't let her leave it on the floor, even though she was sure she wasn't the first to fall victim to the dilemma. She vied for another option and stuffed it into the side pocket of her purse.

She cleared her throat, still waiting for a response from her knock. Nothing. What to do? If she banged louder on the door frame or the Plexiglas, the vibration would probably knock the rest of the damned letters off the window. She had to do something. She couldn't just stand there in the hallway. She had an appointment. She wasn't some shopper looking for a bargain. She was here for a reason—to investigate the cold case, a very personal cold case, but they didn't need to know how personal. That was no one else's business but hers. It had haunted her thoughts and given her nightmares since she was eighteen years old.

She turned the thick brass handle, slowly opened the door, and leaned in, not spying anyone. "Hello? Anyone here?" She stepped into the waiting area. Air conditioning. Cool, blessed air conditioning. She fanned the welcome chilled air to her neck. The room was about what you'd expect for an art dealership. A comfortable-looking brown leather couch, a polished wooden coffee table in front of it, and two small tables adorned with beautiful green and gold porcelain lamps on each end of the sofa. Several original oil paintings hung on the walls, scenes of Savannah city life back in the late fifties, or maybe it was the early sixties. Those days were long gone now. Moving to the painting nearest her, she studied it more closely, recognizing the artist. Herbert Randel, whose best work had been mostly done in the mid to late 1950s. A dark, ornate oak reception desk was squarely aligned with the back wall. The room smelled like coffee and something else sweet and overpowering. Licorice. She mentally congratulated herself on the revelation.

A stout woman, not as tall as McConnel, fiftyish, her short salt-and-pepper hair tortured into tight curls, shuttled into the office from the adjoining room on the left. Frowning, she stopped dead in her tracks. "Hey. What are you doing here? I told you reporters we don't have anything to say."

"I'm sorry. I'm not a reporter. I did knock. I stood out there for a while, but no one answered."

"Well, what do you want?"

It was a good thing McConnel wasn't a customer, or she'd have turned around and left. Right after she told the woman to kiss her ass. "I'm FBI Special Agent McConnel."

The woman stood stoic, a blank stare on her face.

"From Toledo, Ohio. The cold case?"

No response.

Was this what humans acted like when they were exposed to ungodly heat twenty-four hours a day? She took another breath, then forced it out, along with the irritation that was rapidly accumulating. It had started the moment she stepped off the plane. The unbearable temperature, the impatient drivers who had no clue how to drive in a civilized world, the incessant jabbering by everyone she encountered, the car rental staff, the hotel clerk, the people waiting to check in after her, and essentially everyone she'd met. She was here for a reason, and she just wanted to get to it. She wasn't usually this easily irritated. It must have been the circumstances. This entire experience was overwhelming and unexpected.

She thought she'd prepared physically for the change in climate, but she obviously hadn't. She should have worn a light summer cotton skirt, not pants. A sleeveless blouse, absolutely not silk, would have helped, and she should have consumed more water instead of the alcohol on the plane and at the hotel last night. Her mouth was so dry her lips were sticking to her teeth. She handed the woman her business card. "I spoke with a Ms. Ashburn. She told me to be here by Tuesday afternoon. And, well…here I am."

"That's me. Lilly Ashburn. Hiya." Lilly reached for McConnel's business card as she looked her over from head to toe. And then she snorted. McConnel couldn't believe it. She honest-to-God snorted.

Lilly made a half turn and yelled out of the side of her mouth toward the open office on the far right. "Hey, Bitsy. Your agent is here." She tossed the card onto the desk, not looking at it.

A tall, slender woman appeared.

It was her.

McConnel knew her. Well, knew of her. She recognized her from the newspaper pictures and case files. She hadn't realized she was called Bitsy. She knew her as Mary Elizabeth Hanover, forty-one, a year older than McConnel, who tried not to stare. She readjusted her focus to the gray, mottled plush carpet, but then she couldn't help herself and looked at her again.

Hanover stepped a couple of feet from her and stopped. Her sea-green eyes moved over McConnel like she was exploring every part of her. A faint smile crossed her full lips.

If McConnel hadn't disliked her so much, she might have enjoyed this meeting.

The woman held out her hand toward McConnel and said hello. "I'm Mary Elizabeth Hanover. Bitsy."

Her Southern voice was sexy and clear, melodic, like saxophone music in a dimly lit nightclub. It threw McConnel off guard. She wasn't expecting that voice, or for her eyes to be so vivid and soft.

"I'm FBI Special Agent McConnel. If you don't mind, please call me McConnel." She'd croaked the words out, her mouth still so dry she felt like she'd been sucking through an empty straw. It was embarrassing. She was more nervous about meeting her than she'd expected. So far, she wasn't the cold, heartless, uncaring bitch McConnel had imagined, but the day wasn't over yet.

Mary Elizabeth Hanover, or Bitsy, as she'd said, was standing in front of her, after all these years of reading about her, studying the case, scouring every detail repeatedly. McConnel had never spoken to her for any length of time, only long enough for Bitsy to hang up on her five times about six years ago. McConnel had tried to arrange a meeting to talk with her about Hallie Lynn's abduction, but Bitsy wanted no part of it. To be fair, though, McConnel hadn't identified herself as an FBI agent back then. Bitsy had no idea who *she* was, and there was no reason to think she would recognize her now. They lived states apart, and their lives were not similar in any way, except for the cold case. That's what connected them, more than Bitsy could possibly imagine.

McConnel shook her hand, trying to focus. She'd blamed her for so long for not remembering what she saw the night of Hallie Lynn's abduction that it seemed like a paradox to be this close to her and not feel the resentment and anger that had stuck to her all these years, like dandelion puffs on a blanket. If Bitsy had remembered what she'd seen the night Hallie Lynn was taken, the authorities could have found her, saved her. Now the cold case had been blown wide open by the discovery and identification of her remains. She needed Bitsy to remember. One little detail might break the case and identify Hallie Lynn's killer. Bitsy had remained silent about it all these years, refusing to discuss it. It was locked in her mind somewhere, and now that Hallie Lynn's remains had been found, McConnel was determined to pry the information she needed out of her, any way she could.

"Come on back," Bitsy said.

The smile disappeared, and a deep sadness replaced the musical lilt in her voice. McConnel wasn't expecting to hear grief in her tone. After all, it'd been thirty years. She assumed she'd let go of the tragedy long ago and moved on with her life, unlike McConnel, who'd been consumed by it from the moment she'd found out her own relationship to Hallie Lynn Peeples.

Bitsy was beautiful. Delicate fingers and perfectly styled mid-length wheat-colored hair. The defined muscles in her arms stood out against the spaghetti straps that hung loosely over her shoulders. She was slightly taller than McConnel and put together nicely, but the sorrow in her eyes made her look like she hadn't had a decent night's sleep in a long, long, time.

Bitsy turned and started toward what must have been her office, then halted suddenly.

McConnel almost stumbled into her.

"Lilly, if Bo calls, tell him I said he better get that contract signed and back here by three o'clock. If he doesn't, tell him there will be no bonus. That ought to make him move a little faster."

Lilly nodded, then left the room.

Bitsy motioned for McConnel to follow her, walking with a graceful sway.

McConnel found herself enjoying the show. Pleasant sensations associated with Bitsy Hanover were foreign and unexpected, but as enjoyable as they were, McConnel pushed them aside. The pressure was on to find the killer, and she needed to focus all her efforts. Interviewing a critical witness was just one of many tasks. Would it help or hinder if Bitsy knew who McConnel was? Would she be able to figure it out? Should McConnel keep it hidden? What was the best thing to do? One thing was clear. If the Bureau discovered who she was, she'd be suspended, fired, or worse. Everything had a price. How much was she willing to pay to solve this cold case?

CHAPTER THREE

Bitsy sat behind her desk and motioned McConnel to one of the cushioned chairs in front of it. She could have sat on the couch or one of the two overstuffed chairs and encouraged a more intimate and less businesslike atmosphere, but she wanted to keep as much distance from this cold case investigator as possible. Something seemed familiar about her, but she didn't understand exactly what. She didn't know her. She didn't want to know her, and she certainly didn't want to invest in what was about to happen. That way the emotional upheaval wouldn't consume her.

This woman in front of her, although very cute, with her short, curly dark hair and beautiful curves, had no personal interest in this case. It was simply another job. Curiosity. She was after a story like the gaggle of reporters and other thrill seekers banging on Bitsy's door, hounding her.

Her palms became moist. That sinking feeling rushed in. Her heart rate quickened. She massaged her left temple, trying to relieve the pressure headache. She hadn't eaten dinner last night or breakfast this morning. She needed to take better care of herself. She checked the time on the wall clock.

McConnel stared at her.

She hated that. Why couldn't people just glance, or nod, or look around the room and go about their conversations? Bitsy had dark circles under her eyes, and her skin was pale. Everywhere she'd gone this week people had gawked at her. In the grocery store. At dinner when she and Lilly went to lunch the day after they'd positively identified Hallie Lynn's remains. At the beauty shop when she got her hair highlighted, and when the TV reporters shoved microphones in her face on her way to her car. She cringed, sick to death of the endless questions. *How do you feel about the discovery? Were you surprised?* And the mother lode—*What do you remember about that night?* Every time the question surfaced, her heart skipped a beat, she tensed, and her head felt like it would explode. She wanted to remember. Couldn't anyone understand? She wanted to recall that night and what had happened, but she couldn't, other than seeing Hallie Lynn near the side street. That was it. Everything else was like trying to see fish in a muddy pool of water. All these years she'd kept hoping her memory would clear, but it never had.

She'd seen something critical to the case. She wanted to recall it, but for some reason she couldn't. Hypnotism, therapy, endless counseling. Nothing helped. She hated herself for it. The guilt and shame haunted her dreams, but the harder she pushed herself, the darker that night became. She'd shoved it all away. That was easier. Self-loathing consumed her every time thoughts of it returned. If McConnel asked her *that* question, she'd throw her out.

McConnel cleared her throat. "I can see you're upset. I'll try to make this as easy as possible."

Bitsy took a deep breath. Finally, someone who at least was a little sensitive. "You look so familiar. Have we met before?"

McConnel glanced at the floor, then settled her gaze on Bitsy.

Bitsy studied the gold flecks in her deep brown eyes. No. Her right eye was deep brown, but the other wasn't quite as vivid and didn't have the gold flecks.

"Heterochromia," McConnel said. The corners of her mouth turned up in a shy, hesitant smile.

It was charming. Bitsy relaxed a little.

"It's pretty rare. One in ten thousand people," McConnel said. "When you see it, it takes a minute to adjust."

"Does it affect your eyesight?" Bitsy regretted the question. "I'm sorry. I shouldn't have asked that." It was none of her business. The heat of a blush pushed up her neck and settled into her cheeks.

"It's okay. The condition doesn't have anything to do with my vision."

Bitsy leaned into her chair and pushed against the leather backing, wondering if they'd found Hallie Lynn's glasses at the crime scene. "So, *have* we ever met?"

McConnel slowly shook her head.

The vague feeling of familiarity drifted away, like the faint scent of pine on a breeze. "It's very difficult for me to talk about Hallie Lynn," Bitsy said.

McConnel reached into her leather case and retrieved a file folder. Was it Hallie Lynn's information? Her brief life's story reduced to a few facts.

McConnel shuffled slowly through the papers. "I've read everything you've said, the police report, interviews, everything on record. I've been told you were at the recent crime scene."

Bitsy nodded. "Yes." She gritted her teeth and prepared herself for *the question*.

"I'm sorry. It must have been difficult for you."

It didn't raise its ugly head. Relieved, Bitsy drew in a cleansing breath. "It was hard, but I think I needed to be there. Closure, maybe. I don't know. Have you been yet?"

McConnel looked away. "Not yet."

A strange reaction from an agent with no personal stake.

Bitsy leaned back again, clasping her hands in her lap. The gesture anchored her, gave her the stability she needed at that moment. Every law enforcement professional she'd ever talked with wanted answers and couldn't wait to be on their way, but McConnel didn't. Why? Maybe she wasn't the enemy after all. Maybe she *was* someone who could solve the crime this time. Would she be patient and listen to what Bitsy had to say? Or would she stalk off in a frustrated huff like everyone else because Bitsy couldn't remember and didn't have the answers they wanted?

Bitsy shifted and placed her folded hands squarely on the desktop. "It's not just a crime." She paused. Expressions about Hallie Lynn didn't come easy. She'd pushed thoughts of her away for so long she felt like she was reaching into an endless void. "It's a violation of human existence. Murder is such an ugly, foul word. I've never faced the possibility of Hallie Lynn's death. I've always hoped and imagined she was alive somewhere, living a different life. A piece of me was taken with her that night." The tears welled. Bitsy couldn't stop them.

She covered her face, embarrassed as they slipped down her cheeks. She wanted to control herself but couldn't. The stark reality of Hallie Lynn's death forced her to face what she'd avoided for thirty years.

"Here." McConnel whispered the word so softly Bitsy almost didn't hear it. She handed her a tissue from the desk.

Bitsy took it with a shaking hand and dabbed at her eyes, then tossed it into the waste can under her desk. "I'm sorry. I'm usually stoic at these interviews, but since the discovery of Hallie Lynn's remains, it's like reality bitch-slapped me. I'm still in shock."

McConnel adjusted in her chair. "I'm sure this has been a horrible week for you. Let's set another time to meet. Perhaps tomorrow?" She slipped the papers into her satchel.

"Yes. Thank you."

McConnel's sensitivity once again skewed Bitsy's preconceived idea of her. She wasn't the cold, annoying interrogator Bitsy thought she'd be. She was nothing like she'd expected.

Bitsy reviewed her crammed schedule on the computer, searching for a block of time. She scanned each day carefully. Usually, with investigators or reporters, she'd stall, tell them she'd have her secretary call, and then she wouldn't. McConnel was different. How different Bitsy didn't know, but she hoped this time the interrogation would go better. She reviewed the next day again. "I don't have any time until tomorrow evening. I'm sorry." She hesitated, then dared herself to ask, the question gushing from her mouth like water from a pump. "Why don't you come to my house? Say eight?" She wrote the address on the back of a business card and handed it to McConnel, shocked that she'd invited her to her home. Was it too late to take it back? Should she keep her at a distance? Would that make it easier?

McConnel took the card and eyed it. "That's fine. Would you like me to bring supper? I can stop by one of the restaurants and pick up something. What do you like?"

"How thoughtful. I'll get the meal. You bring the wine. A full-bodied red would be good."

McConnel smiled and stood, placing the card inside her purse. She picked up her satchel. "Tomorrow night, then."

Bitsy walked her through the lobby and stopped to open the door for her, noticing the letter A was missing from the Plexiglas. "Damn it. Not again. I've got to get different lettering."

McConnel fidgeted. "See you tomorrow evening." She quickly walked down the hall.

Had that been a slight blush that pinkened her cheeks?

Bitsy summoned Lilly as McConnel left. "Call Bowman's and get them to paint the letters on this damn door." She suddenly felt exhausted, drained of any emotion, and feeling like she could finally sleep. "Cancel the Renard Group meeting and reschedule it for three this afternoon. I'm going home for a while."

Lilly moved closer. "I'm glad. You look like you could use a few hours' rest. Eat something while you're gone."

Bitsy started the car just before she left the office. She slung her purse onto the front seat when she got in and inspected herself in the rearview mirror. She looked as tired as she felt. She squinted. Black mascara was smudged under her right eye. She licked her finger and wiped at it. She'd broken down right in front of McConnel, and on top of that, she'd invited her to the house. "What was I thinking?" She watched the dash cam as she backed out.

Thirty minutes later she opened the garage door of her home—a two-story, four-bedroom estate in Richmond Hill. She'd grown up in Pine Grove, north of Savannah, but this had been home for the last ten years. Maybe when all this was over, she'd go somewhere else to live. She didn't have to be in Savannah. It might be good to move from the area, maybe even leave Georgia entirely. Make a fresh start. But her three older sisters and their families and Momma and Daddy were all here. She couldn't bear the thought of not having them around her. Most of the time. "Oh, hell. Momma? I forgot to call her." She laid her phone on the kitchen counter as she passed by. "Later."

She trekked up the stairs to her bedroom and slipped on her favorite silk nightshirt, then slid between the soft, cool bed sheets and drifted off to sleep.

CHAPTER FOUR

McConnel stared at the building she'd just left. Nothing had been what she'd expected. The feelings she'd had while she was with Bitsy were confusing and unsettling. She'd blamed her for so long for not being able to find Hallie Lynn, she didn't know what to feel now. Bitsy had disarmed her, stripped her of her ammunition, then broken the wall she'd put up to protect herself. She'd read and studied everything she could about her over the years, but they were only facts, glimpses. She didn't know Bitsy as a person. Maybe it was time to let go of the discontent and anger. But could she? Bitsy seemed genuine in her feelings about Hallie Lynn. It was clear in her eyes and the way she acted when she talked about being at the crime scene.

McConnel unlocked the car and opened the door. The blast from the heat blew back against her with such force it almost knocked her over. "Oh, my God!" She auto-started the car, then stood beside it, waiting for the air conditioning to make getting in bearable.

The more she thought about Bitsy, the more uncertain she felt, making it difficult to know what to do. Her anger had become a blanket of comfort, but now she saw the damage it'd done. Every relationship she'd ever had was empty and hollow. She'd had several women in her life, but each relationship had ended within a year. They'd all told her the same thing: "There's no room in your heart for anyone else." She had lots of excuses. There wasn't a deep enough attraction. She couldn't commit to them because they didn't understand her. Now she questioned all of it. Were they right? Was she so full of anger and bitterness she didn't have any room in her heart for anything deep or meaningful? Forty wasn't young anymore. She'd carried her feelings of ill will and discontent for over twenty years. They'd encased her like vines on a wooden fence.

She slipped into the car, relieved the air conditioning had done its job. The steering wheel was warm but manageable. She grasped it and stared at the now-empty dock. If she discarded the hatred, where would her emotional protection be, that shield guarding her from the pain and loss? If she let go of all of it, maybe she could totally focus on finding who killed Hallie Lynn. *Killed her. Not kidnapped her.* The thoughts burrowed into her mind. She reached under the collar of her blouse and lightly touched the pink stone teardrop pendant. She vaguely remembered getting it when she was about five or six. She'd worn out five gold chains since then. She brought it to her lips and kissed it, then returned it to its position against her chest. A crime scene photo of one identical to it was in Hallie Lynn's file. It was around her neck when they found her remains. That's when McConnel had decided to withhold who she was from the FBI and asked to be assigned to the case. Emotion swelled, as it always did when she thought of her. Now that Hallie Lynn's death had been confirmed, McConnel couldn't have any more fantasies of her being alive.

McConnel had been raised in a loving home by her adoptive parents, but her real mother, a drug addict, had given her away when she was a month old. McConnel had convinced herself, at eighteen, after the shock of finding out who her biological mother was and that she'd been robbed of a relationship with her fraternal twin sister, that if she'd been there with Hallie Lynn, maybe she could have stopped what happened to her. Maybe if they'd been walking home together, the abductor wouldn't have taken her.

Hallie Lynn's mother hadn't picked her up from school that night after the play. The report said she had to work at the local restaurant and couldn't get off. Why hadn't she arranged for Hallie Lynn to go home with someone else? Her mother had said in her statement, "Our apartment was only six blocks from the school. She walked home all the time, and nothing ever happened to her. Why would she need someone to be with her?"

Why? Because she was ten years old, that's why. Her mother was unfit. McConnel's adoptive parent—her biological mother's best friend—and her husband should have taken both the girls, not just her.

McConnel reached into her purse and pulled out the wallet-sized photo of Hallie Lynn that her adoptive mother had given her the day she told McConnel the truth. She held it tightly, gazing at it. Hallie Lynn was seven at the time of the picture. She grabbed the other worn, faded snapshot she always kept with it, one of herself at the same age, and placed them side by side. "You and I. Twins." They had the same expressive smile and bone structure, but Hallie Lynn's hair was not as curly, and their eye color was different.

Since the day McConnel found out who Hallie Lynn was, she hadn't stopped trying to find her. A part of that journey was over now. She finally knew where Hallie Lynn was, but she had to uncover the rest of it. Who killed her and why? McConnel gripped the steering wheel tighter. Whoever murdered her would pay. That was an absolute.

Bitsy wasn't the enemy after all. She obviously cared deeply about Hallie Lynn and had also mourned her loss, even longer than McConnel had. Bitsy's life was entwined in Hallie Lynn's disappearance and death. McConnel would untangle all the threads, even if it took her the rest of her life.

She planned to visit the crime scene next and then go on to the sheriff's office in Effingham County, the jurisdiction where Hallie Lynn's body was found. She returned to the hotel in downtown Savannah, changed into a cotton blouse, then made the trip to the park, just over the county line.

The car lot was almost empty. She stepped out, clipped her badge onto her belt, and walked past the benches surrounded by oak trees draped with pale-gray moss. She continued near the north side of the park on the path leading to the area with yellow crime scene tape. No one was there. All the evidence needed had been gathered in the days before. Now it was only disturbed ground, cold and empty, void of any hint that Hallie Lynn had been there all this time. She carefully walked around the site, inspecting the soil. They'd found little evidence due to the years of decomposition. Why here? Why put her in this place? The abduction had happened at the school in Springfield, about a thirty-five- or forty-minute drive from the park, which was isolated, and most likely covered more densely with brush thirty years ago. She walked to the edge of the woods and scrutinized the secluded tree line. It had to have taken time to dig the grave. Did he carry her to this spot after he killed her, or had he brought her here and then murdered her?

"Hey!" A deep male voice echoed in the stillness.

She turned.

A sheriff's deputy in his mid-twenties angled toward her, his hand resting on the gun at his hip. "No one's supposed to be here."

McConnel pointed to her badge and walked toward him. "Special Agent McConnel, FBI, assigned to this case."

The deputy eased his stance. "Why FBI? I thought you people didn't care about cold cases."

She ignored his statement.

The deputy moved toward her and offered his hand.

McConnel shook it.

"We're all stunned," the deputy said. "I'm Graham Newton, Effingham County deputy."

McConnel nodded.

He inspected the bare ground. "I'll be glad when this whole mess is over. Anything I can do to help?" He moved around the dig site, then came back to stand beside her.

"I think I have everything I need. I plan to talk with the sheriff as soon as I'm done here. Do you know if he's in his office?"

"He was an hour ago. I can't speak for him now. We're a small department, just the sheriff and three deputies, including me, and Grace, the dispatcher." He scuffed a small pile of dirt with his shoe. "I imagine you've got your work cut out for you. I heard they didn't find anything that would solve the case." He bent, reached for a handful of sandy soil, sifted it through his fingers, then stood. "I wish you luck in your investigation."

"Thank you. I can use all I can get."

He tipped his hat. "I need to get back on patrol." He turned and left.

It was quiet, only the sound of a few birds in the trees. She surveyed the remains of the gravesite once again, then hiked back and auto-started the car before she got near it. She wouldn't make that mistake again.

The Effingham County Sheriff's Department, located in the city of Springfield, was in a small, dark-red brick building. A dispatcher looked up from her console and greeted her. Her name badge identified her as G. Ellington. Grace?

"Hey. May I help you?"

"Hi. I'm FBI Special Agent McConnel. I'm working the Hallie Lynn Peeples cold case." She indicated her badge. "Is the sheriff in?"

Grace nodded. "One minute. I'll let him know you're here." She walked to the back of the room and knocked on a door, then peeked in. She returned a few seconds later. "Go on back." She pointed behind her and returned to her station.

McConnel entered the sheriff's office.

He stood. In his fifties, about six foot one, he had an impeccably groomed head of thick, dark hair, graying at the temples and at the top. A jagged scar the size of a nickel marred his right cheek, just above the jawline. His uniform was spotless and perfectly pressed. His name was Gerald Atwater, and he'd been a deputy at the time of Hallie Lynn's kidnapping.

"Glad to meet ya." His Southern drawl was thick and heavy on his tongue. He shook her hand. "Have a seat." He gestured to the two sturdy, worn wooden chairs in front of the desk as he returned to his seat.

She slid into the one on the right.

"I'm afraid we can't help you very much."

"Thanks for taking the time to see me, Sheriff. I understand you were one of the deputies at the time of Hallie Lynn's disappearance." It was hard to say her name out loud.

"Yes. That was a long time ago. I'd only been on the job about a year. It's tragic to find her body after all this time. We all hoped she'd lived through the ordeal."

His eye contact was intense, penetrating. What was he looking for?

"The department only handles incidents outside of the city limits, so she was in our jurisdiction, but we didn't investigate the Peeples case. The Springfield city police chief took over because he had more expertise. Back then there was only me, another deputy, Jasper Watkins, and the sheriff at the time, Mason Tucker."

"Were you involved in it?"

"What?"

"Did you take part in the investigation?"

The sheriff shook his head. "I was only in on the tail end of it because I was off for a couple of days and had gone to Cameron, fishing on the Savannah River with a buddy of mine."

"Is Mason Tucker still alive?"

"No. He died of a heart attack about ten years ago, and Jasper, the other deputy at the time, moved to Athens, Georgia, in 1998. He's a professor at the University of Georgia." He rubbed the side of his nose. "I suppose that's the pitfall of a cold case. Everything's changed. The Springfield police chief, Owen Gibson, who led the investigation, is still around. He lives with his daughter and her family in Tusculum, just up the road a way." He typed into his computer and then wrote the address and phone number on a yellow sticky note and handed it to her. "Other than being called when the body was discovered, the sheriff's department wasn't involved in this current part either. Mostly we kept everyone clear of the scene so the state forensic people could do their job. We don't have the expertise to investigate. Now the state routinely brings people in for those kinds of things."

"Have there been any other disappearances in this county over the years?" She knew the answer but wanted to see his reaction.

"No. Thank goodness. You workin' the investigation by yourself?"

McConnel nodded. "For now." She rose and shook his hand. "Thanks for the information."

The sheriff stood. "Any time. Sorry I couldn't be more helpful."

The next stop was the Springfield police station, on the other side of town. She talked with the chief and was permitted to scour what records they had, but it was nothing more than a review of what she already knew.

Her last stop for the day was to see Owen Gibson, retired Springfield police chief. She found the address and parked on the street just past the house, a two-story, older home, surrounded by beautiful magnolia trees and live oaks with moss hanging everywhere. She couldn't stop looking at it. There was something serene and mystical about it, like stepping back in time.

An older woman, maybe in her early sixties, came to the door, her pleasant smile lighting up her face like someone had held a candle next to her. "Are you the investigator? Sheriff Atwater said someone might be stopping over."

"I am. FBI Special Agent McConnel."

"You ain't from around here, are you?"

"No, ma'am. I'm from Ohio."

The woman laughed. "Well, I guess we'll have to let you in anyway. Come on in." She opened the door wider and motioned for her to enter. "I'm Peggy, his daughter. Daddy's in the back yard."

She led McConnel through the living room and dining room and then to the glass French doors at the back of the kitchen. She opened it and pointed. "He's by the river, just there."

McConnel thanked her and made her way down the steps and out to the edge of the water, where an older man with snow-white hair was sitting in an Adirondack chair with a long bamboo pole by his side, trying to bait a hook.

"Chief Gibson?"

He turned toward her, his blue eyes bright and clear. "Are you the FBI agent from up north?"

"Yes, sir. Special Agent McConnel."

"Take a load off."

She sat on the bench beside his chair.

He finished baiting the hook and tossed the line into the river. It splashed, disturbing the reflection of the setting sun on the water. He leaned back, stuck the pole in the holder in the chair, and then reached down beside himself and raised a large glass mug of what looked like tea. He took a gulp and set it on the arm of his chair and pointed. "See that big boulder out there on the far side of the riverbank?"

She looked where the chief was pointing. "That darker one?"

"Yeah, that one. It's been there since before I was born. This is my parents' home. My daughter and her family live here now. That boulder will be here long after I'm gone." He gazed at it, then swatted at a mosquito that looked like it needed a saddle. He sighed deeply and slowly shook his head. "Damn whoever killed that child."

McConnel kept quiet and listened.

"Some things you take to the grave with you," he said. "I don't want that sweet little girl's death to be one of 'em." He looked across the water as if searching for something. "That night there was a stillness in the air. The minute I left the school I could feel it. When I got to the Peepleses' home, Ms. Peeples was crying and screaming about someone taking her daughter. I think she was so full of guilt and shame she couldn't help us. I thought it might have been her boyfriend, Curtis

Stillman. It's usually not a stranger. They'd had a fight that morning, and he'd skedaddled. We finally found him drunk in a bar a couple counties over. We held him for two days, but I couldn't get anywhere with that knucklehead. I brought him in for questioning three different times and never did get anything useful out of him. I don't think he did it. He was killed in Atlanta about a year later, knifed outside a bar. We just didn't have any suspects. There was no trace of her. Not until her remains were found last week." He ran his hand through his thinning white hair. "There just weren't any suspects." He said it like an excuse. He stood and brought the line in from the river, then laid the pole beside his chair and sat again.

"Our best hope of finding who took her was Bitsy Hanover. Still is. Somewhere locked inside that pretty girl is the answer to who killed Hallie Lynn. You want to find the killer, get inside Bitsy Hanover's head." He took another drink from his mug. "She and Hallie Lynn were thick as thieves. Couldn't separate those two with a wedge. Saturdays I'd see 'em all over town. They were sweet kids. Bitsy was never the same after that night." His voice lowered. "She withdrew. The spark went out of her. I thought I'd find who took her or find Hallie Lynn, but never did. Now we discover she'd been here all this time." His expression seemed to change from reminiscent to matter-of-fact. He adjusted in his chair toward McConnel. "Don't suppose you know if there's goin' to be a funeral?"

"No. Not right now. Her remains are being held at the state crime lab. They can't be released until my investigation is closed."

"I wish you well," the chief said, "but I don't put much stock in you being able to find her killer." His eyes were moist and red.

McConnel needed a few more questions answered. "Do you think it was someone local?"

"Now that we know where she was all this time, I think the choice of where she was put is interestin'. The killer didn't just wander into it. You'd have to have known the area to find that specific spot. It's got perfect cover. No one would see him there."

"Him?"

The chief pursed his lips. "I believe so. Do you know how long Hallie Lynn was alive before she was killed?"

McConnel mentally reviewed the report. "The coroner estimates she was killed shortly after she was taken, but he stated it was an educated guess. Remnants of her clothing were found on her remains—a white sundress with yellow daisies. A part of one of her shoes was still on her left foot. The description matched the report when she was taken, and the shoe size was correct. She had a pink teardrop necklace around her neck." The weight of McConnel's identical one lay heavy against her chest.

"Do they know how it happened?" he asked.

"Broken hyoid bone, so strangulation. One other thing, the first two fingers of her left hand were broken."

The chief cringed. "She was a feisty little thing. I imagine she put up quite a fight."

"Chief, do you remember what Bitsy said to you when you questioned her the first time? You wrote in your report she stated it was dark and she couldn't see any details."

He nodded. "Her words were jumbled, and what she said didn't make much sense, so I summarized in the paperwork. I remember it like it was yesterday. I was the first one to interview her. Her family lives not far from here. Her parents called me and wanted me to come over. Bitsy was crying and pacing. It was about one in the morning by the time I got to their house. I'll never forget it. She was wringing her hands and shaking. She said, 'Hallie was there and then she wasn't. The shiny dark took her.'"

"Shiny dark?"

"Yep. That's what she said, and then she had nothing else to say about it."

"How far away was she when Hallie was taken?"

"As near as we could figure, it was around two hundred yards."

"And she didn't say anything else."

"Nope. That's all she ever said."

They both sat without words and stared off at the river, ambling on its way.

McConnel finally rose and thanked him.

He shook her hand. "You find who did it. You're our only hope now. I'm too old, and no one else gives a damn."

"I'll do all I can."

She left. She wanted to get something to eat and put the day behind her. She was even more sure now that Bitsy was the key, but how to help her remember?

CHAPTER FIVE

The morning sun broke through the window. Bitsy was barely awake when her phone squawked in her ear. She rolled over and put it to the side of her face. "I'm sorry, Momma. I was going to call you last night."

"You weren't going to call me, Mary Elisabeth. Lord, you're an obstinate child. Why don't you come home for a few days?"

"Momma, I can't. Not now. I don't want to be there."

"Would you like me to come there?"

Bitsy rolled her eyes. "NO! I'll be fine."

"Darlin', I'm just worried about you, and so are Daddy and your sisters."

Bitsy didn't want to deal with all of them. She loved them, but she had no patience or inclination to share anything with them right now. "I need some space. I'll come see y'all some other time, but not now. I can't face it. I can't bear the thought of being at the house. All it does is make me sick to my stomach. Why don't you come in and we'll go to lunch? Maybe Monday."

"Monday! Mary Elizabeth, that's too long. Don't you want to come home and be with the family, darlin'? It'll be good for you."

"I'm meeting with an FBI agent this evening, and I'm swamped at work. I'll be home sometime next week. I need to go. Please understand. Love you, bye." Bitsy hung up as fast as she could. Any probing of how she felt would throw her over the edge.

Anxious dread at the thought of questions and endless speculation filled her so full it seeped out into the corners of the room and drizzled down the walls. Could she help McConnel find Hallie Lynn's killer?

Was it too late? Had too many years gone by? All this time Hallie had lain in the dank earth nearby.

The bile rose in her throat again. Her hands were clammy, and her heart pounded. She didn't want to think about any of it. She immediately stripped off her silk nightshirt and took a shower, letting the hot liquid relief flow over her shoulders and back until the water began to cool. She dried and dressed, made one cup of coffee, and then forced herself to eat a scrambled egg and a piece of toast. The only thing that made it bearable was the homemade grape jelly her sister Janie had made.

She rushed to the office. Bo Reynolds was waiting, slumped near the reception desk. He followed her in, close behind, hands stuffed in the pockets of his dress pants. He'd been buying and selling art for Bitsy for four years, since right after he graduated from college. Most of the time he did his job, but every so often, like now, he got that defeated attitude because he didn't like confrontation with customers.

"I told him you didn't want any debate about the price," he said. "Ripped me a new one and told me he'd be damned if he was going to pay that much. Not a penny more than ten thousand forty-two." He plopped into one of the purple-cushioned chairs in front of her desk, crossed his lanky legs, and ran his finger down the arm rest.

"Bo, you know he's just saying that." Bitsy sat and began rummaging through the mail Lilly had placed on the desktop. She had to encourage him about every six weeks because his confidence waned from the haggling and customers not wanting to pay premium prices. Everyone wanted a deal, so she had to push him to stand his ground.

Bo frowned. "He won't budge."

"Yes, he will." Bitsy tossed three unopened letters into the trash. "Go back and tell him he's getting a great deal. I'm not budging on the price. If he wants the painting bad enough, he'll meet it. If not, it's his loss. He knows as well as I do what it'll be worth in two more years."

"He's a stubborn old man, and besides that, he's cheap."

"I know he is, and he knows I know, so push back."

Bo was a loyal employee, but sometimes he needed strong direction. He brushed the thigh of his tailored dark gray pants. "I hear the cold case investigator got here."

Bitsy looked up from the mail and glared at him, then went on with her task, hoping he'd gotten her message.

"What's she like?"

Bitsy wasn't expecting that one. She ran the letter opener through the envelope of the electric bill, trying not to stab at it. She pulled the invoice out and scanned the itemized statement, avoiding eye contact with Bo. "She seems very competent." She tossed the bill onto the desk and picked up another one.

"Is she cute? You could use a little cute in your life."

She ripped through the edge of the paper. "Bo, mind your own business."

He glanced out the window and then back. "Every one's sayin' she's gonna find out who did it. She's already been to Effingham County and talked with the sheriff and police chief. She even went over to Chief Gibson's house and talked with him. I heard she did a little fishin', if you know what I mean." He smiled.

Bitsy stopped and looked at him. "Are you done?"

He shrugged. "Just sayin'."

Bitsy pressed her tongue against her teeth to relieve the irritation, a habit she'd had since childhood. "I'm sure she's good at her job. Yes, she's cute. She's coming over to the house tonight for supper and to talk. Now get out of here."

"Talk? Right." He stood. "Do you want to offer his honor anything else if he decides not to get the *Seaport*?"

"He'll get it. Just baby him. I need you to go up to Atlanta on Monday. Waverly Corp is looking for some paintings for their lobby. Find out what they're interested in, and then on the way back, stop at Mr. Pellmont's and give him this check for the *Clairton*." She handed him a cashier's check and envelope.

"Hallelujah! Ol' man Pellmont is finally going to sell." He snatched the items from her hand.

"I already have a buyer for it, but someone else is also interested." Bitsy offered a thin smile.

"Who?"

"Nun ya. Run along. I'll tell you Monday."

"Are you all right? I'm sure this situation is hard for you."

The concern in his eyes was genuine, but Bitsy couldn't talk about what he wanted to know. "I'm fine. Go on now. No speeding tickets."

He left without looking back.

Bitsy faced the window. The port was bustling with deliveries like any other day. The discovery of Hallie's remains was old news. People went on with their lives. Should she let it go? Get on with *her* life? Hallie had been found, and the chances of discovering who killed her were slim to none. But she couldn't give up. Whoever did it had to pay. They couldn't go on with their life as if Hallie's life didn't matter.

The sky was beginning to cloud. A storm was brewing.

By six twenty, when Bitsy picked up their meal at the Carriage House, rain pelted the road so hard it looked like the water was dancing. Deep pools had already gathered in low-lying areas.

The cashier handed her the two large plastic bags of food. "Make sure you warm it up in the oven, not the microwave. Follow these directions." She slipped a small card into one of the bags.

Bitsy thanked her, gathered the items into her arms, and made a dash for the car. By the time she got in and closed the door, she was soaked, but the food didn't get wet. The scent made her drool all the way home. French moules marinieres, cornbread batons, seasoned green beans, Vidalia onions with fresh maple bacon and lemon, and garlic shrimp linguini.

At home she organized the meal according to the directions, then took a shower and dressed. Four times she wondered how the night would go. She faced the mirror. How would they be with each other? How many questions would McConnel ask? How would she feel when *that question* was asked, because she knew it would be? Would it make a difference if McConnel was the one to ask it? She raised her fist as she defiantly stared into the mirror. "You can do this. You can do this no matter how hard it is. You can do it for Hallie. For you."

The doorbell rang at seven minutes past eight.

A drenched McConnel stood on the porch, a bottle of wine cradled in one arm and her light brown leather satchel in her other hand.

"Oh, you poor thing. Get in here." Bitsy guided her into the house.

The storm was still going strong.

"Does it always rain like this?" McConnel handed her the wine and then slipped off her soaked sweater and held it out, clearly unsure where to place it.

"Not always, but when it does it's a corker." Bitsy took the garment from her. "I'll block it in the laundry room. Hopefully we can save it." She set the wine on the counter, then opened it so it could breathe. When she returned from laying the sweater out so it wouldn't lose its shape, McConnel was shivering and running her hands over her arms.

"Let me get you something dry to put on." Bitsy went upstairs, grabbed a long-sleeve cotton pullover from her dresser, and brought it to McConnel. She pointed to the bathroom off to the side of the kitchen. "You can change in there. Do you need some pants?"

"I'm afraid they're wet also."

"No problem." Bitsy returned with a pair of black casual slacks. "These should keep you warm."

"A thousand thank yous."

Bitsy laughed. "Supper will be ready in a few minutes. Would you like a glass of wine? Whiskey? Beer? Juice?"

"Ice water would be great. I'm dehydrated."

"Ice water it is."

Bitsy got her the requested drink and set it on a coaster by the sofa.

McConnel emerged from the bathroom. "That's better. Thank you so much. I didn't have an umbrella. I'm afraid I made a mess of myself trying to avoid getting soaked at the liquor store and then making a mad dash to your porch."

"Well, you look good now. I love your hair. Is it naturally curly?"

"Yes. My hairdresser always wants to cut it a little too short."

It hung in wet ringlets, nestled close to her neck. Bitsy didn't want to notice how good McConnel looked, but she did. She was the same size as Bitsy but about an inch shorter.

McConnel sipped her water.

"Are you sure you don't want something else to drink?"

"This is perfect. I made the mistake of drinking alcohol on the plane and then at the hotel when I got here. Georgia's heat is taking its toll. I tend to get a migraine when I'm dehydrated, so I want to be extra careful."

"You don't mind if I have some wine, do you?"

McConnel raised her hand. "Of course not. Please do."

Bitsy returned with a glass of the cabernet McConnel had brought and sat at the opposite end of the sofa, not wanting to get close. "I'll be honest with you. I'm dreading this conversation we're about to have."

Would McConnel respond like all the other investigators, focused on the case, nothing more? It was going to happen no matter how long Bitsy put it off.

"Let's eat first. Supper's ready."

CHAPTER SIX

McConnel eased back onto the sofa. Bitsy seemed more relaxed after they finished their delicious meal, especially after she'd had two full glasses of wine. But no matter how McConnel worded the questions, Bitsy would pay the toll for the answers. She began the conversation, trying not to be invasive with what needed to be discussed. She decided to ask something Bitsy hopefully wouldn't get anxious about. "Tell me how you met Hallie Lynn."

Bitsy curled her legs under herself as she took another sip of wine. She rubbed her thigh, then touched the side of her hair, tucking the strands behind her ear. "I met her in kindergarten, and we became instant friends. She was shy but quick to smile." Bitsy laughed. "She had such a wonderful spirit about her. I remember how she'd wave to me when I'd get on the school bus to go home. She'd move her hand back and forth and flit it like a bird flapping its wings." Bitsy's eyes sparkled as she talked about the memory.

This was good, non-threatening, and it seemed easy for her to discuss it. McConnel looked at the beautiful oil painting hanging above the fireplace, a field of daisies mixed in green grass below a gorgeous cloudy blue sky. She couldn't help staring at it. "What artist did that piece?"

Bitsy glanced at it, then back to McConnel. A broad smile crossed her face. "I did."

"You?"

"Yes. About ten years ago. I also painted the one in the kitchen of the daisies in the vase."

"What was your inspiration?"

"I don't know. I've always felt drawn to daisies for some reason."
It hit McConnel like someone had slapped her on the back of her head. Had Bitsy realized what she'd painted? Did she remember what Hallie Lynn was wearing the night of her abduction? Fragments of her white and yellow dress with daisies had been recovered with the remains. Bitsy hadn't read the forensic report, so she wouldn't have known. The paintings were a massive indication that Bitsy did recall something, even if she wasn't aware of it. "Do you have other works? I'd love to see them." McConnel couldn't wait.

"Only about forty." Bitsy laughed.

"Will you show them to me?"

"Now?"

"Yes, please."

"They're better viewed in daylight. I need to warn you, they aren't that good."

"I'm sure you're being hard on yourself." McConnel couldn't wait to wade through them. They might be a treasure chest of Bitsy's memories. She hoped she'd be able to glean some bit of insight into Bitsy and what she'd seen that night.

Bitsy finished her drink and held on to the glass, then motioned for McConnel to follow her. "They're in my bedroom-changed-into-a-studio. It's a mess. I didn't expect to take anyone back there."

"Don't worry. I won't judge."

Bitsy set the empty wineglass on the kitchen counter, then led McConnel through the hallway to the last room. She opened the door and switched on the lights.

It was exactly what McConnel expected. Lots of windows, stacks of finished and half-completed canvases, paintbrushes in cans and others in plastic containers or placed on the stands. The wood floor had paint drippings everywhere, and there were rags covered in bright yellows, blues, white, some with darker mixtures, the lingering scent of turpentine filling the air.

Bitsy gestured in a swooping motion. "What would you like to see?"

McConnel couldn't contain her excitement. "Everything."

"Wow! No one's ever been that interested in my work before." She pointed. "Okay. Over here are the ones I put the most time into. Lately all I do is stare at the empty canvas with my brush in my hand."

They moved to the completed work arranged side by side at the far wall.

"If you don't mind, I'd like to see them in the order you painted them."

Bitsy gave her a puzzled look. Was it an odd request, or was she just suspicious of McConnel's enthusiasm?

Bitsy sorted through the paintings, rearranging a few. "It's best to see them at a distance. From Atlanta would be good."

McConnel chuckled and settled into a wooden chair next to one of the easels. Bitsy had a great sense of humor.

As she showed her each painting, one thing was clear. Daisies were included in many. In a vase, fields, arrangements, flowerpots, but the one place they were never found was on a dress. Six had women in them, but not one had daisies on their clothing.

McConnel had no training in the arts. All she knew was two things. She enjoyed the paintings, and clearly Bitsy subconsciously remembered something about that night. Now McConnel hoped she had a chance to bring it to the surface.

"Your work is good. I'm no expert, but I know what I like."

"You're very kind. Thank you."

They returned to the living room, but not before Bitsy stopped in the kitchen and poured herself another glass of wine. "Are you sure you wouldn't like something besides water?"

"I'm good," McConnel said.

Once settled in their original seats, McConnel began to formulate her plan to extract what she needed from Bitsy's memories. She reminded herself to go easy. Otherwise, the whole thing could backfire and explode. "So, you paint, you run an art gallery, you're gorgeous. Who else are you?"

"You're such a sweetheart." Bitsy sipped her wine. "I wrote in college and after for a few years. Lesbian fiction novels. Two of them were published."

"Really?"

"Yep. But I stopped."

"Why?"

"It just got too complicated. My momma didn't approve. It was a constant source of irritation between us and put a strain on our relationship. It became more work after I wrote a story than writing it. I haven't written in almost fifteen years."

"Do you think you'll ever do it again?"

"I don't know. Maybe, but not anytime soon."

She was beginning to slur her words. McConnel needed to ask the question. "Do you remember what you told Chief Owen Gibson the night of the abduction?"

Bitsy straightened, took another drink, then set the empty glass firmly on the end table. She clutched the arm of the sofa, inhaling a deep breath and nodding.

"Will you share it with me?"

"Didn't you read it in the report?"

"I did, but I'd like to hear it from you."

"I said something about a dark figure and shining light."

"You said, quote, 'Hallie was there and then she wasn't. The shiny dark took her.'"

"I said that?"

"Yes. When you said *dark*, what did you mean?"

Bitsy had a faraway expression and was silent.

McConnel didn't want to interrupt her thought process. She waited for what seemed like three or four minutes.

Finally Bitsy brought her hand to her chin and rubbed gently. "Clothing. Dark Clothing."

"That's great. Good job."

Bitsy shook her head. "I don't remember anything else." She waved her hand. "I wish I could tell you more. I want to help."

"I know you do. You know what I think?"

"What?"

McConnel moved closer to her for emphasis. "I think you saw more that night, but it scares you so badly you block it each time it tries to come to the surface. I want you to know you're safe. It's okay to remember. Hallie has been found."

Bitsy clasped her fingers together and didn't speak.

McConnel placed her hand on top of hers.

Neither spoke. The silence wasn't uncomfortable, more like a cozy blanket of acceptance they could share.

McConnel withdrew her hand from hers.

Bitsy's shoulders relaxed. "I believe you. I believe every word. She has come back in a way, hasn't she? She's safe now."

"Yes."

"Did anyone say anything to you about her funeral?" Bitsy asked. "Does she have any living relatives?"

McConnel's lips burned, and her body recoiled as she spoke the half-truths. "I'm not sure. I know they're holding her remains at the state crime lab until the investigation is completed."

Bitsy clenched her fists. "He can't hurt her anymore."

"No," McConnel said. "*He* can't."

It was a male. They'd all suspected it, and he was wearing dark clothes. Bitsy had seen him. Maybe not his face, but she'd seen enough to know it was a man. But why had it traumatized her so badly? Did she witness Hallie Lynn being forced into a vehicle? Did Bitsy know him? Did he gesture to her in some way? Did he threaten her somehow?

McConnel touched her shoulder. "You've done so well. Thank you for making the effort. I know it's hard to do this. We'll stop here and let you get some rest. I'm sure it's been exhausting." She passed her a tissue from the box on the end table.

Bitsy wiped under her eyes and straightened. "I'm sorry for the emotional display."

"No. You don't have anything to be sorry about. You did great."

"I don't know what I said that was so apparently good."

"An outsider can sometimes see things those involved can't because they're too close to the situation. A forest-for-the-trees kind of thing."

"You're the one who's great. I feel so comfortable around you. You should be thanked. Not me."

"It's been my pleasure." McConnel needed to go back to the hotel and sift through what she'd gleaned. "Is there anything I can do for you before I go?" She stood.

"You're right. I'm exhausted." She peeked out the window. "The rain has stopped. Wear those clothes home and bring them back the next time we meet."

"Thanks. We can exchange yours for mine then. I'll call you tomorrow to work something out."

Bitsy accompanied her to the door. "I look forward to it."

"Good night." McConnel left and got into her car.

Bitsy waited in the doorway until McConnel pulled into the street. The drive to the hotel wasn't as dreary as the one to Bitsy's home. McConnel entered her room, set the satchel beside the TV credenza, made herself a cup of herbal tea, and then took her notebook out and began to write.

> *Male, dark clothes, possibly threatening. Did he force Hallie Lynn into a vehicle, or did she enter willingly? Did he threaten Bitsy in some way? What was "the shiny"? Will Bitsy remember more if we go to the school or her home? Can she do it? Can she break through her fears???*

There were questions to ask and questions to solve. McConnel had enjoyed the evening with Bitsy, but how would she react when McConnel pressed her for the answers she suspected were inside her?

CHAPTER SEVEN

Bitsy locked the front door as McConnel drove away. She cleared the table and put the dishes into the dishwasher, then turned out the lights and headed upstairs. Exhaustion overtook her. She barely had the energy to undress and put on her pajamas. She turned off the lamp and crawled into bed.

Her alarm sounded at six a.m. She swung her feet over the side of the mattress, put her face in her hands, and moaned. "Oh, God! How much did I drink, and why?" After stumbling to the bathroom, she rummaged through the cabinet until she found the Tylenol, shook two from the bottle, filled a paper cup with water, and swallowed, choking them down. She made her way to the kitchen for coffee and began to get ready for the day.

Lilly greeted her when she entered the office. "You look like shit."

As if Bitsy didn't know. "Thanks so much."

"What'd you do, pull an all-night slut-fest at Jimmy B's?"

Bitsy tried not to laugh. Even smiling hurt.

"Your momma called me last night."

"Frost my socks. No, she did not."

"Yes, she did. She was worried about you."

"What'd you tell her?" Bitsy sat in her chair and squeezed her eyes shut. The headache was less intense but still hovered like a vulture circling roadkill.

"I told her you were hooking up with the female FBI agent and not to worry." Lilly grinned.

"Sure you did." Bitsy cut her a sideways glance and slowly shook her head. "Go back to work. Who's first on the chopping block today?"

The morning dragged on.

At one o'clock Bitsy called McConnel and left a message. "Hey, this is Bitsy. I've managed to free up the evening and should be done here by nine. I know it doesn't give us much time to talk, but it's the best I can do. If that doesn't work, we can get together at ten tomorrow morning. I can meet you here at my office. Call me."

McConnel returned her call a half hour later. "Hi. How are you?"

"A little stressed, but otherwise good. How about you?"

"Good. I'm going out of town this afternoon, so I can't meet you this evening, but I can come over to your office in the morning at ten."

Bitsy was disappointed. Why? She didn't know what she was feeling, let alone why. "Um, okay, that's fine."

"You sure?"

"Yes. That'll work."

"Can you arrange a couple of hours?" McConnel asked. "If you have time, we can go out to lunch when we're through."

"Sure. That's fine."

"Okay. See you tomorrow." McConnel said good-bye and ended the call.

Had Bitsy distracted her? Was she in the middle of something? She didn't sound as friendly as she had last night. Bitsy was probably reading something into this that wasn't there. Why did she care? Why was she feeling this range of emotion? Given everything she was going through, why wouldn't she?

Her office phone beeped.

"Bitsy, it's your momma," Lilly announced.

"Not now. Tell her I'm in a meeting and I'll call her later."

"All hands on deck. She's headed your way."

"She's here? Good Lord!"

Her office door burst open.

Bitsy gripped the edge of the desk.

There she was—Oakley sunglasses, a sleeveless sundress that hugged her curves like it'd been painted on, four-inch heels, and not a strand of her artificial dark auburn hair out of place. She was sixty-seven years old but looked like she could have been Bitsy's older sister, a fact many people stated when they were out together.

"Mary Elizabeth, I swear I don't know what to do with you."

"Momma, I'm forty-one years old. You don't have to do anything with me."

"That remains to be seen."

Lilly peeked in and cringed as she shut the office door.

Momma claimed one of the cushioned chairs.

Bitsy trailed over to sit beside her. "I appreciate your concern, Momma, I genuinely do, but this is not a good time for me. I have to go to a meeting in ten minutes."

"You're just saying that to get me to leave."

"Momma, I swear I'm not. It's true."

"I hear Mr. Pellmont is finally selling."

Bitsy glared at her. Momma wasn't pulling the wool over her eyes any time soon. "You talked to him, didn't you?"

Momma smiled. "He was a pushover."

"Thank you for that, but I would have gotten that painting without your help."

"Maybe when he finally croaks, but who knows how long that's goin' to be. His daddy lived to be a hundred and two."

"Momma, I wish you'd stop interfering in my business."

"I'm only trying to help."

"I know, but it's exasperating sometimes."

"I'm only returning the favor."

Bitsy didn't want to but chuckled.

Momma grabbed her hand. "Honey, are you okay? You look awfully tired."

Bitsy patted hers. "I'm okay." Then withdrew her hands.

"How's the FBI agent? I hear she's cute."

Bitsy sighed. "I know perfectly well how you feel about my choice of companions, Momma."

"It's true I'm not thrilled, but I want you to be happy, sweetheart."

"She's nice. We met last night for a couple of hours."

"Well?"

"Well what?"

"Well, hell, Mary Elizabeth. How'd it go?"

There wasn't a chance Bitsy would give her any ammunition. McConnel was smart, sensitive, and as sexy as a long-lost lover on a Saturday night. "I have a splitting headache. Could we discuss this when I come home?"

Momma stood and straightened the bottom of her dress. Her red heels shone in the sunlight coming through the window. "I can see more than you know. If you close yourself off like you have recently, you're going to die a lonely, worn-out old woman. Promise me you'll take some time to get out and enjoy yourself for once." She tucked her clutch purse under her arm.

Bitsy rose. "Why all this sudden interest in my social life?"

Momma waved her hand. "I can't bear it when you're sad. Promise me you won't hole up in your house, Mary Elizabeth. I won't leave until you do."

"I promise."

"Promise what?"

"That I'll get out and have some fun. Whatever the hell that means."

"Don't be a sourpuss." Momma kissed her on the cheek, then wiped the lipstick mark with her thumb. "I'll expect you home by the end of the week. Bring that agent with you. I have some questions for her."

"I bet you do."

Momma opened the door, then turned toward Bitsy. "I suspect by the end of this you'll feel differently about life."

"I don't see how."

"Oh, you will. Trust me. Hydrate, darlin'." She blew her a kiss and left.

Bitsy plopped into her desk chair and swiveled toward the window. She stared out at the harbor and sighed. "I don't see how."

The day wore on. Clients came and went. She managed to go through the motions of the tasks at hand. At eight thirty she went home to an empty house and cold food.

She ate her meal in front of the TV, watching a movie, but shut it off after twenty minutes. She changed into a pair of old slacks and top, then went to her studio. She slipped on the cherished stained large yellow shirt with cut-off sleeves that Daddy had given her years ago. Then she set up her easel and paints and stared at the canvas.

"At some point you're going to have to actually paint something." A flash of light from the window caught her attention. She put her brush and palette down, crossed the room, and peered into the night. She could barely see the street. She went through the kitchen to the living room and spotted three parked cars—two underneath lights on her side of the street, and one across and down from the house, in the shadows. There was movement from the driver's side.

Bitsy jumped back, snapped the curtain closed, and stood against the wall to avoid being seen. Was she being watched?

It was irrational, but reason couldn't stop the sensation of the room spinning and her sinking into a pit of quicksand, flailing desperately to get out. She screamed when her phone went off in her blouse pocket. She fumbled for it, then almost dropped it, trying to see who it was. McConnel? She stabbed at the button. "Hello?"

"Did I catch you at a bad time? You seem out of breath."

That panicked feeling was back. She clung to the wall, not knowing what to do or say. "I…I." Should she tell her? She tried to calm herself, but the attempt only added fuel to the fire. She'd think she was an idiot.

"You there?"

She thought better of it. McConnel had probably already surmised she was a nut job.

"Bitsy, are you okay?"

She finally got control. "Yes, I'm…fine."

"I just wanted to confirm for tomorrow at ten."

"That's good."

Silence.

"O…kay. Um, I'll see you tomorrow morning, then?"

Bitsy didn't want her to go, but she couldn't figure out what else to say to keep her on the call. She searched for an excuse. "How'd your day go?" Her heartbeat slowed. She moved from the wall to the chair and then tucked her legs underneath her and curled up with a lap blanket.

"Good. I was in Athens."

"Did you have FBI business?"

McConnel laughed. "Yes."

"Can you talk about it?"

"I was doing some witness interviews for the case. Are you sure you're okay?"

Bitsy glanced at the covered windows, then eyed the front door to make sure it was secured. All the doors were locked and had a dead bolt. She knew it, yet she wanted to run to each one and double-check.

"Yes. I'm all right. Did you find out anything?" It was probably better if they didn't discuss the case. It'd give her nightmares, and she was sure she wouldn't sleep much tonight as it was.

"It's always productive when you can interview witnesses. Listen, I'm driving, so I better get off."

"Oh...okay. Have a good evening. See you tomorrow." Bitsy ended the call, not waiting for any other comments. McConnel must've not wanted to talk.

Bitsy stared at the curtain until she got enough courage to peer outside again. The car that had been parked in the dark area was gone. She breathed a sigh of relief.

She went into the kitchen and began to make herself a cup of herbal tea.

Several minutes later her front doorbell rang. It was ten thirty. Who the hell would be coming over this late? She peered through the stained glass, holding her breath, her trembling hand on the latch. McConnel? Relief rushed through her. How did she know? She swung the door open and pulled her in. "I'm so glad you're here."

McConnel frowned. "What happened? I know something did."

Bitsy was so relieved she was there she didn't say anything, just led her into the living room and sat beside her on the sofa.

McConnel took her hand and held it, rubbing her thumb over her knuckles, looking at her.

Bitsy felt safe. FBI agents always had a weapon. Where did she keep it? She hadn't seen it on her so it must be in her purse.

"You want to tell me why you're so upset?"

"It's ridiculous."

"No. It's not."

"I saw a flash of light and went to the living room to get a better look." She told her about the cars. "I feel so stupid now. I overreacted. I know I did. I go into these panic modes for some reason."

"I think you're hypersensitive to everything around you, and I think it's a natural reaction, given the circumstances."

"Do you really think so, or are you just saying that to try to make me feel better?"

McConnel laughed. "I'm trying to make you feel better, but I do think it's true." She removed her hand from Bitsy's.

Bitsy tracked the ceiling, embarrassed to look at her.

"Hey." McConnel touched Bitsy's chin and moved her face tenderly toward her. "It's okay."

Her eyes were beautiful. At that moment her expression was full of acceptance.

Before Bitsy could stop herself, she ran the back of her fingers over McConnel's cheek. Warm and soft. The desire and urge were there, strong and intense. Why not follow them? She moved closer.

McConnel's lips parted slightly, inviting her in, but then she stopped and stood, her expression unreadable. "If I remember correctly, the bathroom is that way." She pointed toward the kitchen.

"Yes, just there." Bitsy motioned.

McConnel left the room.

Bitsy went to the kitchen, warmed the herbal tea, and waited for McConnel to join her, anxious at the thought of how the night would go.

CHAPTER EIGHT

McConnel leaned toward the bathroom mirror. "You almost kissed her. What are you thinking? You can't do this."

Bitsy probably had a misplaced attachment to an authority figure. It wasn't uncommon in McConnel's line of work. Bitsy was vulnerable. She hadn't stopped crying since their first interview, and now she was having panic attacks. Even if Bitsy did have a genuine attraction to her, it didn't give McConnel license to take advantage of her. She had to stay focused.

The self-reprimand jolted her back to reality. She freshened herself and returned the hand towel to the rack, then squared herself in front of the mirror. "You can do this."

She opened the bathroom door.

Bitsy was in the kitchen, making tea, and turned toward her. She placed a cup on the bar in front of her and motioned to the stool. "I put a little sugar in it. I hope you like apple and cinnamon." She smiled softly.

McConnel sat and sipped the herbal drink, enjoying the soothing scent and flavor as she glanced at Bitsy with hesitation.

Bitsy leaned on the counter. "I don't know what's wrong with me. One minute I'm fine, and the next I'm falling apart. I'm so sorry."

"No need to apologize. You're going through a lot. You'll feel differently when this is all over."

Bitsy squinted. "That's so odd. My momma said almost the same thing this morning."

"Well, there you go. Believe it. It's true."

Bitsy moved around the counter and sat next to her. "You're very sensitive for someone in law enforcement." She eased closer.

McConnel recognized a come-on when she saw one. She took Bitsy's hands. "I...We can't do this."

Bitsy straightened, a blush spreading across her cheeks.

McConnel released her. "It's not that I don't find you attractive. I assure you, I do. But you're a witness."

"Not a very good one."

Her sense of humor was disarming. McConnel couldn't stop her smile but recovered quickly. "Nevertheless, you're a witness, and it's unethical for me to take advantage of you in any way. I don't want to hurt you, or embarrass you, or make you feel uncomfortable, but I want to be clear—this can't happen."

"Ever?"

"Well, not under these circumstances."

Bitsy sighed and nodded. "I understand. I don't like what you're selling, but I understand."

McConnel took another drink and saw the time on the stove clock. It was later than she'd thought. "I should be going. Will you be all right?"

Bitsy glanced toward the kitchen window and stroked her throat. "I'll be fine."

"You don't sound very convincing."

Bitsy shifted.

"I can stay a while longer if you'd like?"

"Would you mind? I promise I'll behave myself."

"No problem."

"Let's go into the living room and talk." Bitsy clutched her cup of tea and walked toward the couch. She sat at one end while McConnel settled onto the other.

Bitsy offered a blanket, draping it over them as they got comfortable. She sipped her drink. "Tell me about yourself? You seem to know a lot about me, but I don't know anything about you." She laughed. "Except you follow the rules, and I assume you have a gun. How long have you been in the FBI?"

McConnel cringed. Her secrets were going to get in the way. What should she do? Tell Bitsy who she was? What would happen? How would she react? Best to just answer her questions and not elaborate for now. "I joined the FBI at twenty-six. Fourteen years ago."

"Did you always want to be in it?"

No, she didn't. She'd originally joined to better her skills at finding her sister or her killer. "I thought it would be a good career path."

"Are there a lot of female agents?"

"A few, but not as many as you'd think. I scored first in my class on the physical and intelligence tests. I'm a skilled marksman, so they couldn't get rid of me."

Bitsy chuckled. "I bet. Have you always worked cold cases?"

McConnel was stumbling over the questions to keep her secrets. "I worked in financial fraud for a while, after that in domestic terrorism, and then in cold case investigation. This is my third cold case." She felt relieved. All of that was true.

"Did you solve the other two?"

"Only one."

"Can you talk about them?"

"One was a murder of a bank president in Seattle, Washington. His stepbrother did it for the family inheritance. The other was the killing of a woman in Detroit who owned a chain of grocery stores. Never solved it, but I think the manager of one of her stores did it. We finally got him for embezzlement but couldn't pin him down for her murder."

"Why Hallie Lynn's case?"

There it was! McConnel took a deep breath. She'd rehearsed what she'd say. "There've been similar cases over the years in several different states. We have a task force because we think they're connected." So far, she'd managed to tell the truth, but then she lied. "I was assigned to Hallie Lynn's when they discovered her remains." It spilled out so easily. She was careful to tell Bitsy only what she needed to satisfy her curiosity. She tried to convince herself it was more true than false, but when she measured it out, the lie tipped the scale.

"So, did you grow up in Ohio?"

"I did." McConnel relaxed, glad to have finished the difficult questions.

"Where'd you go to school?"

"I got my bachelor's at Bowling Green and my master's from Cleveland State."

"What did you get your master's in?"

"Criminal justice."

Bitsy nodded. "That makes sense. Do you have any brothers or sisters?"

McConnel tensed. So much for being done with the difficult questions. What could she say that wasn't a full-blown lie? That she had a sister, but she passed away? That would just encourage more questions. "I was an only child." Her stomach knotted, but she managed to rationalize a half-truth.

"At least you didn't have to share like I did." Bitsy grinned. "I have three sisters."

That'd been in the case file, but McConnel wasn't going to mention it.

Bitsy yawned.

"I should go." McConnel started to get off the couch.

Bitsy grabbed her arm. "Don't go. Stay and watch a movie with me. I'll make some popcorn."

Obviously, she was still uneasy. McConnel parted the drape and surveyed the street. "Everything looks ordinary out there, but I'd love a movie and popcorn."

Bitsy arched an eyebrow. "Lots of butter?"

McConnel nodded.

"What's your favorite genre?"

"Something funny."

"I've got just the one."

They both fell asleep halfway through it.

McConnel woke when a dog barked. It was three thirty. She carefully rose and tucked the blanket around Bitsy, then wrote a note and put it on the kitchen bar. She left as quietly as she could and locked the door behind her, scanning the street before she got into her car. Nothing had changed.

❖

The rays of the early morning sun were dancing on the hotel carpet when McConnel's alarm sounded. She turned it off and rolled over, grazing her hand over the empty bed space beside her. It'd been the right decision, but it was a hollow comfort.

The phone chimed. FBI Field Office, Toledo. "Special Agent McConnel."

"Did you sleep well?" Terrill Jenkins, the special agent coordinator for the combined operation, was always irritatingly too chipper in the morning.

"Alone, but yes."

"I wanted to bring you up to date on your counterparts in North Carolina, Alabama, and Tennessee. Unfortunately, the news is not good. They're at a standstill. They have no bodies and nothing concrete to go on. How about you?"

"I'm making some progress. My main witness is cooperating. I'm meeting with her this morning. I have a few ideas about how to help her recall. I'd like you to check on a name that came up in one of my interviews, a boyfriend of the mother. Curtis Stillman. He was stabbed to death in Atlanta sometime in 1996. I need all the details you can get."

"Anything else?"

"Not right now. Any new cases?"

"No reports that meet our criteria in the last thirteen months in Tennessee, North Carolina, or Georgia. Alabama had one, but we're not ready to add it to our list just yet. It's questionable."

McConnel breathed a deep sigh of relief. "I've confirmed it's definitely a male. I've got my report ready and will send it in a little while."

"No surprise there," he said. "The profile workup was specific. Male, white, between the ages of twenty and thirty at the time of the Peeples kidnapping. Keep in touch."

"Will do. Is there any reason to eliminate the hypothesis that Hallie Lynn Peoples was the initial case?"

"No. Given the time of the disappearance, we still feel she was his first victim."

"Let me know as soon as you have anything about Stillman." McConnel ended the call.

She showered, dressed, and began to sort through the case information in the boxes, arranging what she thought she'd need for her meeting.

A text from Bitsy came in at seven forty-five. *Meet my house 10:30. C u then.*

At nine thirty McConnel gathered what she needed for the day, stopped at the bakery, then drove to Bitsy's.

She flashed the white paper bag in front of her when Bitsy opened the door.

Bitsy's eyes widened. "Ooh. Doughnuts?"

"No, sorry. Bear claws."

Bitsy's face lit up. "Even better." She motioned for her to come in. "They'll be great with the coffee."

McConnel stepped in, anxious to see how the morning would go.

CHAPTER NINE

Bitsy allowed herself a quick once-over of McConnel before closing the front door. From the first time they'd met, she'd appreciated her subtle curves, but after letting her thoughts review the previous night, and actually trying to kiss her, she seemed to have grown more appealing. *Guess you can't unring the bell.* She pushed all her thoughts aside and led McConnel to the kitchen.

She didn't want to discuss Hallie Lynn, but she was much more comfortable with McConnel now. "I can't thank you enough for last night. It was so sweet of you to stay. I'm sure you didn't get much sleep."

"Did you?"

"Thanks to you, I did get some. I walked through the door right before you pulled in. I'll just be a minute. Pour yourself some coffee." She reached for two cups and placed them on the counter, then went to her room, brushed her teeth again, freshened her makeup, and returned to the kitchen. Then she plated the bear claws and handed one to McConnel.

They ate in silence, accompanied by awkwardness, hesitancy. Bitsy wasn't sure if it was from McConnel's rejection the night before or if it was real or imagined.

When they finished their snack, McConnel gazed intently at her. "I think we need to talk."

Bitsy took a deep breath, unsure of what she'd say.

McConnel folded her hands in her lap. "I'd like you to go with me to the school."

Bitsy recoiled. Not *that*. She stood. "I told you I'd help, but I'm not going there. Ask me anything you want, but I won't do that."

McConnel moved close to her. "I need you to do this."

Panic crept into Bitsy's gut. Her palms began to sweat, and her heart rate increased. She backed away. "I can't. I won't put myself through that." She thought she'd made it clear that she could do only so much to help.

"Bitsy, I can't go any farther in this investigation unless you do this. I've got to have your assistance."

"Please don't ask me to do it. I can't."

"You can't, or won't?"

It was a fair question, but Bitsy didn't know the answer. She felt so much fear and anxiety at the thought of going to the school she couldn't delve deep enough past it to find the answer. "I'm not sure if you know this, but I've never gone back there after that night. My parents transferred me to a private school. I don't even drive by it."

McConnel's expression softened. "I wasn't aware. I'm sorry. Give me a minute. I want to get something from the car. I'll be right back."

She left before Bitsy could say anything more and returned a few minutes later with two large boxes and set them on the kitchen bar. "Come on." She motioned to the living room and then walked over and sat on the sofa, patting the cushion beside her.

Bitsy followed and sat.

"I'm sorry," McConnel said. "I thought after last night, you'd trust me enough to go with me, but I can see you're not able to do it. Let's try something else."

"What?" Bitsy filled with skepticism.

McConnel smiled. "We won't leave the house. I promise."

Bitsy's heart rate began to slow. "Okay. What is it?"

"I've taken photos and had them printed. Chief Gibson was able to help me with the location where you were standing when the abduction happened. I took them from that angle. Would you be willing to look at them?"

Bitsy rubbed her lips and glanced away. That was almost as bad as asking her to go to the school. She'd refused to look at any pictures during the original investigation. How hard would it be? Could she deal with the emotion of it? Was she ready? She wanted to do something significant, something meaningful to contribute, but what would it cost her?

"I'll help you through it. I'll be right here with you."

It was time to step up and help, even if she had to force herself. Bitsy turned toward her and nodded, determined to do what she felt she should.

The room was quiet and still. No cars on the street in front of the house. No dogs barking. No birds chirping.

"I'll help you," McConnel whispered.

Bitsy strained, holding back the anxious dread. She balled her fists and began to shake. She wiped at the tears as they spilled from her eyes.

"We're going to find out who did this and make him pay," McConnel said. "From now on, everything you do is for Hallie. Not the abduction. Not the murder. Not for him. Not to help me, but for her."

It *was* for Hallie, and Bitsy didn't have to do it alone. As comforting as the thought was, all she could do was nod.

McConnel guided her to the kitchen. "Sit here on the stool."

The tense strain in Bitsy's neck and shoulders subsided, and the trembling stopped.

McConnel went to the sink and washed her hands, then dried them with a paper towel. She reached into one of the boxes and pulled out a paper tablet and a few photos. "We'll start slow." She held up the notebook. "This is called a murder book, or cold case file. All the facts are in here. My notes, thoughts, speculations, hints, hunches, evidence, everything. I want to walk through some of this first. Then we'll come back to the schoolyard and what you saw. Okay?"

It sounded reasonable. Bitsy nodded.

"What did you do the day of the abduction?"

Bitsy eased into the memories, gathering them like pieces of broken glass on a sidewalk. "We had school." She cautiously searched for another. "I rode the bus home. That evening Momma and Daddy took me to the play."

McConnel nodded.

"I was excited to see Hallie in her part. She was a pumpkin." She smiled recalling the image. "Momma had made her costume because Hallie Lynn's momma didn't sew."

"Why weren't you in the play?"

Bitsy stopped. "That's a good question." She gazed at the ceiling, searching for the discarded memory. It appeared slowly, first obscure, then coming into focus. "I'd been sick and missed the practices, so I didn't get to be in it."

"When did the play end? How late was it?" McConnel turned pages in her book.

The anxious dread returned. "I don't remember what time, but it was late and dark." Her heart rate increased. She couldn't catch her breath.

"How dark?"

She clinched her fists. The queasy feeling began in her stomach, then slithered into her throat. She wanted to leave the thoughts behind, push them away. Do what she always did when it became too uncomfortable.

"Stay with it, Bitsy."

She swallowed, trying to get the acidic taste out of her throat. She sucked in a deep breath, making time to clear a path for the memories.

McConnel reached into the container and pulled out a photo, placing it in front of Bitsy on the counter—an old picture, somewhat faded. Perhaps an original from the crime scene.

"This is looking out past the parking lot from the school," McConnel said. "Can you show me where it happened?"

Bitsy clasped her hands, holding them as tightly as she could until her knuckles blanched. She forced herself to examine the photo, inspecting every detail. The lot was to the right. The sidewalk led past it to the main road, illuminated by a streetlamp. She inspected the rest of the picture. "Here." She indicated with a trembling finger. "It happened on the side street where there was no light."

"How did you see Hallie being abducted if it was so dark?"

Bitsy peered out the kitchen window above the sink, as if to catch a glimpse of that night. "There were some lights, but it wasn't a streetlight?" She strained to recall. She made herself look at the photo again.

McConnel placed another one in front of her. It was a view of the side street in late evening. "You're correct. In that year, there were no lights on the side street. I photoshopped them out to make it look like it did back then. It's dark, Bitsy. How did you see anything?"

Bitsy stared at the picture, then placed her finger on the street, going over it repeatedly, searching. And then it came to her. "Taillights. That's how I saw it. The taillights from a car were on."

McConnel placed her hand over Bitsy's and patted it but didn't say anything. She placed another photo in front of Bitsy.

"This is a view of the side street from where you were standing that night."

Bitsy grazed her lower lip with her teeth and looked away, closing her eyes. She fisted her hands. It was an unspeakable memory. How could she ever explain it to McConnel?

McConnel stood silent, not moving.

Bitsy could feel her watching her. She became aware of the grandfather clock ticking in the living room. *For Hallie. For Hallie.* She turned, quickly eyeing the picture, like swallowing some bitter medicine her momma had given her as a child. "I saw his pants in the taillights. They were black."

"Maybe jeans?"

"No. They were black. Like dress pants. Loose at the bottom, not tight like jeans."

"Did he walk behind the car?"

McConnel was still there, right beside her.

Bitsy looked into her warm and welcoming eyes. "Must have."

"Let's suppose he did get out of the car," McConnel said. "Why would he walk behind it? If the taillights were on, that meant the car was still running. That makes sense. He's planning to leave quickly. Did you see him walking or standing?"

Bitsy looked out the window again. "He moved toward her." The bile rose quickly, forcing its way into her throat, the acidic taste gagging her. She couldn't swallow it down. She jumped from the stool and ran to the bathroom, slamming the door shut behind her. She violently threw up in the toilet, retching, choking. When it was over, she rinsed her mouth and washed her face, trying not to smear her makeup but not caring if she did. Her hands shook. Her image staring back from the mirror was pale and drawn. There was nothing she could do about it. McConnel would see her at her worst.

She returned to the kitchen.

McConnel had poured her a glass of wine. "Drink this. You should have as much as you want."

Bitsy drew back, suspicious. Why would she tell her that? Was it going to get worse?

"I think it'll help with the next part," McConnel said.

"I can't continue. I have to get ready for a meeting at two."

"Clear your schedule for the rest of the day. You're so close, Bitsy."

"If I don't have that meeting, I could lose a lot of money."

"I understand." McConnel continued to watch her.

Did she really expect her to do it? "I'm not kidding. I can't miss that meeting."

McConnel pulled out a stack of papers stapled together. She placed them over the pictures.

Bitsy glanced at it. *Forensic Report.* Terror stuck. No way she could go into that much detail. She shook her head emphatically. "Please don't ask me to do this. I can't."

Did McConnel expect her to do it?

CHAPTER TEN

McConnel squinted in the afternoon sun, shining through Bitsy's kitchen window. She hated putting her through this. Was she pushing her too fast, too soon? Would she retreat again? The memories Bitsy had locked inside her were needed now, not later. It was true, Hallie Lynn had been in that grave for thirty years, but her murderer was most likely still out there, and possibly still killing. The joint operation in Tennessee, North Carolina, and Georgia had linked Hallie Lynn's killer to possibly twenty-two other similar cases over the years. Of all the ones lost, Hallie Lynn was the only one found. McConnel and the members of the operation were sure the other young girls had been killed and buried in a similar manner to Hallie Lynn, but they had no concrete evidence, nothing but speculation.

If Bitsy couldn't get through these next few minutes and make the needed breakthrough recollections, McConnel would be at a dead end like the team members in the other states. She had very few gathered facts that could help her. She knew how Hallie Lynn had died, approximately when it happened, where she was abducted, but McConnel didn't have enough evidence to uncover who did it. If Bitsy couldn't get past the trauma and remember what she saw, the case would never be solved. Their only other hope was if other victims were discovered. But it was a slim chance. Finding Hallie Lynn had been a fluke accident and luck.

Bitsy had to walk out on that ledge and stay there. She was obviously on the verge of recalling something critical, McConnel sensed it, and if they stopped now, Bitsy would shut down.

She tapped the report. "It's important to read this, Bitsy. It's important for you to know."

Bitsy violently shook her head and gripped the counter. "No. It's not. I don't need to know the details."

"Yes. You do. For Hallie. For you."

Bitsy leapt to her feet and stabbed her finger at the front door. "Get out of my house."

It took a moment for McConnel to realize what was happening. She'd never expected Bitsy would react so harshly, although it was always possible a witness would retaliate when confronted. She'd pushed her too far. She had to help her know she wasn't alone in her pain. She went to her. "Bitsy, you can do this."

"You don't know me. You have no right to interfere in my life. Who do you think you are?"

Bitsy had snapped shut like a steel trap right in front of her. McConnel understood. She'd done it herself when others got too close to her truths, but she refused to let Bitsy push her away. "It's not your fault Hallie Lynn was taken."

Bitsy retreated. Her muscles were so tight in her hands and arms that her veins were bulging. "I said get out." Her voice went up an octave as she continued to shout and point toward the door.

McConnel backed away to give her space. She suspected Bitsy didn't want *her* to get out. What she wanted and needed was to *get out* the pain she was feeling. "Bitsy, I'm here with you. You can do this."

Bitsy lunged toward her, fists drawn.

In that moment, McConnel understood her like she'd never understood anyone before. Bitsy wasn't attacking her. She was attacking *him*. Everything was skewed and twisted and jumbled so badly, Bitsy didn't stand a chance of getting through it without help. And she desperately needed it, right here, right now. McConnel planted her feet and prepared for what was coming.

Bitsy came at her hard and pounded her shoulder, then pummeled her arm.

McConnel blocked a blow to her face.

Bitsy started screaming. "Let go. Let go of her." Her face was contorted and red with rage. She tried to shove McConnel, but McConnel stood firm. Bitsy raised both her fists.

McConnel grabbed them and then slid her arms around Bitsy, holding on to her as tightly as she could. "It's okay. It's not your fault."

Bitsy writhed and tried to break free, but McConnel held on.

Bitsy screamed. "He took her. That son of a bitch took her. He looked at me and ran his finger over his throat and pointed at *me*. He took her and I didn't do anything." She started to drop to the floor.

McConnel steadied her and lowered her until she was on her knees, then released her.

The deep pain and anguish etched in Bitsy's face made it appear to be chiseled in stone. She screamed, "He took her, and I didn't do anything." She buried her face in her hands and sobbed.

McConnel drew her close and stroked her hair. "You were a child, Bitsy, not an adult. *He's* responsible, not you." She guided her from the floor, walked her upstairs to her room, and eased her onto the bed. Then she handed her tissues from the box on the nightstand and wrapped her in her arms.

Bitsy laid her head on her chest. "He killed her."

McConnel cradled her. "I know."

Bitsy moved closer to her. Her muscles relaxed. She lay in McConnel's embrace for over an hour, and finally her breathing became even, with only an occasional stuttered breath. When McConnel was sure she was in a sound sleep, she slid from her bed, went to the kitchen, and made a call.

"Lilly, this is McConnel. I'm with Bitsy. She won't be in the rest of the day. She's upset."

"Did she talk about it?"

"Yes, but it was traumatic."

"Well, you've gotten farther with her than anyone else ever has. Can I speak to her?"

"She's exhausted and asleep."

"Tell her when she wakes that I'll send Bo to the meeting. He can work with the clients and get another time to close the purchase. I'll also clear her schedule for tomorrow in case she needs it. She won't like it, but she'll get over it."

"I'll let her know."

"You'll stay there with her? You won't leave her alone? If you need to go, I can call her momma to come over."

"I'll be here with her. I won't leave until I'm sure she's okay."

"That's good. Tell her we all send our love."

"I will." McConnel ended the call.

She imagined Bitsy would sleep for a few hours. She placed the papers and photos into the box and moved them to the end of the bar. She ordered soup and toppings, and after it was delivered, she lay on the sofa, covered herself with the blanket, updated her notes, and waited for Bitsy to wake.

She startled when a horn blasted. The glare of the setting sun shone through the window. How long had she been asleep? She peered through the glass. Cars were in the driveways and parked on the street. She climbed the stairs and went toward Bitsy's bedroom to check on her but heard the shower running. She returned to the kitchen, where she warmed chicken noodle soup in the microwave and cut some French bread.

Bitsy walked in dressed in her night clothes and wrapped her arms around McConnel. "This isn't a come-on, I promise."

Her hug felt so good, McConnel almost wished it were. She smelled of coconut and lavender.

"I'm so sorry. Did I hurt you?" Bitsy inspected McConnel's arms, then lightly touched her shoulder.

"No. Not at all. How are you?"

She looked into McConnel's eyes. "I'm okay. Are you sure I didn't hurt you?"

"I'm fine. Are you hungry? I had soup and fresh bread delivered. I hope you don't mind."

"Do I mind? It smells wonderful. I'm famished."

Bitsy retrieved bowls from a cupboard and knives and spoons from a drawer, then set them on the bar. She lit a candle and put on soft music. The mood was relaxing and peaceful.

"I talked with Lilly," Bitsy said. "Thank you for letting her know what was going on. It was very thoughtful."

They sat.

"I hope you didn't lose as much money as you thought you might."

Bitsy shook her head as she swallowed a spoonful of soup. "Actually, it seems everyone's pretty understanding right now. Bo was able to reschedule for next week." She grew quiet, stopped eating, and took McConnel's hand. "I'm not ready to talk about the case again just yet, but I want to tell you I'll never forget what you did for me today. This entire experience with you has been the hardest thing in my life, but it's brought the greatest peace I've ever felt. It's a paradox at every step. But I'm not sure how to process all of this. I'm so confused. I can't seem to work through what I'm feeling."

How would Bitsy react if she knew who McConnel was in relation the Hallie Lynn? It would certainly complicate things. The dread of Bitsy finding out crept into McConnel's chest from somewhere in the shadows. She didn't have to know. Did she owe that to her, or was that something beyond this association? Was it an *association*? It felt like something deeper, and certainly more complex. The potential for a far more personal and intimate relationship was there, but obstacles, seemingly insurmountable, existed, and then there was the timing, and the situation itself. McConnel wanted a connection with her, but she didn't know Bitsy, not really. How could anyone know someone without spending time with them? Who was she? McConnel ached to get close to her, but did she have the right? And could she get that close without telling Bitsy who she was? Reveal all of her, not just a part? Bitsy wasn't the only one confused. "I should probably go."

"No, don't. Stay with me."

"I need a bath and a change of clothes."

"You can shower here, and I've got lots of things for you to wear. Stay. Only one thing. No talk about the case."

"If I stay, I want to know more about you."

"Okay, but nothing related to the investigation."

"I have to stay focused on it," McConnel said. "Don't forget it's why I'm here. I won't mention details if you promise to tell me everything you can about yourself."

If Bitsy could relax and just talk, she might reveal even more insight into what she had seen, whether she consciously realized it or not.

"I have more questions for you also. Quid pro quo."

McConnel stiffened. What if Bitsy asked her questions she didn't want to answer? She'd avoided earlier ones. Could she do it again? All of it, no matter how she responded, felt like lies. She expected Bitsy to answer her questions. McConnel would answer hers, but probably with only a portion of the truth. The thought of her deception gnawed at her stomach.

"I'll lay out some nightclothes for you on the bed in the guest room while you take a shower."

They finished their soup.

"I love the idea of you staying over. This is going to be fun."

Maybe. McConnel would have to ease into whatever they talked about. Bitsy was exhausted, emotionally and physically, and McConnel was wary. She'd have to be careful on both fronts. She showered and changed into a pair of lightweight cotton pajamas Bitsy had provided.

Bitsy sat curled on the couch when McConnel came to the living room. "I made some tea." She pointed to the iced glass on the coffee table, then sipped her own.

McConnel nodded and sat opposite her, needing separation. What questions would Bitsy ask? How detailed should she be with the answers? She'd worried the entire time in the shower.

They sat in silence for a few moments.

Bitsy inspected the glass in her hand. "How long will you be on the case? What happens if you don't get anywhere? How do you decide when to drop it?"

McConnel chuckled and leaned back into the sofa. "I thought you didn't want to talk about the case."

Bitsy rewarded her with a smile. "I don't want to talk about *my* part in the case."

"I see. I'm going to have to learn to keep up with you." McConnel took a drink, then placed the glass on the end table, giving herself time to formulate the answers. "I'll be on the case until I either find the killer or feel there's no longer a chance."

"Is that normal?"

"It's pretty typical."

"How did you get on it?"

"I asked to be assigned." That was a truth. McConnel reminded herself to tread cautiously.

"Why? You're from Ohio, not Georgia."

McConnel saw the red flags and caution tape around the question. She ran her hand over her thigh as she retrieved the lie. Tucking one leg underneath herself, she settled into the cushion. "I first heard about the case in a criminal justice class my freshman year of college, and it intrigued me. So, when the news about the discovery of Hallie Lynn's body became public recently, I asked my supervisor if I could be on the task force. They were happy to give the assignment to me."

"Really?" Bitsy tilted her head.

Perhaps it was the fear of losing something McConnel valued that kept her from sharing her truth with Bitsy. At that moment she realized Bitsy's interest in her was important to her, but one lie leads to another, like the twists in a cord. This she knew. She'd seen it time and time again. Now she was building a relationship on sand. She could stop it. Stop it right now and come clean, but what would Bitsy do with her whole truth? Maybe she could risk a portion of it.

Bitsy gazed at her with those soft, vivid eyes. "Are you all right? You're a little pale."

McConnel cleared her throat. "I want to tell you something, but it's personal, and it only complicates things when it gets personal."

"Are you worried about us getting too close?"

"Bitsy, you're nothing like I expected."

"You're nothing like I expected either. I pictured you like all the others—cold, calculating, just another investigator banging at my door, looking for answers no matter the cost. But I couldn't have been more wrong. You really seem to care about me, not just what I know or don't know."

"I do." McConnel ran her hand through her hair. Was she really going to say it? "I think about you in connection with the case, but it's more than that. I feel drawn to you."

Bitsy set her glass on the table and moved toward her. "It's been a long time since I've felt this attracted to anyone. We can keep things reasonably simple if you want. No obligations."

"Bitsy, I don't know if it's that simple for me. I'm not talking just about sex. I mean, yes, I'm very attracted to you in that way. But like I said the other night, I can't go there as long as you're a witness in a case I'm investigating. But I do want to get to know you more."

Bitsy looked at her hands. "I'm not talking only about sex either. I didn't mean to make it sound that way, and I understand it would be unethical for you to get involved with me while you're still trying to find Hallie Lynn's killer. So, what if we just take this time to learn more about each other?"

Bitsy's words reached into McConnel's heart. "That's a perfect idea." The guilt swept over her. Bitsy would tell the truth, and McConnel would hold back and lie. How would they ever be able to build anything?

Bitsy grinned and stood. "Want to start with popcorn and a movie again, and this time we stay awake?"

McConnel looked up at her. It was a start. She'd just have to trust that the right time to tell Bitsy her secrets would reveal itself.

CHAPTER ELEVEN

Bitsy stared out the office window. It'd been eleven days since she met McConnel. She rehearsed each one in her mind. It had to have been longer. Wasn't it at least a month? She folded her arms and leaned closer to the glass. A great blue heron waded in the shallow water at the far bank of the river, then struck with its powerful beak and captured its prey, probably a fish or frog. It was hard to know from this distance.

McConnel was in Atlanta for the day, meeting with the state forensic specialists and interviewing witnesses. She was a closed book when it came to telling how the case was going. Tonight, Bitsy would ask her to go home with her for the weekend to meet Momma and the girls. Daddy was in Macon for meetings with the governor's cabinet members on environmental issues and wouldn't be home for a few days. Bitsy laughed out loud. *Momma.* Her stand on banning plastic bottles from Georgia was the driving force behind Daddy's appointment to the committee. They were both on a first-name basis with the governor and practically every leader in the state, their home county of Effingham, and the city of Springfield.

Daddy was a stabilizing force in Bitsy's life. He had a way of calming things when she and her sisters got out of hand, and they usually did when all four of them were together. But most of all, he stood by her, no matter what.

Being with Momma and her three older sisters would probably do Bitsy and McConnel in, but Bitsy needed to go home. She'd put Momma off as long as she dared, and she needed McConnel with her because she couldn't face them alone. They'd ask too many questions. McConnel could screen the interrogation much better than Bitsy could. After all, it was her job. Bitsy would much rather listen to her than answer the probing questions Momma and her siblings would certainly ask, and McConnel would be able to answer them without the emotional trauma it'd cause Bitsy. They'd get to the heart of the case immediately and wouldn't let up until they'd wheedled every possible detail out of McConnel. Bitsy smiled at the thought of McConnel being grilled by Momma. She could hold her own, Bitsy was sure of it.

She didn't leave the office until nine that evening.

McConnel arrived at the house an hour later with another box and set it on the bar.

Bitsy peeked inside. More pictures and files. "Are we going to look at photos again?"

McConnel didn't answer. "How was your day?"

"Good."

McConnel touched the box. "I can't stay late. I need to get up early and review what's in these files."

"I hate that you have to drive over here all the time. Would you like to stay here for the rest of your investigation? It's much better than a hotel, and you'd have some company."

McConnel blinked and moved away slightly.

Bitsy stepped toward her. "You've got to be sick of that hotel, and it'd be easier on you to have all that information in one place and not have to drive back and forth all the time."

"That's thoughtful, but I don't think you'd like the murder board or pictures all over your house."

"You can put everything in one of the guest rooms. I won't go in there."

"Are you sure?"

"Yes."

"I'll think about it. That's very kind. Thank you."

"I have an idea." Bitsy approached it carefully. "It may help you to meet my momma. I'd like for you to go home with me to Springfield for the weekend."

McConnel frowned. "I'm sorry. I can't. I've got new information in that box, and I need to review it."

"You can bring it along. Besides, Momma will be a great source of information. She may remember something that could help."

"Are you sure?"

"I have to go home. I've put it off long enough. If I don't get back there soon, Momma's going to be here banging on my door. If you go with me, she and my sisters will lighten up on me and direct their inquisition at you." She laughed.

"Oh, thanks a lot."

"You can handle it. You're an FBI special agent."

"You enjoy saying that, don't you?"

"Very much."

"You've got three sisters and you're the youngest, right?"

"Yes."

"The baby! I bet you were spoiled rotten." McConnel smiled. "Okay, as long as you don't mind me digging into that box and you answering a few more questions." McConnel glanced at the container.

Bitsy already dreaded the thought. "I'll do my best."

It was possible the weekend wouldn't be what Bitsy wanted and needed. Her sisters could be relentless in their probing, and Momma could be a pistol. Yet they did know how she felt about it all and were protective, most of the time. They might even be thrilled to have a real live FBI agent to grill.

If she had to go home, she'd much rather have a buffer. McConnel would do nicely.

McConnel sat at the kitchen counter, seeming lost in thought.

"How'd the day go?" Bitsy asked.

McConnel nodded. "Okay."

"Did you get what you were looking for?"

"Partly. Unfortunately, it just added more confusion and reminds me I need a break to solve this case."

"Are you at all close to finding who did it?" Bitsy wanted to help more than ever, in spite of the anxious dread that searching her memories caused.

"I may need to bring in some help."

"How will you do that?"

"A call to the Bureau. They'd send me an additional agent."

"Can you tell me anything about what you've found out?"

"Not really. I'm sorry."

Frustrated, Bitsy wanted to do more. Her memories were important, but how much of what she saw was critical? McConnel had said, "Everything and anything." She'd try harder to remember. Maybe being home would help her more than she thought.

CHAPTER TWELVE

In the morning, as McConnel drove Bitsy to Springfield, she experienced the full ambience of the South. The large, majestic trees, moss clinging and dangling from their branches, mile after mile of pine trees, and the reddish dirt. She rode with her window down, taking in the scents. "My drive to Atlanta consisted pretty much of housing developments, but this is beautiful. Did you grow up here?"

"I did." Bitsy directed McConnel to turn right onto a divided highway. "Our house is technically in a small town called Pine Grove, but about three years ago it was annexed into Springfield. It's kind of sad that it doesn't exist anymore. We all still consider the area Pine Grove. It's a touchy topic with Momma, so don't bring it up. My sisters went to school here. I took the bus to Springfield because Momma and Daddy thought it was a better school, and then I went to a private academy. My sisters are touchy about that subject, so don't bring it up either."

McConnel laughed. "Anything else off-limits?" She didn't know Southern culture, but she'd already learned firsthand that things were much slower paced here. You couldn't just ask for information. You had to stop and discuss the weather, your family, and the neighbors. "How's your mom 'n 'em?" was a requirement, like cornbread or grits with your meal or sweet tea in the afternoon. "What are your sisters like?"

"They're Colliers. Full of piss and vinegar, unafraid to tell you what they think, and very pushy when they want something. We all have Daddy wrapped around our little fingers, but Momma is a whole 'nother world."

"Do all your family members call him Daddy or just you?"

"We all do. Most people down here refer to their parents as Daddy or Momma. Mary Ruth, my sister Tilly's daughter, calls him Pa-paw."

Bitsy's family was fascinating, and McConnel hadn't even met them yet. "Tell me about your sisters?"

"Tilly's the oldest, then Louise, Janie, and me. I don't know who'll stop by the house this weekend. Tilly lives just up the street with her husband Clifford and their daughter. Louise and her husband, Bobby Ray, have a gaggle of kids. They live about thirty minutes away. And Janie and her husband, John Henry, have three children and live on the other side of Springfield."

"How many children do Louise and her husband have?"

"Five."

"Yikes."

"I know. She shouldn't have had any. All I can say is, if she's there this weekend, take anything she says with a grain of salt."

"I suppose you aren't as close to her."

Bitsy frowned and shook her head. "Slow down and turn right onto that one-lane road."

McConnel did as directed. No lines on the pavement, so she opted for the middle.

"Louise is an entity all her own."

"Who are you closest to?"

"Probably Tilly. She's always accepted me no matter what I did." She looked over at McConnel. "And I've done some things I'm not proud of."

McConnel shrugged. "Haven't we all. Want to share?"

Bitsy laughed. "Not really. I've always been able to talk with Tilly about anything. She's six years older than me. Louise, on the other hand, is opinionated, stubborn, judgmental, and irritates the hell out of me."

A deep sadness engulfed McConnel. It was hard to relate to Bitsy's feelings about her sisters. She'd always wondered what it would have been like to have Hallie Lynn in her life, but *he* took her. She squeezed the steering wheel.

Bitsy touched her arm. "You okay?"

McConnel relaxed her grip. Bitsy was a nice diversion.

"You said you were an only child?"

That wasn't exactly what McConnel had said, but she wasn't going to draw attention to it by correcting Bitsy. She nodded. "There were just me and my mom, and dad. My mother passed when I was eighteen."

Bitsy furrowed her brow. "I'm so sorry. That must have been horrible. What happened?"

"Breast cancer."

Bitsy patted McConnel's forearm. "Is your daddy still alive?"

"Yes. He moved to Florida. I haven't seen him in over a year."

"You aren't close?"

"Not really."

"That's too bad. Daddy is such a rock in my life. He's gone for a few days, so you won't get to meet him." Bitsy pointed. "Turn left here."

McConnel pulled onto a long, shell driveway. "Good grief, Bitsy."

The white house with its red roof and shutters was huge—a two-story with a wraparound porch. A veranda? It looked like something out of a magazine for Southern living. Moss covered the magnificent live oak trees, stone pillars stood on the four sides of the yard, hanging flower baskets adorned both the first- and second-floor porches, and the hedges were perfectly manicured.

McConnel turned off the car. "Holy crap!"

"I know. It's a little intimidating at first. You'll get used to it." She pointed. "My room's up there on the second floor, facing front. Yours is next to mine."

An older version of Bitsy stood at the screen door. Momma? Same cheekbones and height, but her mid-length hair was darker than Bitsy's. She wore a light tan-and-black flowing dress with a leather belt and leather heels, her glasses secured by a gold chain around her neck. She was gorgeous. She opened the door and waved, her hand floating in the air.

Bitsy sighed. "Remember, stand your ground no matter what. Just keep telling yourself it's only for a few days."

McConnel sucked in a breath. How would Bitsy's family react to her? Why did she care what impression she made? She'd be gone in a matter of weeks and never see these people again. But for some reason their opinion was important. She straightened and stood beside Bitsy, facing the house. "What's your mother's name?" she whispered.

"Call her Mattie." She returned the exact same wave to her mother. "I brought someone for you to meet."

McConnel got the fleeting impression Bitsy was offering her up like a lamb to the slaughter and enjoying every minute of it.

"I see that," Mattie said. She swung the screen door open wider and stepped out as she smiled. Not a full grin. More like she held part of it back.

Bitsy covered her mouth. "Don't mistake that look. She's luring you into her lair."

McConnel's laugh was nervous, mixed with a smidge of anxiety and hesitation. It was silly to feel this way, but she'd mostly worked with men and was more comfortable around them. For a lesbian to say that was probably odd, but it was the way she felt. These women were feminine and stylish. McConnel was out of place and out of her comfort zone. It reminded her she had some growing to do. Maybe that was one of the things that attracted her to Bitsy. Among her many fine qualities, she had a sense of elegance and was different from all the other women McConnel had been with over the years.

They stepped onto the veranda.

Mattie hugged Bitsy. "Darlin', I'm so glad you're home."

"Momma, this is FBI Special Agent Cecilia McConnel. She likes to be called McConnel, so please don't call her Cecilia or CeCe."

Mattie frowned. "I won't. Although Cecilia is quite a lovely name. I'd think she'd want to use it."

"Momma!" Bitsy chirped.

"It's wonderful to meet you. I'm Mattie Collier." She offered her hand.

McConnel shook it gently. "The pleasure's mine."

They carried their luggage into the house.

"Just leave your things there," Mattie said, pointing to the floor. "Harold, our hired man, will take them upstairs in a moment."

Her home smelled of honeysuckle, wood, and furniture polish. A beautiful, full bouquet of pink and white roses sat on an antique side table against the far wall.

"Bitsy, what are the sleeping arrangements?" Momma asked.

Bitsy looked at McConnel and smiled. "She's next to me."

"That's good to know." Mattie eyed McConnel.

Heat rushed to McConnel's neck and cheeks. Bitsy wasn't kidding. This woman had balls of steel. She had to say something to redirect her attention. "Tell me about your beautiful home."

Mattie turned toward her, looped her arm in hers, and led her through the house. "It was built in the 1940s by my momma and daddy. The original homestead is next door, where my sister, Tallulah, lives."

"She's not stopping by, is she?" Bitsy asked. "You never know what's going to happen with her. She's about six slices short of a full loaf."

Mattie stopped and glared at Bitsy. "That is enough, young lady."

Bitsy grinned at McConnel.

At that moment McConnel knew the weekend was going to be an eye-opening experience.

"This house has six bedrooms, five full baths, and lots of areas for entertaining," Mattie said, continuing to lead McConnel.

"What's your favorite?" McConnel asked.

"Well, sweet you for asking." Mattie's green eyes lit up.

Bitsy chuckled. "That'd be the Card Room."

"Mary Elizabeth, hush." Mattie removed her arm from McConnel's. "It's the Gathering Room."

"That's where Momma and her friends *gather* to gossip and play Texas Hold'em until all hours of the night." Bitsy motioned to her left. "In there."

The room was open and light, with floor-to-ceiling windows on the east wall, edged by laced, flowered curtains. A round, ornate wooden game table with four plush chairs occupied the center, and a light with a multicolored stained-glass lampshade depicting birds in flight hung above it. Original oil paintings decorated the walls.

McConnel recognized Bitsy's style in the one above the fireplace and moved closer to get a better view. A walkway lined with flowers and lush trees that seemed to go on forever. On each side of the path were beautiful bushes dominated with purple blooms, topped with various colors of blue, yellow, and white. It was breathtaking. "Bitsy, did you do this?" She leaned closer. Bitsy's signature was on the bottom right, just above the frame. "It's gorgeous."

Bitsy stood beside her. "I can't believe you guessed before you saw my name."

McConnel clasped her hands in front of her. "It's impressive."

"You girls hungry? We'll have lunch out on the veranda." Mattie left the room.

Bitsy leaned closer. "Momma's secretly glad we're staying in separate rooms. She's come a long way over the years, but she has her limits. She probably thinks we're sleeping together."

"Are you going to tell her we're not?"

"Maybe." Bitsy laughed and rubbed her hands together. "This is going to be fun."

In late afternoon, Bitsy took McConnel on a stroll around the grounds. The grove of pine they walked through was quiet, the forest floor soft beneath their feet.

"Bitsy, were you able to let go of Hallie Lynn after a time?"

Bitsy reached for a cluster of needles on one of the branches and plucked them off, bringing them to her nose and sniffing. Then she tossed them into the air, took in a deep breath, and folded her arms tightly across her chest.

A protective response McConnel knew well.

Bitsy walked a few more steps before she spoke. "I think I've never let her go. I just shoved thoughts of her deeper into my heart so I could get on with my life, but she's always there to some degree. I'd like to bury her at the cemetery here with my people. Her mother died a few years after Hallie Lynn was taken. Do you know if she has any other family? Do I need to talk to someone about it? How can I get her remains to bury her?"

McConnel hadn't expected those questions. As Hallie Lynn's only living relative, she'd have the right to claim her remains if she established their blood connection. But if she did, her job would be in jeopardy because she'd kept her ties to Hallie Lynn a secret from the Bureau. She wouldn't have been able to work the case if they'd known she was related. Should it be Bitsy who laid Hallie Lynn to her final rest? McConnel had never known her sister. They'd never met, never interacted. But Hallie Lynn and Bitsy had. They were best friends, went to school together, spent the night with each other, played together, loved each other.

At that moment McConnel wanted to tell Bitsy who she was, but she'd withheld the information this long. How would Bitsy respond? To reveal that she'd lied could cause a reaction she wasn't prepared for. Bitsy could rebuff her and withhold needed information. It was a troubling thought and loomed over her, lingering. Why tell her if she didn't need to? Of course, Bitsy might find out. If McConnel petitioned for Hallie Lynn's body, all Bitsy needed to do was contact the state forensic office, and they'd tell her who claimed the remains.

McConnel stopped walking. "Would it bring you peace to have her here with you?"

Bitsy turned toward her. "It would. Very much." Tears filled her eyes. "Can you check for me?"

McConnel nodded. Maybe she could avoid having her secret discovered. Maybe the killer was already dead. But what if he was alive? Because of the other similar cases in other states, chances were he was alive and still killing. If he was caught, there'd be a trial. She'd have to testify. Right now, she was walking a tightrope trying to keep her identity a secret from both Bitsy and her employer. The connection from Hallie Lynn to McConnel was obscure, but if someone in the FBI dug deep enough, they could find out Hallie Lynn was a twin and what had happened to her sibling. And if they discovered that, they'd know she'd lied about her reasons for wanting on the case. She could get fired for not revealing that she was Hallie Lynn's relative. As hard as it was to uncover a secret, it was even harder to keep one. Her stomach soured. The evening cool brought a chill that swept through her.

After supper, McConnel had planned to go to her room and sift through the box she'd brought with her, then remembered what Bitsy had said about her mother possibly having some information she could share. "Mattie, would you be willing to go over some pictures of the case I brought with me and give me your thoughts on some things?" she asked.

Mattie grinned and rubbed her hands together. "I'd love to. Let's do it in the kitchen."

McConnel brought the container marked number three and set it onto the table, then pulled out the pictures and placed them in front of Mattie.

Bitsy excused herself and left the room.

Mattie sat next to McConnel and shuffled through the photos. Then she picked up an eight-by-ten of the officers involved and pointed. "That's Sheriff Atwater and that deputy. What was his name?" She put her hand to her cheek. "Watts...Water...?"

"Jasper Watkins?" McConnel asked.

She stabbed at the photo. "That's right. Gerald Atwater started out as a deputy a year or so before Hallie Lynn was taken. He and Jasper didn't get along, and Jasper constantly complained about him. Said he never knew where he was half the time."

"What do you know about them?" McConnel asked.

"Jasper's folks are from the next county over. Nice people. His parents passed about five years ago. He was a likable kid. I knew the sheriff at the time, Mason Tucker, and he didn't like Gerald too much either. Said he always got too involved with the back end of the law."

"What do you mean?"

Mattie laid the photo on the table and exchanged it for one of Tucker. She tapped the picture. "He went to his grave blaming himself for not finding out who took Hallie Lynn. So many people blamed themselves." She looked toward the entranceway of the kitchen, then lowered her voice. "Most of all Bitsy. I thought she'd never get over it. Still hasn't." She clutched McConnel's arm. "You've got to find out who killed Hallie Lynn. You have to, or Bitsy's never going to have any peace."

McConnel redirected her to the deputies. "What about Gerald and Jasper?"

"Oh! Sorry." She patted McConnel's arm. "Sheriff Tucker used to come to our house now and again with a few of the other officials from the county. They played poker with my husband Albert, Bitsy's daddy. He told us one night that Gerald took things from crime scenes and that he'd caught him once sitting in his car for five hours outside the apartment of a waitress from the local diner when he was supposed to be on patrol. It infuriated Tucker."

"Why didn't he fire him?"

"Deputies were hard to come by."

"What'd he do about it?"

Mattie shrugged. "I don't know. I guess he called him to task. He never brought it up again."

"What about Deputy Watkins? Any trouble with him?"

"Jasper?" She pressed her lips together. "If anything, he was the opposite of Gerald. He got the hot seat for not writing *enough* speeding tickets. I used to fly down I-29 like I was haulin' white lightnin'." She grinned. "He stopped me at least five times and never once gave me a ticket. He was a sweet kid. Have you talked with him?"

McConnel nodded. "Several times. He lives in Athens. Works at the university."

Mattie held the picture of both deputies standing side by side. "This must have been taken at that car crash site about a month before Hallie Lynn's disappearance." She pointed to the wrecked car in the background. "That was a mess. Two drunken teenagers." She offered the photo to McConnel.

McConnel inspected the images of the two men and then set it aside.

Mattie sifted through the photos and held another one with the two deputies and several others gathered in a circle, discussing something. She passed it to McConnel. "This one was taken three days after Hallie Lynn disappeared."

"How do you know?"

"It's in front of the school." She pointed. "See the date on the information board on the far right?"

McConnel looked closely, inspecting the group. Gerald was turned to the right, with his back almost to the camera. "They look like they need a note from their mother to be in police work."

Mattie laughed. "They were young, for sure. Gerald came over to the house a couple of times to check on Bitsy. I didn't let him see her."

"Why not?"

"Bitsy was in such a state, we didn't let her talk with anyone, other than Chief Gibson, who was in charge of the investigation. Did you interview him?"

"Yes. We've spoken several times."

"He's such a dear man. He's another one that almost died of a broken heart because of the case."

"He's been a great help to me."

"Tell me about the forensics. Anything revealing you can share?" Mattie asked.

"I can't. It's an open case."

"Can I see a copy of it?"

"Sorry, no."

"I have connections. I can get a copy if I want to badly enough."

McConnel admired her intimidation tactics. "Nice try."

"May I ask some questions about it?"

"Yes."

"Could they tell how she died?"

"A broken hyoid bone indicates strangulation."

"Oh, my. Were there any other injuries?"

McConnel shifted nervously in her chair. How much should she tell Mattie? "Two fingers were broken on her left hand."

Mattie rubbed her chin just the way Bitsy did. "Hallie Lynn was left-handed."

"Are you sure?"

"Yes. I remember. The girls were here in the kitchen." She pointed. "At this very table, coloring."

McConnel stroked the surface. She was left-handed also. She imagined Hallie Lynn holding a crayon, laughing and talking with Bitsy.

"I'd made cookies, chocolate chip, their favorite, and set the plate on the table. Hallie Lynn laid the crayon down from her left hand and took one. She had the sweetest little smile. You know, you remind me of her when you smile. Isn't that odd?" She put the photos in the box and sighed deeply.

McConnel's heart skipped a beat. They weren't identical twins, but their features must have been similar enough that Mattie could recognize and make a subconscious connection. What if she saw other similarities and guessed who she was? That wasn't realistic. No one even knew Hallie Lynn had a sister, let alone a twin, and she was never able to grow to adulthood. McConnel had to get a grip on her fears. In some ways Mattie's comparison was comforting because it brought her closer to Hallie Lynn. It was like someone had said, "You look just like your sister."

"How's Bitsy doing with your questions?" Mattie asked.

"It's difficult for her, but I think she's doing all she can."

"Oh, good Lord. What time is it?" Mattie grabbed her phone and pressed the button. "I've got to get next door to check on Tallulah. See you later." She stood.

"Thanks for the information, Mattie. You've been very helpful."

Mattie cupped McConnel's cheeks. "Sweetheart, thank you for all you're doing. Take care with Bitsy. She's precious and oh so delicate right now."

Mattie left through the back kitchen door and descended the steps.

McConnel closed the box.

Bitsy came into the kitchen. "Are you through for the night?"

McConnel nodded.

"Do you want to have some fun?"

"Sure. What's up?"

"Tilly and Janie are coming over. We'll get Momma to play Texas Hold'em with us. You do know how to play?"

"Yes. How much for buy-in?"

"Twenty bucks, and I'm telling you right now, Momma loves to bluff, but you can't tell when she's doing it. Don't trust her. Ever!"

"My momma always said don't gamble with strangers." McConnel laughed.

"Good advice. Janie never bluffs and never bets big unless she has a good hand. Tilly, you never know what's going on with her."

"What about you?" McConnel grinned, waiting to hear what she had to say.

"Me? I'm just an average player."

"Sure you are."

A night of distracting entertainment would be good. Soon it would be time to approach Bitsy with an important question, one that might be the most difficult for her to answer. What was the shiny in the *shiny dark*? McConnel suspected Bitsy knew the answer.

CHAPTER THIRTEEN

Sunday morning Bitsy lay under the covers and listened to the shower. McConnel was in there naked. Images of her body next to her grew more vivid, bringing frustration and longing. She got out of bed and dressed. When she was sure McConnel had finished and was fully clothed, she rapped on her door.

"Come in."

McConnel's hair was still wet and hanging in ringlets around her ears. Adorable.

Bitsy moved toward her. "I'm going to call the state tomorrow and see if I can get Hallie Lynn's remains. I want her buried here."

The smile left McConnel's face. "The state won't release her yet."

"I thought they have all they need."

"Not necessarily. You never know what will turn up in an investigation. I may find something that needs confirmation or review. She may have more to tell us."

Bitsy didn't want to wait. Hallie Lynn had been away long enough. "What if you don't find who killed her? Will she just stay there? Won't I ever be able to bring her home?"

McConnel sat on the unmade bed and tossed the pillows aside. "A large percentage of cold cases are never solved, but I'll find him. I won't stop until I do."

"But what if you don't? What if time runs out and you have to quit the case?"

"Well, there's always that possibility, but I'm close. I just need a break, something that will bring it a little closer. I'd like to stay here another day, if it's possible. I need to try something."

What did she want to do? "I don't think I can remember anything else. I don't see the point." It was good to be home, but it was time to leave because unpleasant thoughts were beginning to creep in. Twice when she'd walked through the hall, she caught a flash of Hallie Lynn racing her down the stairs.

"I'd like to meet with you and Chief Gibson here at the house. He's the one who initially interviewed you, and it might be productive to get you two in the same room, especially here, and I think your momma could also help."

"Why? I don't see that happening." She sat beside her on the bed. The contentment she'd felt moments ago had vanished, and now anxiety and dread were beginning to push their way in. "I don't want to meet with him. Do we have to?"

McConnel repositioned and looked her straight in the eyes. "I think you still have some memories locked inside that will help me. Please, Bitsy. I know it's hard, but I need this."

"Why?"

McConnel clasped her hand. "I see what happens. Every time I ask you to remember, you get a panicked look on your face. I'm not oblivious to what you go through. I know how hard this is, but I need to be able to ask the people who were involved spontaneous questions. I need you two to be in the same room. Who was here at the house with you when the chief interviewed you early that morning?"

Bitsy withdrew from her touch.

"I care very much about you," McConnel said. "I empathize with what you're going through, but I have to push to get every possible speck of information I can from you to solve this case. Please trust me and know that I wouldn't ask if it wasn't vital. I assure you that you're helping. You're the key to unlocking this case. The chief cares a lot about you too, and he wants to help. You'll be in good hands, and of course I'll be there too."

McConnel wasn't going to stop probing.

"I want to help, but it's so hard."

"I know. I'm sorry to have to put you through this again. Your mother's going to be perturbed."

"Why's that?"

"Because I've made you cry and upset you."

The angst subsided. McConnel's words had eased her mind. "Don't worry about her. Momma's…What can I say? Momma."

McConnel slid from the bed. "I hope you don't mind, but I need to spend some time alone, going over the files. It's no reflection on you. I just need to concentrate. I feel like I'm not seeing something in the information."

Bitsy stood. "I get it."

McConnel looked more stressed than usual. *Usual.* Had they spent enough time together that Bitsy recognized what was usual for her? Did they have the beginnings of something special? How involved with her did she want to be? "Would you like breakfast?"

McConnel scrunched her face. "Not right now."

"I'll check on you later." Bitsy left her room.

At breakfast, she poked at her scrambled eggs and grits, and glanced at the empty chair beside her, a twinge of abandonment gnawing at her.

Momma stopped eating. "Honey, what's wrong? You haven't touched a thing. Are you ill, or just frazzled? Will the sleeping arrangements remain the same?"

It was none of her business what she and McConnel did or didn't do. Bitsy placed her fork on her plate. "Honestly, Momma."

"Will you be staying a few more days? Daddy gets home late Tuesday evening."

Momma had deliberately changed the subject, and it was just as well. Bitsy didn't want to fight. "I think probably another night." She sipped her coffee, then set the cup on the delicate china saucer. "Momma, I think I'm…in trouble."

Momma grabbed her hand. "What kind of trouble could you possibly get into? You don't do anything but work."

"Heart trouble."

"Oh! That. How can that be anything? You haven't known her long enough."

Bitsy withdrew from her grasp. It was risky discussing this subject with her. She should be talking to Tilly, but she and her family had gone to an Atlanta Braves game, so who knew when she'd be available. Bitsy needed someone to listen right now. "Momma, there's just something about her." She pressed into the back of the chair. "You're right. We only met less than two weeks ago, but I know the important things about her. She's gentle, and kind, easy to talk with, thoughtful, and I feel safe with her." She folded her hands in her lap. "More than safe. Confident. But this isn't logical. The only thing we have in common is Hallie Lynn." She rubbed her hands together. "I asked her to stay at my house until she's through with the case."

Momma's eyes widened. She placed her fork on her plate. "No! You did not. I can't believe it." She patted the corners of her mouth with her napkin, then placed it in her lap. "You were involved with that Kerrie or Karren woman for almost a year. You never asked her to move in with you."

"You know perfectly well her name was Katrina. It was three years ago, and you're right. I didn't ask her. McConnel's not moving in, just staying at the house until the case is over."

"First you fell in love with that Irish woman, Rebecca, and ran all over the country with her. Then you married Sondra Hanover, and we all know how that turned out." She flitted a wave. "Then *Katrina*. Bitsy, I can't keep track of all the women who meander through your door."

Bitsy slapped the table, instantly enraged, regretting she'd brought up the subject. She'd known better and had done it anyway. It was her own fault. After all these years she still wasn't sure if Momma insulted her on purpose or not. "That's not fair, and you know it. I've had three relationships in my entire life. It's true none of them lasted for any significant time, but I assure you women do not *meander* through my door."

Momma motioned for her to stop. "All right. I get the point. I'm sorry. But honey, you need to be careful these days. Did you see her identification? Is she who she claims to be?"

She'd put Bitsy in a defensive position. She had no choice but to stand her ground and fire back. "How can you ask that? You've been with her. You see how she acts and what she does."

Bitsy recalled her first meeting with McConnel. No, she hadn't seen her badge. All she saw was the business card she'd left with Lilly. She squirmed in the chair and stared straight ahead.

"Bitsy, stop that. You're ruminatin', darlin'."

Bitsy immediately picked up her napkin and wiped the corners of her mouth. "Momma, excuse me. I believe I'll go upstairs."

"You aren't going to finish your breakfast?"

Bitsy pushed away from the table and tossed her napkin onto the chair. "I'm not hungry." She left the room, feeling Momma's eyes on her all the way to the staircase.

McConnel's bedroom door was half open. Bitsy couldn't see her anywhere in the room from her position in the hallway. She knocked softly and entered without waiting for an invitation.

McConnel sat on the floor by the far side of the bed, pictures and files spread around her. She hesitantly looked up like she was concentrating deeply.

Bitsy immediately regretted disturbing her. It was obvious she'd broken her train of thought. "I'm sorry. I thought you might be hungry. May I get you something?"

McConnel didn't answer, just stared at her, then came back from wherever she'd been. "What?"

"I said, would you like something to eat?"

"Do you want me to come downstairs?"

"Do you want to take a break?"

McConnel reached for her phone. "It's ten. Now that I think about it, I am kind of hungry." She stood and stretched, then went to the window and peered out, moving one of the curtains aside. "Bitsy, what shape were the taillights of the car that night?"

Bitsy slid into the cushioned chair and gripped the armrest. The question wasn't too invasive. She'd have to force the memory to appear. She'd spent so many years pushing them out, it seemed unnatural to invite them in. She closed her eyes and tried to bring the image center stage, but it wouldn't appear, and she wasn't willing to spend the time and waste the emotional effort to recall it. "You know, I just can't remember. May I see your FBI badge?"

"What?"

"Your badge. I'd like to see your identification."

McConnel crossed the room to her purse and reached into the side pocket, hesitated, then lifted her empty hand. "Why?"

"I've never seen it."

"What's going on?"

"Nothing. I just want to see the damn badge."

"You don't need to see it."

"Yes, I do."

McConnel stepped toward her, stopping before she reached her. "No, you don't."

Bitsy glared at her, the way she'd always done when she demanded something and refused to back down. It was a dependable tactic and had worked on everyone else: Lilly and Bo at work, her ex-wife, customers who wouldn't pay her price. She intensified the stare and then balled her fists for effect. That *always* worked.

McConnel didn't budge. She stood rigid, eyes fixed on her. "Bitsy, what's going on?" Her voice was soft, full of concern.

Hearing it tempered Bitsy. She stood. "Nothing. I just want to see your badge."

"Are you upset because I needed to be alone for a while? Silence helps me work through my thoughts. The information is jumbled, and I can't get it organized the way I need to. I'm sorry if I offended you."

That's all it took to render Bitsy defenseless.

She looked into McConnel's eyes. Care and warmth were there to greet her. How could anyone she'd known for such a short time look at her that way? Was it real? Did Bitsy imagine it because she'd been so lonely for so long? Could she trust it? "Who are you?"

CHAPTER FOURTEEN

Bitsy's question pierced McConnel, exploding like a stick of dynamite, penetrating every cell.

The possibility of something special with Bitsy was there. It was in the way she responded to McConnel, the way they interacted, their tender, intimate moments. But the closer they seemed to get, the deeper the harbored secrets wedged between them.

It was not a time to risk losing Bitsy's confidence and trust. If she wasn't going to tell Bitsy who she really was, then she needed a diversion. She returned to her purse, pulled out her badge, and handed it to her.

Bitsy inspected it closely, running her fingers over the raised gold letters. "If you expect me to trust more, then I need some questions answered."

"Fire away." It was a dangerous response because it left McConnel open and exposed, but she was a good liar. It was part of her skill as an agent. She'd been proud of it, until now. Not with Bitsy.

"Why would an FBI agent from Ohio be assigned to this case in Georgia?"

Careful! "That's confidential. I can't share that information with you." At that moment McConnel hated her job. In addition to her own secrets, there was this. As an agent, she could share very little with anyone. How would she ever be able to have any type of meaningful, intimate relationship, especially with Bitsy? No wonder she was alone. The familiar ache in her stomach grew stronger.

"Are you by yourself on this case?"

"Yes. Until I need more help." It wasn't a lie, at least not a full one. She wasn't alone. She had the states of Georgia, North Carolina, Tennessee, and the entire force of the FBI behind her. Because of the other cases in those states that were possibly connected to this one, it was much bigger than anyone could imagine.

"I don't understand. How can you be from Ohio and have jurisdiction in Georgia?"

"FBI has interstate authority."

"So, all the evidence you gather, the state of Georgia can use against whoever killed Hallie Lynn?"

"Yes. Kidnapping is a federal crime. Because Hallie Lynn was taken, and then her body found thirty years later, that falls under both federal and state laws."

Bitsy didn't say anything for a moment, as if deep in thought.

McConnel was glad for the break. The conversation was dangerously close to her truths. "I assure you my authority to work this case is legitimate."

Bitsy nodded, then rubbed her thigh. "Okay, thanks. That helps."

McConnel wanted to grab hold of her, whisper who she was and why she was here. Bitsy deserved the truth. She deserved to know the secrets. The pit of lies McConnel had dug was so deep now she got dizzy looking into it. Every time she thought of the possible consequences of withholding the truth from Bitsy, it sickened her, and the more time they spent together, the more difficult it would be to tell her the truth. But she had to do her job. She'd never imagined she'd ever feel like this about Bitsy. If anything, she was sure the intense negative feelings she'd had for her since she was eighteen years old would carry her through all of it.

Many people were depending on her to solve this crime, including Bitsy. It'd been a mistake to let their personal interaction go this far. No amount of rationalization would ever justify her not doing her job. It was time to stop thinking about what she wanted and focus on her obligations. It was the only way she could get through this investigation without her heart being ripped apart when Bitsy found out her secrets. Whatever was between them would be over, and she'd better get ready for it. "I'd like to invite Chief Gibson here so you, he, I, and your momma can talk. Would you be up to it? I know it won't be easy, but it'd help me a great deal."

Bitsy rubbed her eyelid. "I suppose."

"I'll call him and set it up. Will your mother mind?"

Bitsy grinned. "Are you kidding? She'll be in her glory."

"Was your dad with you that night?"

Bitsy looked at the ceiling. "He was there. I remember him cradling me in his arms, but I don't recall who was in the room with me when Chief Gibson asked questions."

"Let's ask Mattie," McConnel said.

In the living room, Mattie sat in one of the overstuffed chairs, doing something McConnel had never seen. She held two small paddles and was pulling thin thread between each one. The process made a clicking sound.

Mattie stopped the motion. "What are you girls up to?"

"We're going to get something to eat," Bitsy said. "Would it be all right with you if we invited Chief Gibson over this evening?" She pointed to McConnel. "The FBI agent here would like to have a conversation with you, me, and him." She smiled.

Mattie placed the paddles and thread in her lap, removed her glasses, and peered at McConnel. "Is that right?" She shifted her gaze to Bitsy. "Do you think you're up to it, Mary Elizabeth?"

Bitsy nodded, "Yes. I'll do it."

"Well, this is going to be interesting." Mattie's eyes lit up.

Bitsy poked McConnel and led her to the kitchen.

"What was your mother doing with that thread?"

"It's called tatting. It's intricate lace work for collars and doilies, and things like that. It's made with knots and loops."

McConnel leaned on the counter as Bitsy opened the refrigerator. "It looked interesting. I've never heard of it."

"It's kind of a lost art here in the United States. Momma has always loved it and has been doing it since she was little. She tried to get us girls interested in it, but I don't have the patience. Tilly does it."

Bitsy seemed to relax as she talked about her family history. McConnel would have to remember that fact.

❖

Chief Gibson and his daughter, Peggy, arrived at seven. She walked him to the veranda, visited briefly with Mattie, and then kissed the chief's cheek. "Call me when you're ready to come home." She waved to the others, then drove away.

Mattie slipped her hand through the crook of the chief's arm and led him to one of the cushioned chairs, then sat beside Bitsy on the sofa.

"It's been a long time, Mattie." He looked at Bitsy. "I swear you get prettier every time I see you." He eyed McConnel. "Hello again, young lady." He smiled. His pale blue eyes sparkled in the light of the setting sun shining through the windows.

She returned a smile. He looked like everyone's grandpa should. "Nice to see you again, Chief."

McConnel sat in the chair next to him.

He leaned back and rested his hands in his lap. "I went over the case notes to remind myself how it went that night. How would you like to proceed?"

The room wasn't exactly right. It wasn't the middle of the night, or completely dark, but this would have to do. Her container with the information she needed was on the coffee table, with an easel and a corkboard set up at one end. She stood and faced the small group. "I'd like the three of you to take a few minutes to remember that night. Mattie, where were you and Bitsy when Chief Gibson got here?"

Bitsy shifted.

Mattie reached for her hand and held it. "Upstairs in Mary Elizabeth's bedroom."

"Who was in the house?"

"Albert was with us." Mattie said. "I made the other girls stay upstairs. We walked Mary Elizabeth down to this room."

"You and Bitsy's father?"

Mattie nodded.

"I know it's hard, but I believe it will help if we review some things first." McConnel reached into the container and withdrew pictures of the school and the abduction site from thirty years ago. She tacked them to the top of the corkboard. "Chief, what were you hoping to find out from Bitsy that night?"

"Several things, but mostly if she'd seen who took Hallie Lynn, or if she could give me any descriptions or details of what she saw. She was pretty upset, as you can imagine."

"Of course. Mattie, what did Bitsy say to you at the school?"

Mattie squeezed Bitsy's hand, then let go. She licked her lips. "She told Albert and me that Hallie Lynn had been taken."

"Where were you that you didn't see what happened?"

Mattie tilted her head for a moment. "Albert and I were talking to one of our neighbors just inside the gym. Bitsy had gone out."

"I went to wave good-bye to Hallie," Bitsy said. She cleared her throat and closed her eyes. Her cheeks paled.

"How long were you out there before you saw her taken?"

"It took me a few minutes to find her."

"Why?"

Bitsy opened her eyes. "Because she'd already walked to the side street."

McConnel nodded to the chief, indicating for him to take over.

"Bitsy." His voice was gentle but strong. "What did you see? What was the shiny dark?"

McConnel had asked him to bring the question up to put it into Bitsy's mind. She didn't expect to get the answer right away.

The sun had gone down and cast shadows into the room. Mattie reached to turn on the lamp beside the couch, but McConnel motioned for her to stop. It would be easier for Bitsy if she could hide in the semidarkness.

Bitsy rubbed her hands together and peered out the window. She didn't answer the question, just stared off, as if lost in the past.

The chief spoke again. "Bitsy, he had on dark pants. What was the shiny that you saw?"

Bitsy stiffened. "It was a flash of something in the light." Her voice quavered.

"What light?" the chief asked. "It was dark on the side street. Where did the light come from?"

Bitsy shook her head slightly. She clenched her jaw and squinted. "A car passed. A loud, ratty old green clunker. Its headlights flashed on him. He raised his arm."

"I remember that vehicle," Chief Gibson said. "It was Curtis Spillman's, the mother's boyfriend. Did the car stop?"

Bitsy hesitated. "No. It slowed a little but never stopped."

"When the man who got out of the car raised his arm, was he greeting someone or covering his face?" The chief looked at McConnel and shrugged.

He was on the right track. She was sure of it. She nodded.

Bitsy shifted on the couch, then touched her chin.

"Was he greeting someone or covering his face?" he asked again.

Bitsy continued to strain. She balled her fists.

McConnel held her breath. *This* was all new.

Bitsy blew out a deep sigh, obviously discouraged. "I don't know."

"Was something shining on him or somewhere else?"

Bitsy cupped her cheek. "It was on him. Something on him."

"Where on his body?"

She grimaced, then slumped in her seat. "I don't know. Above his waist? Maybe?"

McConnel's heart pounded. They needed just a little more. They were so close, but she didn't dare push her any further on this new piece of information. "That's okay, Bitsy. That was great." She made sure her disappointment didn't come through in her tone.

Bitsy looked up at her, an apology in her eyes.

"Would you be able to talk a little more about the taillights?" McConnel asked. If Bitsy could remember that small, non-threatening detail, chances were other memories would come to the surface.

"I'll try."

McConnel placed another picture on the board, a snapshot of obscure red taillights from a car in the dark. She nodded to the chief.

He leaned forward in his chair. "Bitsy, were they round or square?"

McConnel moved closer as Bitsy focused on the board.

Bitsy gazed at the pictures once, then twice. She stopped and relaxed her hands. "They were round."

The chief sat back and gave McConnel a thumbs-up.

Everyone was silent.

Bitsy inhaled deeply and looked at McConnel. She licked her lips. "That wasn't so bad."

"We're through for the night. You did great." McConnel touched her shoulder.

Mattie stood. "This calls for some pecan pie."

"I'll help." Bitsy followed her into the kitchen.

McConnel sat near the chief.

"I've got to tell you that was some fine manipulation," he said. "You're gifted."

"I'm worried I'm pushing her too hard."

"She's stronger than you think. You may know a lot about her, but it takes time to understand her." He stroked the arm of the chair, then straightened the delicate white lace doily over it. "She's carried a lot of baggage since she was a child." He pulled his cell phone from his pocket and started tapping the screen. "My daughter, Peggy, will be here in about twenty minutes or so. Hope I have time to eat that pie."

"Chief, are you sure it was Stillman's car Bitsy saw?"

"Oh, I'm sure. Everyone knew that piece-of-crap car. You could hear it a block away."

"I think I'm getting closer to finding the killer. I just need a little more to put it together."

"That reminds me," he said. "I found a few additional snapshots I took myself that you might be interested in. I meant to bring them, but I forgot. Sorry."

"I'm very interested." She'd already seen hundreds of photos, but his might reveal something new, just like Bitsy had tonight. "I can stop by tomorrow and pick them up, if that's all right?"

"That'd be fine." He looked toward the kitchen, probably concerned his pecan pie wouldn't arrive in time.

McConnel hoped she was a step closer, but time was running out on her secrets, and the risk was getting higher that Bitsy would find out who she was. It was becoming too complicated, but she was sure Bitsy still had the key piece to the case locked inside her.

CHAPTER FIFTEEN

The evening was finally over. Bitsy had gotten through it without any tears or a panic attack. Progress at last! The ordeal had been unsettling, but at least she'd remembered something, although she wasn't sure how important it was. What did it matter if the taillights were round or square? McConnel had assured her it did but didn't explain why. She never talked about her progress in the case, only asked questions. Always questions. It was irritating. How close was she to finding the killer? How much longer would she be here? Being around her was comforting, most of the time. She had an enjoyable sense of humor and an even temperament. She was easy to be with, but it was difficult to get to know her. She rarely talked about herself.

Bitsy slid onto the bed, fluffed one of her pillows, and lay watching the white lace curtains dance on the night's breeze through the open window. The day's frustration and emotion began to drift away. Flashes of that night long ago appeared again, but this time the anxious dread wasn't as intense, and the memories weren't as consuming and overpowering. It was as if she was experiencing them from a distance. Was she finally letting go? She'd spent years with psychiatrists, forcing herself to talk about them, but the apprehension and fear always clouded her mind, and the best she could ever do was wring her hands and rock back and forth. She'd learned quickly in those beginning days after the kidnapping that it was less painful to block it all. What was different now? The passage of time? Finding Hallie Lynn? McConnel had certainly played a part in the process. She'd brought a support with her that Bitsy hadn't realized she'd desperately needed until she had it.

A soft rap on the door caused her thoughts to fade. "Come in."

McConnel entered the room and sat on the bed. She looked at the floor, then at her.

Bitsy tried to read her expression. Was she disappointed? Anxious? She couldn't tell.

"I don't know if moving into your house is such a good idea. We should talk about it a little more."

Bitsy repositioned, placed the pillows against the headboard, and scooted back against them. "Why? I thought we'd already decided."

McConnel averted her gaze. "I'm going to be in and out a lot, and I don't want to disturb you at all hours of the night."

If McConnel had that much concern, maybe she shouldn't stay with Bitsy, but again, maybe she should. Her own feelings were clear. "I think you should move in. I know it's only temporary, but I'd love your company, and I think it'd be easier for you. Besides, you've got to be sick of that hotel."

"I haven't spent much time there." McConnel frowned, appearing concerned.

Bitsy touched her arm. "What is it?"

"To be honest, I don't know if it's a good idea to have all that information about the case around you. What if I leave something lying about, and it upsets you?" She paused and inhaled deeply. "That's not the real reason. I'm having a little trouble when I'm with you."

What was she saying? "What do you mean?"

"It's all getting too complicated. I need to simplify and focus, and I think it'd be best if I keep my distance."

"It's a big house."

"I know we said we'd take it slow getting to know each other, but I think staying with you while I'm on the case is pushing it a little. I'd like to think about the possibility for a while longer."

"Of course. Although I'm sure it'd be good for both of us."

McConnel nodded but didn't speak.

Bitsy had looked forward to her staying with her, spending more time together, getting to know her better. Maybe McConnel didn't want to know *her*. After all, Bitsy was a witness.

McConnel looked tense.

"There's no pressure. I'm just saying it might be good for you to be at my house and not that lonely hotel room." Bitsy hoped her words would make McConnel feel more comfortable.

"Thanks for that. I'm sure this evening was hard for you. I hope you know how much I appreciate your efforts." McConnel stood.

Bitsy grasped her hand. "Don't go. Stay a while."

"I don't think that's a good idea. Good night." She started to leave.

"Wait. What's going on?"

McConnel grimaced. "I just think I should go."

"Please don't."

McConnel shook her head. "I have to. Good night."

Bitsy let her leave. If she didn't want to stay, then she shouldn't. Right?

❖

She woke suddenly in the middle of the night from a flash of lightning and then a deafening roll of thunder. She slipped on her robe to go downstairs for a drink of ice water. McConnel's door was ajar when she passed. She peered in. McConnel wasn't in the bed. She searched the darkened room, catching a shadowy glimpse of her standing by the open window, staring out. "McConnel, what are you doing?"

"The storm is beautiful. It seems like the heavens are open."

Bitsy walked in and stood beside her.

The rain drops splashed against the windowsill. The air was fresh and smelled of pine and earth.

McConnel turned to her. "I've had to withhold some things from you in order to do my job."

Bitsy stepped back. "What kinds of things? You aren't married or in a relationship with someone else, are you?"

McConnel's shoulders relaxed. "No." She gazed at the rain.

"Well, are you going to make me guess?"

"I can't tell you what it is right now, but I wanted you to know I've held it back so when you find out you won't be so disappointed or upset."

"Now you've piqued my curiosity. Will you tell me when you can?"

McConnel ran her hand up Bitsy's arm. "Yes, I will."

"Then that's good enough for now."

"It bothers me that I haven't told you."

Bitsy brushed McConnel's hair from her face. "It must be hard being an FBI agent. I'm sure it's lonely keeping all those secrets to yourself. Do you talk to anyone about it?"

"You mean like someone I'm close to?"

"Yes, or a coworker."

"I can talk with other law enforcement personnel about a case, but I don't discuss my personal feelings with anyone."

"So, what you've held back from me is personal?"

McConnel stiffened.

What was she not telling her? Bitsy would never be able to guess. McConnel was like a vault, and it probably came with her job. Would she ever let her in? Did Bitsy want in? What about when the case was solved? What then? McConnel would go back to Ohio. Did she really want to invest in someone who'd be gone in a matter of days or weeks? "I hope you can trust me enough to tell me when you're ready."

"I hope *you* can trust *me* after I do."

It was an odd thing to say. "Why wouldn't I?"

McConnel breathed deeply, walked back to the bed, and sat. "Bitsy, let's not discuss it. It's just too complicated. You deserve answers to your questions, but I can't give them to you right now."

Bitsy positioned beside her. "How can I trust you when you won't let me know you?"

McConnel switched on the lamp by the bed.

It took a second for Bitsy's eyes to adjust.

McConnel looked at her.

Whatever she wouldn't tell her caused a genuine and deep concern. The worry of it was written all over her face. Bitsy withheld the urge to reach out and touch her. "I want to get to know you. It's important to me."

"And I want to know you, but for now I have to keep my distance," McConnel said. "Please try to understand. Once this case is over, then we can get to know each other the way I imagine we both would like, if you still want to."

"It's a tough ask to make me wait."

McConnel smiled and nodded. "I know. I'm sorry."

There was a loud knock on the partially opened door. "Mary Elizabeth?"

Bitsy startled, and she and McConnel jumped up.

Momma looked from one to the other.

Clearly she was upset about something other than the storm.

"What's wrong?" Bitsy asked.

She came into the room. "There's been a horrible accident. I just got a call from one of the neighbors down the road. Chief Gibson and his daughter, Peggy, are dead."

Bitsy covered her mouth and gripped the edge of the nightstand. "What?"

McConnel moved closer to Momma. "What happened?"

"A car accident. Evidently, it was on the way home from here."

"What kind of accident?" McConnel asked.

"They were about halfway home." Momma brought her shaking hand to her cheek. "Bonita, a friend of mine, called and said she and her husband heard several emergency vehicles and decided to go see what happened. She said it looked like the car had rolled and landed upside down in the embankment. It must have been a while before someone drove by and saw it." Momma slouched into the overstuffed chair by the window. She moved the curtain and peered out. "It's just a cryin' shame. That poor family."

McConnel excused herself and left the room.

Bitsy crossed to Momma and placed her arm around her shoulders. "He was such a sweet man. I hope they didn't suffer."

Momma clasped her hand. "I feel so bad. If he hadn't come over here this evening, it wouldn't have happened."

Bitsy kissed the top of her head. "Don't think like that, Momma."

McConnel's voice drifted in from the hallway. "I'll let you know when I get back."

Bitsy left Momma and went to McConnel, who was lowering her cell phone. "Where are you going?"

McConnel's posture was rigid, and one hand was balled. "I need to get dressed. I'm going to the crash site. I need to find out what happened."

"I'll go with you."

McConnel raised her hand in evident protest. "It's not necessary. I don't know how long I'll be."

"I insist. You're not going alone." Bitsy didn't particularly want to visit the scene of the accident, but she didn't want McConnel to be by herself. McConnel was an FBI agent. She dealt with these kinds of things all the time, but Chief Gibson was connected to the cold case.

McConnel had talked about him several times, pointing out what a good resource he was. He was a strong support for her. How would this affect her investigation? How would it affect her?

"No unauthorized personnel are allowed on a scene," McConnel said. "You'd have to just sit in the car, and I don't know how long I'll be."

"I understand." Bitsy nodded. "I'll be ready in a few minutes."

McConnel eyed her. "No. This is official business, Bitsy. I can't let you go." She turned toward her room. "I need to get dressed. Mattie's upset. Why don't you tend to her?"

The rejection stung, making her angry and resentful. McConnel had no right to order her around. But the fury subsided as quickly as it had come. McConnel was right. Momma was a mess, and she needed Bitsy, plus, she obviously wasn't going to go with her. She was determined, though, not to let McConnel shut her out that easily. She'd be waiting when McConnel got back.

CHAPTER SIXTEEN

The rain had stopped, the clouds cleared, and the moon was full. McConnel was anxious to get to the scene of the accident.

No matter how much Bitsy pouted or tried to manipulate her to get what she wanted, she had no business at the crash site. McConnel had questions to ask the police, and she didn't want her getting in the way. It was a harsh thought, but true. Basically, McConnel needed to focus. Was the death of Chief Gibson related to Hallie Lynn? The suspicion had entered her mind the moment she'd heard the news. If it was true, she was much closer to finding the killer than she'd thought.

As she neared the top of a hill, the red and blue flashing lights reflected in the trees and onto the wet pavement. She drove to the last patrol car with its emergency signals on, pulled to the side of the road, and turned on her flashers. Then she grabbed her phone and Maglite from her carry bag, opened the car door, clipped her badge to her belt, and climbed out.

Sheriff Atwater was standing beside a deputy near the twisted wreckage. Glass and debris from the car were scattered from the road to the tree line, about seventy yards away.

"What are you doing here?" He sounded abrupt and loud.

"Can you tell me what happened?"

He shrugged. "They were northbound, probably headed home." He pointed past McConnel. "Skid marks indicate the driver tried to stop a good hundred feet before the car left the road. No clue as to why. Deer, maybe, but no carcass from roadkill. Can't tell a lot about what caused it. It wasn't another vehicle. No other debris. Looks like the car veered right for some reason and rolled several times before it came to rest." He shone his light toward the wreckage. "Looks like they were there an hour or so before someone spotted them."

"Why do you say that?"

"Coroner's assistant got to the scene about forty-five minutes after I called him and made the estimated time of death."

McConnel surveyed the terrain. A secluded area. No houses, only woods and a dark road.

The deputy beside the sheriff wasn't the one she'd met in the park where Hallie's body was found. The name plate on his uniform read *M. Bingham.*

"We got the call at one ten and were here within thirty minutes," Bingham said.

"Who arrived first on the scene?"

He glanced at the sheriff.

Atwater massaged the back of his neck. "I did."

"Where were you?" she asked. "It's pretty late for you to be working. Were you off duty?"

He rested his hand on his sidearm. "Who do you think you are coming here and questioning me? I'm not going to answer. It's none of your business. I'm the one who's investigating tonight, not you. Again, why are *you* here?"

McConnel took a step back to give him space. He was on the defensive. Why? "I was at the Colliers' house with Bitsy," she said. "Her mother told us what happened. Can I do anything to help?"

The sheriff shifted and seemed to relax. He shook his head. "Nope. We got it covered."

"Mind if I look around, take some pictures?"

He waved his hand. "Be my guest."

Had he flinched?

A flatbed tow truck arrived, its yellow flashing lights cutting through the mist of low-lying fog beginning to form on the ground.

McConnel walked the crash site, noting the vehicle's position when it finally came to rest. It was pointed opposite from the direction they would have been traveling. She pulled out her phone and began taking photos, focusing on the rear bumper and trunk compressed and almost even with the wheelbase. If they had rolled side to side, why was the back end so badly damaged? She moved closer, shining her light into the car. Most of the windows were crushed, the front seat and remaining glass smeared with blood.

She returned to the men. "Sheriff, were they both dead when you reached the scene?"

He looked over at the wreckage, back to her, then rubbed his nose. "Yes. They probably died on impact."

McConnel made a mental note that each time she'd asked a question he'd made a gesture—to the back of his neck and now his nose. Could the reaction indicate avoidance? Was he withholding something? "I'd appreciate a copy of the report, and the coroner's finding when it's ready. Give me a call and I'll come pick it up."

"No need," Bingham said. "We can email it to you on the secure network."

She wrote where to send it on a business card and handed it to him. "Thanks."

She surveyed the scene one final time and then returned to her vehicle. The entire thing bothered her. It wasn't so much the actual crash site but the type of damage to the car, and why did Atwater seem so nervous? Was he that intimidated to have another agency at his scene?

It was just twenty minutes back to the Collier house. As she maneuvered the long driveway and parked, she wondered if Bitsy would still be mad. She wasn't sure she was up to another confrontation.

Bitsy came onto the veranda and sat in one of the white wicker chairs. She folded her hands in her lap and smiled wearily.

McConnel got out of the car, made her way up the steps, and sat on the wooden porch swing next to her, leery of what to expect.

The silence between them was deafening.

She needed to say something. In the past, when women she'd been with got irritated or upset, she'd just distance herself from them, but Bitsy was different. McConnel cared about what she thought, how she felt, but there was a cost. Could she afford to pay it right now? It'd be a lot easier to drive away. That's what she should do. Mattie could take Bitsy home.

The humidity hung in the air so thick McConnel's cotton blouse was damp. The cicadas, tree frogs, and other night creatures pronounced that the rainstorm had long passed. Slivers of the moon peeked through the intermittent cloud cover.

"I owe you an apology," Bitsy said softly. "I'm sorry."

McConnel couldn't have been more shocked if Bitsy had stripped down in the moonlight. "What?"

Bitsy unclasped her hands and turned in her chair to face her. "I understand why you didn't want me to go to the crash site. It's police business, and having me there would've made your job harder."

The tension that had knotted between McConnel's shoulders since their disagreement eased. "Thank you. I appreciate that."

Bitsy looked out across the yard into the darkness. "I just don't know what to do with you." She took a deep breath. "I know you're investigating Hallie Lynn's case, and I'm the prime witness, but I feel there's so much more between us, and I think you do too. I know you can't share a lot of things, but it seems like one minute you want intimacy, and the next you push me away. It's confusing and unsettling, and I don't like it."

McConnel had forgotten how demanding it was to have an intimate relationship. "I assure you I wasn't pushing you away."

Self-control. That's what was needed. McConnel couldn't let how she felt about Bitsy get in the way of what she had to do, but at the same time, Bitsy was right. She *did* feel more for her. McConnel wrapped her fingers around the swing chain. She wanted to spend more time with Bitsy, enjoy her company while she could, but maybe she was hiding her feelings better than she'd thought. Truthfully, half the time she couldn't care less about the case now. She went through the motions of working it well enough, but when she was with Bitsy, she could just as easily have tossed it all into the trash. Years of effort to find Hallie Lynn, hating Bitsy for not wanting to help. None of it mattered now that she was getting to know who Bitsy really was. Everything was clouded by how she felt about her. Every moment they were together, McConnel wanted more. It was a raging swell of conflict, and the guilt was crowding in around it. What was happening? Why was it happening? Was it just loneliness? Were the years of shutting out everyone around her finally demanding their price?

The peace and contentment she felt when she was with Bitsy was a respite, a relief from the storms in her life. Was she an escape? Was being with Bitsy nothing more than an opportunity to get away from all the pressure and conflict she'd had for so long? No. She wasn't using her. Was she? The idea was repulsive. She twisted her grip on the cold metal links. It was clear. Bitsy had admitted her feelings. McConnel needed to do the same. "I have something I need to tell you."

Bitsy studied her for a long moment. "It's late, and you look really tired. Are you sure you don't want to get some rest?" She uncrossed her legs.

"I really think we should talk."

Bitsy shrugged.

What was she thinking?

"All right. If you insist." Bitsy pointed toward the house. "I could use a drink. You?"

"Yes. That sounds good. Thank you."

Bitsy opened the screen door, walked in, then hesitated and turned toward her. "Whiskey okay?"

McConnel toed the swing into motion. "Fine. Neat, please."

A few minutes later Bitsy came back with their drinks. She handed McConnel hers and then returned to her seat and sipped her own, staring out into the night.

McConnel swallowed, the smooth burn sliding down her throat, then settled her glass in her lap. "Bitsy, I've got to stop being with you so much."

Bitsy stiffened. "I see. You've gotten what you needed from me, and now you'll go on with the rest of it?"

Her response took McConnel by surprise. Why would she say that? "No. That's not true."

Bitsy set her drink on the wicker table beside the swing. "Then tell me what's going on. I'm confused. We agreed there's an attraction between us and we'd take it slow. I told you I understood why we can't be together. I've tried not to pressure you, so why this sudden withdrawal? You knew perfectly well how hard it would be for me to talk about what happened. Did you decide to romance the information out of me, get what you needed, and then leave?"

"Oh, my God! Bitsy, no. Absolutely not." Where had that come from? She took another long swallow, then looked into Bitsy's eyes. It was obvious she believed what she'd expressed. McConnel didn't want her to be angry. She needed her to understand the dilemma she'd put herself in. Bitsy had done everything McConnel had asked of her, and sometimes at great personal cost. She deserved the truth. "It's nothing like that."

"Then what is it? Talk to me." Bitsy was persistent and relentless when it came to her questions. She wouldn't give up.

McConnel couldn't sidestep her way out of this. Her heartbeat quickened. A moment of panic struck, but she swallowed it down. What if this wasn't what she thought it was? Bitsy had said she had feelings for her, but what if it was some misdirected attachment to McConnel's authority? Should she reveal how *she* felt? Would that make it worse? After the comment Bitsy had just made, she couldn't just sit there and say nothing. She took a chance. "I'm starting to lose my focus on the case because of how much I care about you."

"Oh!" Bitsy revealed a hesitant smile.

Did she find this revelation amusing? Was she toying with her? Was it a Southern thing? She'd managed to knock McConnel off balance.

Bitsy reached for her glass, took a drink, then set it back. "Now I understand why you've been acting like you have. I don't know how you Northerners do it, but normally, here in the South, when this kind of discussion happens between two people, we kiss and get to it. But since you've made it clear that can't happen, I want a promise from you."

For someone who'd had so much trauma in her life and was struggling with all the emotional baggage she was carrying around, Bitsy was unexpectedly stable and composed.

McConnel was almost jealous. "I have to know what it is before I'll do that."

"Promise me when this is over, you'll come to me, and we can start dating." Bitsy reached for her hand.

McConnel squeezed it gently, then released it. "I promise. But you may not want to when this is over. A lot can happen between now and then."

"I'm holding you to it."

McConnel intended to keep her word, but would Bitsy want anything to do with her when this case ended?

"I'll make this easy for you," Bitsy said. "Let's go to our rooms. It's about two hours till daylight, and I have to pack and be at work by ten." She took McConnel's glass, reached for hers, and stood.

"I appreciate what you're doing," McConnel said.

Bitsy patted her shoulder, and they went into the house.

❖

The morning sun shone through McConnel's bedroom window like a welcome friend come to say good morning. It was a beautiful day with a cloudless sky.

She rolled, reached for her phone on the nightstand, checked the time, and made a call.

"Special Agent Jenkins."

"This is McConnel. How'd you sleep?"

"I had a fine woman next to me. How about you?"

McConnel thought of Bitsy. "A glint of hope, but unfortunately alone."

"I'm sorry to hear that," he said. "I've got an update for you." Papers shuffled in the background. "Curtis Stillman was stabbed in the stomach in 1996. The knife was thrust at an upward angle. Whoever killed him must have been taller. There was also bruising on the back of his neck."

"Indicating he may have known his killer," McConnel said.

"Yes. That's my thought as well."

She reasoned it out. "He approached, stabbed him, and then reached around his neck and pulled him closer, thrusting the knife in deeper and upward for effect."

"He gutted him," Jenkins said.

"It wasn't just an argument in a bar," she said. "It was deliberate and specific."

"What are you thinking?" Jenkins asked.

She gathered her thoughts and impressions. "He knew Hallie Lynn's killer. Whoever murdered him shut him up because he may have known something or seen something. From what Bitsy told me, and from information I've gleaned, we can put Stillman at the scene of the kidnapping or at the very least a few minutes before it happened. This confirms my suspicion that whoever killed Hallie Lynn was local. He had to have been around town and known by Stillman."

"Maybe not. Stillman could have been stabbed because he was in the wrong place at the wrong time in Atlanta."

"I don't think so. Chief Gibson, who originally investigated the case and was a great resource for me, died last night in a car accident."

"That's not good."

"I'm sending you pictures from the crash site. I need someone with expertise to look at them. I don't understand why the rear end of the car was so damaged if it rolled from side to side."

"I'll get on it. By the way, I found out that Mason Tucker, the sheriff at the time of the murder who died of a *supposed* heart attack… It's not absolute. I talked with the coroner who did the autopsy."

"Why not conclusive?" McConnel asked.

"Evidently the heart didn't look quite right. He won't say anything else except he can't be one hundred percent sure it was a cardiac arrest."

"Why didn't he follow up?"

"The family pressured him, and there was no reason. Tucker was overweight, had high blood pressure, and his favorite food groups were barbecued ribs and beer."

"That is a recipe for a heart attack," McConnel said. "But if the autopsy wasn't conclusive, I'm going with an unnatural death. That makes three dead connected to Hallie Lynn."

"You mean two."

"No, three. Mason Tucker, Curtis Stillman—the boyfriend of the mother—and now the chief who investigated it. I don't like it."

"It wouldn't have been unusual for Tucker to have had a heart attack," Jenkins said. "You also must consider the boyfriend could have been killed by someone other than Hallie Lynn's murderer, and the chief? Country roads, weather conditions. More likely than not, it was a simple accident."

McConnel understood what he was doing. "I know you're taking the opposite view to help me reason it out, but the facts lead me to believe it's something more. Maybe each event separately is what it appears to be, but combined?"

"That's the problem with a case being open for over thirty years," Jenkins said. "You've got very few people to question. Keep pursuing your line of thought. What's your next step?"

"If the killer is local and did murder the three people involved in the case, then Bitsy is at risk, and so are the two deputies at the time—Jasper Watkins and Sheriff Atwater. I think it would be wise to have Watkins and Bitsy under protection. I'm not as concerned for Atwater because he's trained and carries a weapon, but he needs to be careful."

"Twenty-four hours a day for Watkins and Bitsy. Keep an eye on Atwater?" Jenkins asked.

"Yes. I don't want any of them to know right now. Bitsy's the only one who isn't a possible suspect. We need video and drones. Watkins has a background in law enforcement. It's been years, but he said he's a gun owner. Bitsy invited me to stay with her while I'm investigating so I won't have to be at a hotel. I was hesitant at first, but I've changed my mind. I'm going to accept her invitation. It will be extra protection for her."

"Don't feel pressure to do that. Our contract security people are very good. We'll use the agency out of Las Vegas again, Ralston Enterprises."

"They're good," McConnel said. "I've worked with Kathrine Henderson, their lead coordinator, on several jobs. Send me the details when you've got them. I'll meet with whoever is coordinating the surveillance as soon as everything's in place."

"I'll send the information as soon as I can," Jenkins said. "You be careful. If you're right about this, it could all come to a head soon. Are you sure you don't want more help?"

"I'll have what I need once security is in place. I'll let you know if I need more agents." McConnel ended the call.

Three people connected with the case had been murdered. She was now sure the killer was local, like Chief Gibson had suspected, and if she couldn't find him, she'd somehow have to make him come to her. Bitsy was the most important witness. Likely the only reason he hadn't come after her already was that McConnel was nearby. Had he been watching her the night Bitsy had the panic attack? The closer she got to finding him, the more desperate he'd become. Bitsy needed all the protection she could get.

CHAPTER SEVENTEEN

Monday morning, Bo sat rigid in the chair in front of Bitsy's desk, grimacing. "I never said I didn't get the commitment." He inspected his hand. "What I said was Waverly Corp is willing to make a substantial investment in their artwork, but their CFO wants to meet you before they sign the contract."

Bitsy had gotten only a couple hours of sleep. The death of Chief Gibson and Peggy had been heartbreaking and overshadowed everything, but despite it, she was glad she'd made the effort to go home, and especially that McConnel had gone with her.

"Bo, I'm swamped. I don't have time to go to Atlanta. Besides, I hate driving there. The traffic is horrific, it takes forever to get downtown, and parking is a mess. That's why I sent you." She tried to hold back her grin.

"Tell me about it. It took me twenty-five minutes to get from the exit to Waverly, and then I ended up using valet parking. The only good thing that happened was I got it paid for."

"And now we have a potential substantial contract," Bitsy said. "By the way, if we get it, I've decided to give you a bonus. You did a good job with them." It was a bone to throw him, but he deserved it. Going to Atlanta was a pain in the backside, and if they got the contract, he'd need to go there more than a few times to keep them happy.

He settled into the chair. "I appreciate it. So, should I tell Lilly to set the appointment for you?"

Bitsy gave in and nodded. It dawned on her that Bo was becoming better at getting what he wanted.

He stood. "Pellmont was a pushover."

"That's because Momma softened him up."

"She's my hero. The *Clairton* will arrive by the end of the week."

"Well done."

He left her office.

She continued to sort through the mail.

Lilly peeked in the doorway. "FBI babe is here," she whispered, then winked. "Do you have a minute?"

Bitsy tried to hide her anticipation. "Send her in."

McConnel entered, looking fresh and bright, even though she'd probably gotten less sleep than Bitsy.

"I won't take much of your time."

"No. I'm glad you're here. Please sit."

Bitsy stepped around the desk and sat on the sofa.

McConnel chose the chair next to it. "I've thought a lot about your invitation to stay at your house. If it's still open, I want to take you up on the offer."

Bitsy was surprised. After their discussion, she'd been sure McConnel wouldn't do it. "I've got to ask, why the change of mind? You're not worried anymore about us spending too much time together?"

McConnel half smiled, her soft gaze meeting Bitsy's. "There's always that possibility, but I think it'd help the case, and you're right. It'd save drive time." Now the grin was full.

"That's fabulous. Lilly has an extra key to the house. Stop by her office when you leave and pick it up. Make yourself completely at home. Take one of the bedrooms upstairs on the right, opposite mine. You can use the back one for your work if you need to." She wrote the security codes on a sticky note and handed it to her. "I'm sorry I don't have another garage door opener. Park on the right side of the driveway. That way you won't block my car." She wanted to hug her, welcome her with open arms, but refrained.

McConnel rose. "Thanks, Bitsy. I really appreciate it. It's very kind of you. I promise I'll keep the case information out of your way as much as I can. The extra room will help me get away from it for a few hours."

"Of course. Use however many rooms you need. I have confidence we can work it out. I'm excited to have you there. I won't be home until late tonight. The cleaning service comes on Wednesdays and is usually there from nine to about noon, and the landscaper comes on Thursdays. Other than that, there shouldn't be anyone to bother you."

"Thanks again. It's very gracious of you." She folded the note and tucked it into her pants pocket.

Bitsy noticed her gun on her left side, not in her purse. She stood. "Will you be going to Chief Gibson and Peggy's funeral? The family decided to have just one. I think it will be easier on them. We could ride together. It'll probably be this Thursday. I imagine the church will be packed, so parking will be limited."

"Yes. I'd like to," McConnel said. "I'll see you this evening." She left.

Bitsy walked to the window and gazed out at the few puffs of gray-tinged clouds. Another storm was coming. *See you this evening.* It was a pleasant thought.

❖

At eight fifteen, Bitsy arrived home, tired and hungry, and immediately brightened when she saw the rental car in the driveway. She entered, put her purse on the bar, and reset the alarm system. Table service for two was on the counter. McConnel was in the living room, on the sofa. The sight lifted Bitsy's mood. The scent of something delicious wafted from the oven. "What's that wonderful smell?"

"I'm warming garlic and herb roasted lamb with glazed carrots and red potatoes. Snap pea salad is in the fridge."

"That sounds so good. I'll change and be out in a second." Bitsy's stomach growled all the way to the bedroom. There, she changed into shorts and a light top and returned.

"Do you want to eat at the bar or the table?" McConnel asked.

"Dining room, if you don't mind."

McConnel moved their plates and silverware.

Bitsy retrieved napkins and glasses. "Ice water or something else?"

"Water, please."

"I'll make it two."

The meal was delicious and filling. Bitsy wiped her mouth and placed her napkin beside her empty plate. "I'm stuffed like a Thanksgiving Day turkey."

McConnel laughed.

"Thank you for that, but I hope you don't feel you need to do this."

"Not at all," McConnel said. "I was starved and hoped you'd be also."

"I suppose we should at least coordinate meals," Bitsy said. "Do you eat at certain times during the day?"

"No. Mostly whenever I can stop to grab something. I'm not a fan of a schedule because of the demand on my time. How about you?"

"My workdays can be long, although Sundays are lounge days for me. I usually cook or order in."

"Do you always get food from the same place?" McConnel asked.

"No. It just depends on what I'm in the mood for. Did you buy this from Silver Fork on High Street?"

McConnel nodded.

"Never order the barbecue. It's not their thing. The place for that is Jimmy B's. It's a bar and grill. Fabulous ribs. We'll have to go there while you're here. They have a great band too. Do you line dance?"

"No. Never tried it."

"Never? Oh, we'll have to go for sure."

Nothing was said about the case, and Bitsy was glad. She didn't want to know anything about it. The sooner it was over, the better everything would be, except that McConnel would eventually have to go back to Ohio. She'd promised they could start dating, though, and some couples had successful long-distance relationships. Maybe they could be one of them. "I'll clean up. Let me know what the cost was, and we'll split it."

McConnel pushed her chair out and stood. "No way. You're letting me stay here. It's the least I can do. I'd like to take you out for a meal now and then, when your schedule permits. Let me know when you have some time during the next few days."

"On a date?" Bitsy laughed.

McConnel pointed her finger at her and grinned. "I'm going to work on some notes. Have a good night." She climbed the stairs.

It'd been a pleasant evening, more than Bitsy had hoped for. If it kept going this way, by the time the case was over, they'd be ready to spend some real time together.

❖

Bitsy hardly saw McConnel during the next two days. They passed like shadows on the street. The morning of the funeral she'd arranged to meet her at her office. McConnel got there a few minutes late, wearing a sculpted black dress that showed every curve and then some. She was even more beautiful than Bitsy had imagined. And she'd imagined plenty. She'd already had two sex dreams about her. Her hair was loose and framed the sharp contours of her lovely face. Her makeup was perfectly applied. Her gun must have been in her purse, or maybe she had a smaller one strapped to her thigh. Bitsy wanted to look.

It was no surprise that by the time they reached the church, it was filled. They were lucky Momma and Daddy had saved them room in their pew. Bitsy quietly introduced McConnel to Daddy, and she shook hands with him as they sat.

People continued to enter. By the time the reverend began the service, it was standing room only and heartbreaking to see all the sad faces. Bitsy's only contact with the chief had been through the case, but she felt his family and friends' loss and grief. She held back tears when Peggy's daughter spoke about her mother and grandfather.

McConnel wiped a tear and looked away when her lip started to quiver.

Bitsy was exhausted by the time it was over and they'd visited with the chief's family at their home. She'd rearranged her schedule and cleared the rest of the day.

McConnel changed into slacks when they reached the house and then left, not saying where she was going. She didn't owe Bitsy an explanation, but it would have been nice to have known. Bitsy rested for an hour and then went into her studio, where she readied her materials and cautiously approached the easel. Without thought, she put brush to canvas. The stupor was gone. She knew what she wanted to create.

The time slipped by without notice, and she became aware only when she heard McConnel call out for her. "I'm in here."

McConnel entered and stood beside her. "You're finally painting."

Bitsy began to clean up. "Yes. At last." She checked the time. Ten thirty-two. "You were out awfully late."

McConnel eyed her work-in-progress without comment. "I hope that's not a problem."

"Not at all. Did you get something to eat?"

"I'm not hungry. I had enough at the chief's house. I'm going to shower and go to bed."

Bitsy had hoped for a little conversation. "Everything all right?"

McConnel stopped but didn't face her. "Yes. It's just been a long day." Disappointment colored her voice.

"Anything new?"

"No, unfortunately." McConnel left the room.

Bitsy wanted to help her, but what could she do? The less they discussed the case, the better she liked it. But something was brewing. She could feel it, and from the way McConnel acted, it wasn't good.

CHAPTER EIGHTEEN

McConnel stripped and showered, dressed in her pajamas, then entered the last bedroom on the right, or what she now called the murder room. She tossed the surveillance report onto the bed. "Damn it." After she positioned the pillows, she sat against the headboard, staring at the folding corkboard propped open on the desk in front of her. It was covered with information, but none of it gave her what she needed. The wall was now decorated in crime scene photos from thirty years ago and the burial site. "Who are you? Why can't I find you?" She threw the report toward the board, but it hit the desk, pages scattering everywhere. She folded her arms and squinted, focusing on the display. "I know you're there. I just can't see you." She slid from the bed and paced, trying to work through the facts. Her cell chimed.

"Special Agent McConnel?" a female voice asked.

"Speaking."

"Go secure."

McConnel adjusted her phone.

"This is Kathrine Henderson, from Ralston Enterprises. Our people are on the job for Hanover and Watkins. We have twenty-four-hour security on both of them, two female security teams in twelve-hour shifts for Hanover. Watkins is covered by one male on twelve-hour shifts. Per your instructions, I've not assigned anyone to Atwater. I've just emailed you our photos, identification, and other information you'll need. We're all on secure phones."

Henderson was working point. Impressive. "Excellent. I'll meet you tomorrow morning at eight thirty in the parking lot of the Garden

Market on Chelsie Street." Bitsy usually left the house by seven fifteen. McConnel would have plenty of time.

Henderson gave her the make and model of her car. "See you then. Rest well."

"And you." McConnel breathed easier. Bitsy now had more security. She gathered the papers off the floor, then sat at the desk, continuing to scrutinize the information in front of her. She opened her notebook and began to write.

> *Male, tall, dark pants, round taillights, intimidates, exaggerated sense of importance, white, travels to kill, no jeans, local, knows the area. Georgia boy? Scouts his victims because he took Hallie Lynn at the school and knew she'd be there, knew where to pick her up, probably knew her mother. What was the shiny dark Bitsy saw that night? Reflection? Light against metal? Did he go after Chief Gibson? Lacks empathy. Fights his desire to kill because the twenty-two victims linked to his MO were abducted over a twenty-nine-year period. Remorse? Could there be more cases we haven't identified?*

She picked up her cell and called Jenkins.

"What's bothering you? It's too late for just an update," he said.

She laughed. "I suspect this guy has killed more than we thought. I think we can be confident he buried all his victims in a similar way to Hallie Lynn. I'm still not positive she was his first, but probably. He may have killed in other states, but I think he lives here, a local boy, and probably within a fifty-mile radius of the burial site because he knew the area so well. I'd like to have someone review the kidnappings again. This time include any cases that were in specific situations, not just random. For example, abducted from some type of practice or event where he'd know the victim would be there. He's meticulous and a planner, not random. He stalks his prey before he takes them. He enjoys the anticipation. It's a buildup for him. I think we've scared him and he's in a reactionary mode now. If I can keep the pressure on, maybe he'll make a mistake."

"You be extra careful," Jenkins said. "He knows who you are.

Witnesses won't be the only thing he'll go after. Are you sure you don't need another agent?"

"I'm good. I don't want to give him any hint that I'm as close as I am to finding him. Henderson and her teams are in place. Thanks for arranging it. I have confidence in their abilities to keep Bitsy and Watkins safe. I'm comfortable with leaving Atwater on his own for now."

"Sounds like you've made some progress."

"Unfortunately, it doesn't feel like it."

She ended the call.

She went to the kitchen for water.

Bitsy was turning out the living room lights.

McConnel noticed the time. A little past midnight. "You going to bed?"

Bitsy switched on the night light in the kitchen. "Yes. Are you?"

"I hope. My mind can't seem to shut down." She drank a half glass of water.

"You know, they have things for that. Warmed alcohol, herbal tea, massage. I bet your shoulders are stiff as boards."

"I know my neck is." The tension shot up McConnel's back when she said it. She twisted and heard her neck creak.

"Good grief. You aren't kidding. Go lie on the bed on your stomach, and I'll give you a scented oil massage."

"I'd love it, but do you think that's a good idea?"

"I absolutely do." Bitsy laughed. "I promise, only a massage."

"Okay. I'll meet you in my bedroom."

McConnel liked saying it. But was it a good idea? Her neck and shoulders were so tense she felt like her muscles would snap from her bones. She'd tried to relax when she was in the hot shower, but the water gave her only a small amount of relief. She lay on the bed, a pillow tucked under her chest and arms. And waited. With anticipation. And a smile.

Bitsy came in a few minutes later with a small towel and other items, which she placed on the nightstand. "It's perfectly all right for you to go to sleep. If you do, I'll turn off the light when I leave."

"If I go to sleep while you're doing it, tomorrow night I'll take you to Jimmy B's for barbecue and maybe some line dancing."

"Really?"

Bitsy began to rub the warm, scented oil onto McConnel's shoulders. Honeysuckle or something close. McConnell immediately relaxed, the tension oozing from her body. "Mmm. That feels so good." Bitsy kneaded her upper back and shoulders, and then her neck. Her touch was gentle and soothing, yet firm. The relief spread throughout McConnel's entire upper body. "Bitsy, you have great hands."

The scent permeated the room. It was quiet. McConnel closed her eyes.

She jolted awake. The room was dark. She grabbed her cell to check the time. Three thirty? She couldn't have slept that long. She returned the phone to the stand and rolled over, adjusted the pillow, closed her eyes, and went back to sleep.

The alarm went off at seven. By the time she got out of the bathroom and went to the kitchen, Bitsy had left for work. A note lay on the counter.

> *Hope you slept well. I'll be home by six and ready to go by seven.*
> *I'm holding you to your commitment.*
> *By the way, I'm inviting Tilly and Janie and anyone else who can meet us.*
> *Yes, I'll ask Louise, but I don't want to! Girls' night!*

What had McConnel gotten herself into? She poured a cup of coffee Bitsy had made, sat at the bar, and reviewed her note. It lightened her thoughts to read it. She ate, dressed, and got ready for her meeting.

McConnel pulled into the parking lot beside Henderson's car and unlocked the door.

Henderson scooted into the passenger seat. "Good morning."

They shook hands.

It was good to see her. "Kathrine, I'm glad you've been assigned to this case. How are you?"

"I'm great. How about yourself? I hope you don't mind me being honest, but you look like you could use a vacation."

"I've hit it pretty hard the last several weeks."

Kathrine handed her a folder. "All our information is in here."

McConnel opened it and began to review the contents. She removed a flash drive attached and held it up. What's this?"

"A gift from Rachel Portola, our computer whiz." She pointed to one of the papers in the folder. "That sheet explains what the program does. She'd like you to test it and let her know what you think. Basically, it's an analysis program. Follow the prompts. Enter everything about your case. When you've got it all in there, hit the sequence numbers, and it will give you the results. For example, enter the suspects, and it will provide the probability of them being the perp. Can't decide if something was an accident or not? Enter all the data, and it will tell you the probabilities if it was or wasn't. Can't figure out if it was a murder or accident? Enter the data, get the results. We've started using it, and it's changed the way we run investigations."

"Wow!"

"The hardest part is taking the time to enter all the data. The more input, the better the program works. If you're having problems sifting through your evidence or hunches, I'm telling you, this program can really help clear things up."

McConnel held the flash drive tighter. "I'll use it for sure. Thank her for me. Maybe this will be what I need to break the case. Do you have everything you need?"

"I believe so. I have schedules. I think you should inform Ms. Hanover she's under protection. I understand why you don't want to tell Watkins, but I recommend you inform her. If she knows, it's easier to keep her safe."

"All right. I'll tell her in the next couple of days. Anything else?"

"Not for now."

"Bitsy will be with me this evening around seven. We're going to a place called Jimmy B's, on the outskirts of Savanah. There'll be a lot of people."

"Shouldn't be a problem."

"All right. Let me know if anything's suspicious. Check in by ten in the evenings, and by eight in the mornings. I'm more concerned about Watkins than Atwater. He's probably the least at risk."

"Don't worry. We have Hanover and Watkins well covered." Kathrine opened the car door and got out, then ducked her head back in. "I have some time if you need any help with analysis."

"I appreciate the offer. I may take you up on it."

Kathrine nodded and shut the door, started her car, and drove away.

McConnel eyed the flash drive. Rachel Portola was known for her innovative security program development. If this new one worked like McConnel hoped it would, it could give her a needed boost in the investigation. She couldn't wait to get back to the house and start entering the data.

By six p.m., her eyes were burning, and her shoulders were stiff again. She'd been entering data into the computer for nine hours. It'd be at least another day before she was ready to run the probabilities on the car crash and profile of the killer.

Bitsy had arrived home and started getting ready.

It was too late to get out of her promise. McConnel showered and changed into jeans and a light top. If she was going to line dance and make a fool of herself, at least she'd be comfortable doing it.

Jimmy B's was about what she'd expected. Packed with people, a dance floor, tables everywhere, and lots of noise and music. Four women were waving and motioning to them from their table near the back. Bitsy took the lead as they weaved through the crowded room.

McConnel recognized Tilly and Janie but not the other two women.

Bitsy hugged her sisters, then rested her hands on Tilly's shoulders. "Tilly and Janie you know."

They both said hello.

Bitsy motioned to the other women. "This is Annabelle Sutter, Savannah Assistant District Attorney, and my sister Louise." Bitsy sneered.

Annabelle raised her glass to McConnel. Louise nodded.

"We ordered drinks for both of you," Annabelle said. "Whiskey neat for you, McConnel, and on the rocks for you, Bitsy. Sit. I want to hear everything about you, McConnel, and what you're doing here." She patted the empty seat beside her.

McConnel worked her way around the table and sat between her and Janie. Bitsy sat across from her, between Tilly and Louise.

Annabelle sipped her drink, probably some type of whiskey

cocktail. The unique thing about her drink was it had a fake bullet molded into the side of the glass.

"Ribs will be here in about ten minutes," Tilly announced.

It fascinated McConnel that the four sisters looked so much alike. Each was different, yet they all had similar traits. Different hair color, same thickness of hair and widow's peak, same cheekbones and eyebrows. Their hands were long and graceful. Louise's chin was more pronounced, and her nose was wider. Tilly's face was more rounded, and she had a longer neckline. Janie wasn't as tall as the others, and her lips were fuller. Bitsy looked most like their mother in her facial features, the way she moved, her gestures, and even her voice. Now that they were all together, Bitsy was clearly a cut above the others in her beauty, and her smile was intoxicating.

"I can't stay until all hours of the night." Louise frowned. "I've got babies at home."

"Well, so do we," Janie said.

"And it won't kill Bobbie Ray to take care of them for the night," Tilly said. "We'll make sure you don't get drunk." She laughed. "Too bad Aunt Tallulah isn't here. She'd police us for sure."

Everyone but McConnel laughed. She didn't get it.

"Auntie T isn't a drinker," Bitsy said. "One night Momma and her best friends, Ms. Ester and Ms. Sally Anne, sat out on the veranda at Ms. Sally Anne's, got drunk, and yelled at the people passing by. After they'd done that for two hours, they got bored and decided to go down to the local Piggly Wiggly to protest. She never did explain exactly what they were protesting. Anyhoo, Auntie T came to get Momma and gave them all a twenty-minute lecture on the evils of alcohol. Momma voluntarily climbed into the police car to get away from Auntie T."

Tilly laughed and slapped her leg. "Oh, Lord. What a hoot that was. Momma and her friends got banned from the Piggly Wiggly."

"I don't think it's funny, Tilly," Louise said. "And besides, you shouldn't air our dirty laundry in front of strangers."

"Sing me back to Savannah, Louise." Janie smirked. "McConnel's not a stranger, and besides, anyone who plays poker the way she does deserves to know our family secrets."

Bitsy raised her glass. "Lord knows there's enough of them." She took a drink.

McConnel instantly loved Bitsy's sisters, even Louise.

Bitsy grinned. "You can't keep secrets from her anyway. She's FBI."

McConnel couldn't help but laugh.

Annabelle leaned closer to her. "I'd love to discuss what I think about who killed Hallie Lynn if you have some time tomorrow. I'm in court until three." She handed her a business card with a phone number written on the back.

Bitsy watched them.

McConnel wasn't sure if Annabelle was being nice or coming on to her. Southern women's intentions were hard to know, but from the looks of Bitsy's glare, it may have been a come-on. Annabelle was attractive, but Bitsy had her beat hands down.

The ribs arrived, the biggest slab McConnel had ever seen. Baked beans, coleslaw, hush puppies, a pile of napkins, and lots of barbecue sauce were distributed around the table. It was a family-style dinner, and McConnel hadn't had such a fine meal and great conversation in a long, long time.

After they ate, Bitsy dragged McConnel to the dance floor and guided her into position as everyone lined up.

McConnel felt like she had three legs and no hips. She tried to keep in step, but she had no idea what she was doing. She anticipated and spun right, but everyone spun left. Bitsy kept pointing and encouraging her, but McConnel got so lost she raised her hands and started to walk away.

Bitsy grabbed her arm. "Oh, no, you don't. You can't give up that easy."

Tilly, Annabelle, and the others gathered beside her.

"We won't let you make a fool of yourself," Janie shouted over the music.

"I think it's too late for that," McConnel said, trying to make light of the situation.

All five of them encouraged her and did the steps so she had no choice but to follow. She finally caught on near the end of the song, and when the dance was over, everyone clapped and stood in place.

"I don't think I can take another one," McConnel said.

"Sure you can," Bitsy said. "Just do what we do."

"That's easier said than done." Out of the corner of her eye McConnel caught Kathrine Henderson standing off to the side, grinning. Her team was there, and now she'd embarrassed herself in front of all of them.

"Don't look so stoic. People may think you aren't enjoying this." Bitsy laughed.

She was way too comfortable teasing her. "Go ahead, have your fun," McConnel said. "I'll get even somehow."

"I'm sure you will, but in the meantime, shake your tail feathers." Bitsy placed her hand on McConnel's waist and moved her a few steps to the right.

That's when the line dance took a turn for the worse. McConnel raised her hands. "Oh no. I'm done." She walked away, along with about a third of the crowd.

The music got faster. The moves jumbled together. It was like the elimination round at a shoot-off. Six more people left the group, which was getting smaller by the second. Louise and Annabelle conceded, then Tilly. Janie and Bitsy were in it to win.

Eight people remained when the music ended to loud cheers and applause.

Sweat was pouring down the dancers' faces, but they were all grinning so wide you couldn't see anything but their smiles. And Bitsy most of all.

The crowd dispersed and went back to their tables.

It took Bitsy a few minutes to catch her breath.

"Is it always like this?" McConnel asked. She searched for Kathrine but didn't see her.

"This is about the only place respectable lesbians can let off some steam," Annabelle said. She moved closer to McConnel. "I hope you call. I'd enjoy talking with you, very much."

McConnel felt Bitsy watching her. She tried to be as polite and tactful as possible, yet not give Annabelle any false signals. "I'd be interested in your thoughts about the case. Chief Gibson was a great resource for me, and it'd be nice to have someone like him to talk to."

Annabelle looked puzzled. "Are you serious?"

"What do you mean?"

"Bitsy's daddy knows the case better than anyone in the county. Haven't you discussed it with him?"

Why hadn't Bitsy or Mattie said anything to McConnel about that? "No. He wasn't there at the house. Bitsy said he was out of town."

Annabelle nodded. "You talk with him. You'll get an earful." She stood. "I hate to be the first to break up this party, but I've got court prep to do. McConnel, call me when you want to discuss the case." She turned toward Bitsy and Tilly, then looked at the others. "Girls, it's been fun, as always." She left.

McConnel had another resource. Why hadn't Mattie said something? She hadn't given any indication her husband could add anything to help her with the murder. McConnel needed to hear his story as soon as possible.

CHAPTER NINETEEN

Bitsy was glad Annabelle left. She was notorious for her one-night stands, and if Bitsy had anything to say about it, McConnel wouldn't be one of them. By the time they got back home, she had a splitting headache, so she poured herself a glass of ice water, took two Tylenol, and sat in the dark living room, trying not to brood.

McConnel joined her, sitting at the other end of the sofa. "It was fun. Thanks for making me feel part of the group."

"Yes, it was, but what was that with you and Annabelle? I thought we had an understanding." Bitsy probably shouldn't have asked, but if they were going to move forward, they'd better get things straight right now.

"What do you mean?"

"You were awfully attentive."

"Bitsy, that was nothing. At least on my part."

"Just so you know, she's a womanizer and only wants to go to bed with you."

"I wouldn't do anything with another woman to break your trust. I know we agreed not to pursue our feelings for one another right now, but please know I take our understanding seriously."

Bitsy found comfort in McConnel's words, easing her mind. "I appreciate you being up front about it. I hope you don't think I'm being selfish."

"Not at all. I'd probably feel the same way if the situation was reversed."

Bitsy liked that McConnel spoke her mind. It was refreshing, but was it a Northern thing or her personality? She looked forward to getting to know her better.

"I'd like to stay up and visit, but I'm exhausted," McConnel said. "I'm going to take a shower and go to bed." She stood. "Thanks again for helping me feel a part of things tonight. I had a good time, even though I can't dance." She smiled.

Bitsy stood beside her. "You just need some practice."

"You're too generous."

"Lots of practice." Bitsy laughed.

McConnel grinned and pointed her finger. "I warned you."

"Yes, you did."

They climbed the stairs and said good night.

Bitsy showered and went to bed. Just a few minutes of open conversation with McConnel had made all the difference.

She spent an hour the next morning talking on the phone with Bo about an art piece he'd seen in an Atlanta dealer's office. He tried to convince her they could get it for a song and sell it for a windfall. But she convinced him the price was already inflated and they wouldn't make as much money as he thought. He gave up with his ego intact.

She changed into her paint clothes and went downstairs to her studio, determined to get a good start on the day. She cracked the window and turned on the exhaust fan.

Two hours into it, she heard a gentle knock on the open door when McConnel entered.

Bitsy lowered the brush and turned toward her. "Good morning."

"Morning. I'm sorry to interrupt you, but can we talk?"

Bitsy placed the palette and brush on the bench. "Sure. What's up?"

McConnel's face was taut and drawn. She slowly closed the distance between them. "It may take a little while." She moved to the couch and sat.

"This sounds serious." A little too serious for this early in the morning. Bitsy wiped her hands, slipped off her paint shirt, and placed it on the stool, then sat beside McConnel, whose face remained tense. Had she found the killer? Was it finally over, or was it something else? It was hard to read McConnel's expression.

"Bitsy, I've wrestled with if I should tell you this or not, but I think in the long run it's better if you know."

"I take it we aren't going to discuss what type of doughnuts to get this morning."

McConnel didn't smile, and she should have, but instead she looked at the floor. "I want you to know I've had you placed under security."

"What do you mean?"

"We have people around you for your protection."

"Protection?" It caught Bitsy off guard. This definitely wasn't about doughnuts. "I don't understand. What people? Why?"

McConnel sat straighter. "You have two female agents watching over you."

Bitsy couldn't believe what she was hearing. Why would McConnel do that? Her heart began to race. She couldn't catch her breath. She must be in danger. She couldn't think of any other reason. She jumped to her feet and began to pace. *He* was out there, getting closer now. She had nowhere to go, nowhere to hide. "Are you serious? What the hell is going on? What aren't you telling me?"

McConnel also stood. "Listen to me. It's a precautionary measure. You're my only witness."

"Well, hell. Why don't you just come out and say whoever killed Hallie Lynn wants me dead." The stress and fear pressed inward, building. She tried to control it, push it out, but it erupted, overpowering every thought, spewing out until all she wanted to do was run to get away from it. "What's going on? Tell me. I have a right to know."

"Bitsy, you're an important witness in this case."

"You've already said that. I need specifics."

"Why don't we discuss this, calmly?"

"*Calmly*? You want calm? Hallie Lynn's killer is out there, coming after me now because he thinks I know something. Only the joke is on me. I'm going to get killed because I can't remember. I don't understand what's happening. What's changed? I have a right to know why you have security around me, and you will tell me right now."

"I'm trying to tell you."

"No, you're not. You're not saying anything." Bitsy became aware she'd backed herself into the corner of the room and was wringing her hands. She rubbed them on her thighs and took a deep breath, trying to get control, trying to bring herself to a point where she didn't feel like the walls were crushing in on her.

McConnel reached for her. "Let's sit and talk. Would you like something to drink? Can I get you a cup of coffee or tea?"

"Whiskey."

"Okay. I'll be right back." McConnel left.

Bitsy scanned the room. One window was open slightly, the rest were locked, and the air conditioning was on. He couldn't get into this room unless he broke in. Would he do it? Would he throw something at the glass and climb through the window to get to her? She needed to buy a gun, carry it for protection. She walked toward the couch, determined to make herself sit, but she could only continue to pace. There was only one reason for security. Protection from *Him*. McConnel didn't even know who he was. Or did she? If she did know, why hadn't she arrested him and informed Bitsy? She determined to stop wringing her hands, but the impulse was strong and compelling because she needed immediate relief, release.

She rushed to her painting station and began to clean the brushes. She had to do something. She couldn't just be here in this room. She inspected the ends of the brushes. She could use them as weapons or throw the can of turpentine in his face. Had he been spying on her that night in the car on the darkened street? She should have known he'd come after her once Hallie Lynn was found. Of course he wanted her dead. He probably thought she knew more than she did. She was going to get murdered, and she didn't even know who he was. "Oh, God! He's coming after me." A splash of turpentine hit the tabletop. She stopped stirring, released her grip on the brush, and resumed pacing, legs heavy, each step weighted.

Suddenly McConnel was beside her, the alcohol in her hand. She offered it. "Come sit."

Bitsy reached for the glass and took a gulp, trying to steady herself. She choked, then wiped her mouth with the back of her hand.

McConnel led her to the couch and sat next to her. She took the drink from Bitsy and set it on the end table. "You have to listen to me." Her tone was gentle yet firm. "I've put security around you for your protection as a *precautionary* measure. They're some of the best security in the world. They're professional and know what they're doing. Kathrine Henderson, the one in charge, is coming over in a little while to meet you."

"I still don't understand. Why now?" She looked deeply into

McConnel's eyes to make sure she was telling the truth but, more than anything, to feel the connection between them. She needed it, like oxygen to breathe. She couldn't be alone. Now more than ever she needed McConnel emotionally and physically. She desperately searched for their connection but couldn't see it, couldn't feel it. Was it gone or momentarily obscured?

McConnel clasped Bitsy's hands.

There it was! Bitsy inhaled a cleansing breath. McConnel was with her. She wasn't alone.

"Bitsy. It's a *precautionary measure*. I haven't found him yet. I want to make sure you're safe."

All Bitsy heard were *precautionary* and *safe*. "I'm in danger."

"Honestly? Not with security around you."

"You can't guarantee that. How long have I had protection?"

"A few days."

"What's changed?"

McConnel didn't speak. The muscles in her jaw tightened.

Bitsy had never realized McConnel had a small, perfectly round mole on the right side of her face, near her hair line. It was reddish brown, faint, yet distinguishable if you looked close enough. "Has something happened that you're so concerned now for my safety?"

"Bitsy, I can't talk about that. All I can say is that you're safe."

"Do you know who he is? Has he done something else?"

"Once again, it's a precautionary measure."

McConnel wasn't going to tell her.

Bitsy had to act, do all she could to protect herself, get away somewhere safe. She stood. "I can't stay here. He'll find me, or God help me, he already knows where I live. He must be local. He's local and coming after me."

McConnel rose quickly and put her arms around her. "Bitsy, it's okay. You have two experienced agents outside watching over you. We won't let him get anywhere near you."

Bitsy's heartbeat slowed. The comfort of McConnel's embrace surrounded her. "You promise?"

"Yes," McConnel whispered.

Her voice was full of confidence, and her embrace gave Bitsy a measure of reassurance. She didn't have to go through this ordeal alone. McConnel would be there with her, at least until it was over. Oh, how she wanted it to be over.

McConnel eased away, leaving Bitsy cold and empty.

"It smells like turpentine and something else in here. What is it?" McConnel asked.

"Oil-based paints."

McConnel said nothing more, just watched her intently, like she was expecting something to happen.

"Are you worried I'm going to freak out? I think I already did that." Bitsy took a deep breath, determined to deal with what she had to. She picked up the drink with a shaky hand, swilled the rest of the alcohol, and then returned the empty glass to the table. "What's that security person's name again?"

"Henderson…Kathrine Henderson. Are you feeling better?"

"No, but I think I'm over the initial shock. I've got to make a call." She left McConnel standing in the studio. She needed privacy. She retrieved her cell from her pants pocket as she walked into the kitchen and pushed the number. It took only a moment before he answered. "Daddy, I need to come home."

"Darlin', what's wrong?"

The floodgate opened the minute she heard his comforting voice. She could barely speak in between frantic breaths. "I…I have to come home. I don't want to talk about it over the phone. Will you be there this weekend?"

"Yes. Do you want me to come get you?"

She willed herself to control her emotions but wasn't doing a very good job. "No. I'll drive."

"When?"

"I'll come soon."

"Call me before you leave."

"I love you, Daddy."

"I love you too, Little Bit. Drive safely. I'll see you soon."

Bitsy ended the call and returned to the studio.

McConnel was looking at the paintings in the corner of the room.

"I'm going home for the weekend. You're coming with me." Just saying the words brought her heartbeat almost back to normal. She no longer trembled. The walls weren't closing in.

McConnel raised her hands in protest. "Bitsy, I can't. I have things I need to take care of."

She had to go with her. Bitsy needed her. Couldn't she see it? "You can do them from Momma and Daddy's house."

McConnel stared at her for a long moment, speechless. She was thinking about it. "Okay, but not until after you meet Kathrine. She's outside."

Bitsy could do that, and then she'd pack, and they'd go home. Daddy and McConnel would keep her safe.

The doorbell rang.

"Would you mind getting that?" Bitsy said. "I need to freshen up a bit." She left without waiting for an answer.

She climbed the stairs and shut her bedroom door. They could wait. After all, they were *her* security. She washed her face and applied makeup, changed, then descended the stairs.

The woman standing beside McConnel was tall and athletic looking, her gun visible on her left side. Her hair was gathered in a braid.

She turned and smiled as Bitsy walked toward her.

"Hello. I'm Kathrine Henderson."

Bitsy greeted her, noting her firm handshake. "You're not wearing your badge?"

Kathrine glanced at McConnel, then back to her. "I'm not FBI. I'm with a private agency out of Nevada."

"Why don't we sit," McConnel said.

Bitsy reclined in the chair, McConnel and Kathrine on the sofa.

Kathrine had a pleasant smile and a gracefulness in the way she moved, but was she good at her job? Could she hit her target from a long distance? Was she fast? Strong? What about the others? How many were there? Bitsy offered her something to drink, not out of a desire to make her feel welcome but because that's what you did to be hospitable. She didn't feel it. Didn't want to do it, but it was something she should do.

Kathrine declined. "I know you have questions."

Yes, Bitsy did, and she needed them answered. "What are your qualifications to protect me?"

"I told you she'd want the facts," McConnel said.

Kathrine half smiled. "I went into the Army right after college and served six years in the military police. Then I took a job with the Ralston Agency and have been working in private security ever since."

"How many others? What are their qualifications?"

"We have four women assigned to you, a team of two on twelve-hour shifts at all times. One served in the Secret Service for ten years, The others are former Las Vegas police officers."

They at least sounded like they knew what they were doing. "I'm going home for the weekend. Is that a problem?" She didn't really care if it was.

"Not at all. We'll be near you wherever you go."

"What about everyone needing food and going to the bathroom?"

Kathrine laughed. "We manage."

Bitsy wasn't sure how to word the next questions. "Do I speak to them or acknowledge them in some way? How do I know who they are and not some strangers following me?"

"We can arrange for you to meet them if you'd like," McConnel said.

"Yes. I want to."

McConnel looked at Kathrine.

"We can gather at one of the big hotels in Savannah," Kathrine said.

McConnel nodded. "When do you want to do it, Bitsy?"

"Not until we get back from Momma and Daddy's."

"I'll set it up," Kathrine said. She stood.

Bitsy rose. She didn't care where they were or what they were doing. All she wanted was to go home and be with Daddy and McConnel. They'd keep her safe. They'd protect her. "We need to get ready to leave. Thanks for the information. I appreciate what you're doing. I hope y'all stay safe. Excuse me."

Bitsy couldn't leave the room fast enough and be on her way. Odd how she'd felt the opposite just a few weeks before. But everything had changed. Now what did her future hold? Did she even have a future?

CHAPTER TWENTY

After Kathrine left, McConnel went upstairs and packed. When she came back down, Bitsy was ready and insisted she wanted to drive, but McConnel thought differently. "It's not open for debate." Whether Bitsy acknowledged it or not, she was too stressed and distracted to get behind the wheel of a vehicle.

On the way to Pine Grove, Bitsy kept turning around, eyeing the other drivers.

"I assure you your security is there," McConnel said.

"Which car?"

McConnel searched in the review mirror. "The silver one, a couple of cars back."

"Why are they keeping their distance? So they won't be detected? I thought they'd stay right behind us."

"I'm with you, so they don't need to be as close as they normally would right now." The answer seemed to appease Bitsy, and she settled into her seat. "They don't want to interfere in your daily life, but they will if it's warranted. Their priority is to protect you at all costs."

Bitsy folded her hands in her lap. "*At all costs*?"

McConnel glanced at her. "Yes."

"Does that mean what I think it does?"

"They're dedicated professionals. They risk their lives every day. It's part of the job."

"You too?"

"My oath of office is to uphold the constitution of the United States against all enemies foreign and domestic, but yes, it does require risk of life."

"I guess I never thought about that part. I picture you interviewing people and asking endless questions, not pulling your gun out and aiming it at someone. I mean, I know you carry one, and I saw Kathrine's, but it's not something that crosses my mind."

"To be honest, I haven't drawn my weapon in a while, but I won't hesitate if I have to." She didn't want Bitsy to lose confidence in her.

Bitsy repositioned and shifted toward her. "Have you ever had to fire it?"

McConnel laughed.

"What's so funny?"

"If you want to know, just ask."

"Fine. Have you ever shot someone?"

"I don't discuss things like that."

Bitsy frowned. "Then why did you let me ask it?"

"I'm not sure. I guess to see if you would."

"You've been around me enough by now to realize I'll ask anything."

"That's true." McConnel was getting to know her, and their conversation felt comfortable and natural. "I like that about you, and because of that, I'll answer your question. Yes. I did fire my weapon during an attempted arrest and wounded two suspects in the process."

"Can you give details?"

"All I can say is it was a human trafficking operation, and I had no remorse about it."

Bitsy shivered. "That's a horrible crime."

"I went home and celebrated that night."

Bitsy perked up. "Oh, really? What'd you do, pop open a can of ginger ale and have at it?"

"Hey. I know how to party."

Bitsy laughed. "Sure you do. I bet you party about as well as you line dance."

McConnel enjoyed her teasing. It was light-hearted and endearing, but most of all it took her and Bitsy's mind off the present, even if it was only for a little while.

McConnel was now sure she was close to finding the killer. Unfortunately, the closer she got, the more at risk Bitsy would be. Whoever he was, he was methodical and organized. The discovery of Hallie Lynn's remains had obviously disrupted his routine. Now the

FBI was here, snooping, asking questions, which caused even more chaos in his life. The more she dug, the more desperate he'd get. It was to her advantage

Then it suddenly dawned on her. "You know what?"

Bitsy gazed out the passenger window. "What?"

"The killer dug a grave for Hallie Lynn, so now I'll dig one for him." McConnel gripped the steering wheel tighter.

Bitsy studied her. "I hope so. He deserves everything he gets."

When they arrived at the house, Mattie and a fit, gray-haired man were sitting side by side on the porch swing. They both stood when Bitsy rushed from the car and went to them. The man wrapped his arms around her and said something McConnel couldn't hear.

At that moment McConnel wished she had someone to hold her like he did Bitsy.

Now that Bitsy was with him, McConnel could see it was her daddy. They had four daughters, but it was obvious he and Bitsy had a special bond. It showed in the way he embraced her and his expression when he looked at her. He stepped back and held her at arm's length. "Little Bit, you look like you've been to the county fair and didn't win a thing."

Bitsy laughed and kissed his cheek. "Oh, Daddy! I have to say, I'm full spent."

"Well. We'll get you fixed up directly. Mattie, what're we feedin' these two renegades?" He smiled and let go of Bitsy, then moved toward McConnel. "Hello there. I'm Albert Collier. You the FBI agent from up north?"

The way he spoke was like water over rocks in a mountain stream, smooth and slow, yet rhythmic. The epitome of a Southern drawl, aged in generations before him and steeped in tradition.

McConnel offered her hand. "Hello, sir. I'm Special Agent McConnel."

He shook it gently. "What shall I call you?"

"McConnel is fine, sir."

"You call me Daddy, or Al, if you like." He grinned.

Mattie hugged Bitsy and then McConnel, her embrace warm and welcoming.

Bitsy looked past the driveway. "Where are they? I don't see them."

"See who?" Daddy asked.

McConnel glanced where Bitsy was searching. No other cars were in sight. "Don't worry. They're out there."

"Who's out where?" Daddy's voice was demanding. He must have been the type of man who got what he wanted. He stood a little over six feet, his thick hair peppered gray.

"I have security," Bitsy said.

McConnel wasn't sure if she was bragging, teasing, or just stating a fact.

The smile left his face, and he grimaced. "Was this your idea, McConnel?"

"Yes, sir." Somehow it didn't feel right addressing him as anything but "sir." Bitsy and Mattie had a demanding presence, but it was clear he was king of all he surveyed.

"I take it we have reason to be concerned," he said.

"It's a precautionary measure." McConnel didn't add any qualifiers to the statement. She needed to assess him right away. How would he respond?

"You must be getting close to finding the killer," he said. "You both look a little jumpy." He wrapped his arm around Bitsy. "You're safe here, darlin'."

Bitsy laid her head on his shoulder. "I know, Daddy."

"Well, honey, you rest and relax," he said. "Stay as long as you need to. I believe I'll mosey into the woods with McConnel here. Are you up to it?"

It wasn't really a request, more like a command. McConnel needed to lay out the ground rules with him quickly because she couldn't let him think he oversaw Bitsy's security or the investigation. Yes, this was his home, but she didn't want the situation to turn into a power struggle. She needed all the diplomacy she could muster. "Of course. Just let me freshen up and change into more comfortable clothes." She got the distinct impression he wasn't used to waiting for anything or anyone, but he was too much of a gentleman to deny her request. It was his Achilles' heel, and she'd take advantage of it.

Mattie motioned toward the front door. "You're in the same room as before, McConnel. Make yourself at home."

McConnel thanked her, and then she and Bitsy retrieved their bags from the car.

McConnel changed into jeans and an oversized shirt, refastened her weapon at her side, and started down the hall to the stairs.

Bitsy came out of her bedroom. "You be careful with him. He's a gentleman, but when it comes to his family, he's fierce."

"I'm counting on it. Don't worry about him."

"Don't' judge him too harshly. I'm also concerned about you."

"You're worried about me?"

Bitsy smiled. "I'm always thinking about you."

"That's good to know."

Bitsy grinned. "He's as fierce as Momma. They're a matched set."

McConnel laughed. "I'm sure he is. I don't know how long we'll be. This may take a while."

"You won't go far, will you?"

McConnel saw the fear grip Bitsy again. She cupped her face. "Your dad was right. You're safe here, even if I'm out of your sight. Remember, you've got two other people armed with weapons watching over you. Try to relax."

"Easier said than done."

McConnel continued down the stairs and out onto the veranda.

Bitsy's dad motioned for her to follow him, then slipped his hands into the pockets of his slacks as they strolled through the yard toward the pine grove. "Mattie tells me Bitsy thinks quite highly of you." He studied her, as if surmising all he could in a few seconds. "And that she's taken a liking to you."

McConnel didn't respond, sensing he had more to say.

"Her momma and I are very worried about her, especially with all this business about Hallie Lynn being found. Everything's been brought to the surface again. Are you as close to finding him as I hope you are?"

Him? He had a theory, and his concern for Bitsy was evident in his face.

"I can't tell you very much," McConnel said. "But yes, I believe I'm very close. Do you mind if I ask you a few questions?"

"Of course not. Anything to help."

She was glad for his willingness. It showed trust had been established. "Someone told me you know a lot about the case."

He nodded. "Ever since it happened, I've tried to find out all I can. Not for Hallie Lynn, although someone should have stood up for that precious darlin'. I'm sorry it wasn't me, but Little Bit was and is my priority. All my girls are important to me, but Bitsy's the youngest." He stopped and faced her. "She's never been the same since the night it happened. I always hoped she'd get over it, but she hasn't." His face looked strained as he continued leading her deeper into the woods. "Something's been broken or ripped out of her. I don't know which, but I do know she'll never completely heal until Hallie Lynn's killer is found. So, because of that, I've done my own investigation. Tell me what you know, and I'll see if I can add anything."

A yellow caution light flashed in McConnel's head. She had to be careful. He was the type of father who'd go after the killer if he suspected who he was. Even if he promised he wouldn't, he wouldn't be able to restrain himself. She'd seen it in other cases involving child victims but never in someone whose child was a witness. She reversed his question. "Given the information you've collected over the years, what do you suspect?"

He half snickered. "You're a wily little thing, aren't you?"

"I mean no disrespect, but we have to be cautious in cases like this. There's so much emotional trauma to the family and to anyone close to the victim. I see what Bitsy's been through. I see her pain and anguish, and the fear. I want to help her. I think the best way to do that is to find the killer and bring him to justice."

"So, you do care about Little Bit?"

It was McConnel's turn to stop and look at *him.* How much did she want to reveal about her feelings for Bitsy? They'd declared their attraction to each other. Did Bitsy's father need to know? Was it any of his business, or did he just think it was his right as a parent? She felt sure his question was asked in sincerity, but was it a betrayal to Bitsy if she told him, or would it cause problems later? She wanted to answer out of respect for him and Bitsy. "Yes. I do care about her, very much."

"What are your intentions toward my daughter?"

The question astonished her. Bitsy was a grown woman, divorced, successful, living on her own. She doubted Bitsy ever discussed how she felt about other women with her mom or dad, but then again maybe she did. He acted like she was an eighteen-year-old, dating someone seriously for the first time. Was it a cultural thing? She didn't want to offend him, not only because he was Bitsy's father but because he might know things that could help her. On the other hand, it seemed he was trying to extract more information from her than she'd ever get from him. "Mr. Collier, right now all I can focus on is this case."

"So, what you're really saying is you like her enough to protect your feelings about her from a prying old father."

McConnel laughed as they continued their walk. The air was thick with the scent of pine, and the cool evening brought a sense of belonging she hadn't expected. "I think I'm in culture shock down here."

He laughed. "Could be. All right. Ask me any questions you want, but first answer my questions about Little Bit's security."

"Be glad to," McConnel said.

"How many people you got watching her, and how good are they? Do I need to hire someone myself?"

"We have two teams of two, twelve-hour shifts, twenty-four hours a day. In my opinion they're some of the best in the world. No, I think if you hire more security, it will get in the way of my investigation."

"You're going to smoke him out, aren't you?"

McConnel didn't answer.

He stopped, withdrew his hands from his pockets, and crossed his arms over his chest. "Just so we understand each other, you better not be using my daughter as bait. If I suspect you are, I'm going to send her away until this is all over, whether she wants to go or not."

It wasn't a threat. It was information she needed to know concerning him. She didn't want to go to battle with him on top of everything else she was dealing with. She'd never tell him outright what she was doing. "I gather you think it's a male, local, maybe someone who knows Bitsy?"

He grabbed a few pine needles from an overhanging branch and rubbed them between his finger and thumb, then tossed them toward the ground.

McConnel smiled, remembering Bitsy had done the same thing.

"Yes, I do," he said. "Always have, and I think you and I both suspect that Chief Gibson's death was no accident."

He was right on the mark. "Mr. Collier, I'm impressed."

"You've got to pick something to call me besides Mr. Collier or sir. I have a feeling we're going to get to know each other. My name is Albert Thomas Collier. If you don't like Al or Daddy, call me AC. Some of my closest friends do."

"Okay. AC it is."

"Now, let's talk about the case." He continued toward the house. "I think it's someone local, and I think he knows what's going on in the county. In other words, he has access to information that could help him."

"Like someone in law enforcement?" McConnel asked.

"Yes, or a person in a government office, although I don't think there's anyone smart enough working in government around here who could pull this off for thirty years."

McConnel laughed. He had a good sense of humor. She saw where Bitsy had gotten hers. He thought what Chief Gibson had suspected. Had they discussed it over the years?

"He's most likely done this more than once," he said. "But I think Hallie Lynn was his first. It whetted his appetite, and then he branched out. I've got a list at home of all the similar disappearances in the surrounding states. There's something you need to know." The muscles in his jaw tightened and he frowned. "The chief and I agreed he's probably Southern. True Southerners don't like to go outside their comfort zone. If you're trying to link similar cases, stick to the surrounding states. I doubt he'd go up north. Tying any of those cases to this one would be a waste of time."

"I'd like to compare your list to mine," McConnel said.

"You see. We're on the right track already."

McConnel was sure of it. "I appreciate all you're sharing with me, AC, but I can't return the favor."

"I understand. It's okay. I want to help where I can. I owe it to Hallie Lynn, but more than that, I want this over with as soon as possible for my daughter's sake."

He was a good man, and McConnel was glad she'd spent time with him.

They returned to the house.

That evening, after she reviewed his list of similar cases, she called Jenkins.

"I was just about to email you the reports you asked for," he said. "It looks like your suspicions about the crash were correct. Gibson's car was more than likely rammed from behind. Our expert thinks it was a larger truck with a bull bar, one of those big metal ones, and before you ask, I'm already working on a list of all large-truck ownership within a fifty-mile radius."

"That's great. Thank you. Would you get me a list of all bull bars ordered in the fifty-mile radius? I also need something else if you can get it."

"I will if I can."

"A cross reference of vacation schedules for all the law enforcement personnel in the county and cities within a fifty-mile radius of Springfield, beginning when Hallie Lynn disappeared. I want to see who was on vacation or leave on the date she was abducted and coordinate them with our other similar suspected cases."

"You think the killer is in law enforcement?"

"Or some type of leadership that would give him access to evidence or information about the cases. Chief Gibson, and now Bitsy's daddy, suspected it, and I'm inclined to believe it myself. I'm at the Collier home for the weekend. I know it's going to take time, but let me know as soon as you have anything I can use."

"I'll get our people on it, but it's a big ask."

"You need to be careful not to alert anyone we're looking into."

"Unfortunately, many of those police departments are small and not online and may not have records that go back that far." The concern was evident in his voice.

"Do the best you can," McConnel said. "Anything you can get will be helpful."

After the call ended, McConnel went downstairs. Bitsy and her mom and dad were playing cards in Mattie's favorite room.

Was this what it was like to have a family? To come home and know you were welcome? To be together and enjoy each other's companionship? It was something McConnel had never experienced as an adult. She watched them as they laughed and talked. Bitsy looked relaxed, but how long would it last?

CHAPTER TWENTY-ONE

Bitsy eased onto the porch swing, McConnel beside her in the darkness, the sounds of the tree frogs and cicadas surrounding them. She swung slowly, longing for the familiar comfort their serenade had always brought. Instead, she felt only uneasy, discontented. Where were her security people? Were they watching her right now? Did they use binoculars, or were they close? Was he close? She searched the shadows until they were engulfed by the ebony of the night. The thought of being observed sent a cold shiver of dread through her.

"What's the matter?" McConnel asked.

"Is safety an illusion? A false concept, like being in control? I want to feel at peace, but as hard as I try, I can't. I've felt this discontent for so long I don't know if I ever will be able to feel genuinely comfortable with myself. I'm so tired of trying to keep it together. It's exhausting."

"I wish I could help."

"You are. I feel at least some measure of safety when you're nearby. I hope I'll feel differently when this is all over." Now conscious she'd been rubbing her hands together again, she clasped them in her lap.

They sat in silence.

The gentle motion of the wooden swing lulled her into momentary relief. She rested her head on the back of the swing and closed her eyes.

Suddenly, she jerked awake. Had she drifted off to sleep? "How long have we been out here?"

"About forty-five minutes. Why don't we go in so you can get some rest?" McConnel stood.

Bitsy followed. "I hope I can. I feel bone weary." She hesitated, the vague sense of fear still lingering on the edges of the night. "Would you do something for me?"

"If I can."

"Would you mind staying in my room with me? I know what we're trying to do, but please. I need you beside me, just for tonight."

"How would your mom feel about it?"

"Frankly, I don't care. Daddy will put her in her place."

"If you need me to, I can stay with you."

"I do. Tomorrow, when we go back to the city, I want to meet my other security."

"I'll arrange it with Kathrine."

They walked into the house, Bitsy straining from exhaustion as she climbed the stairs.

When McConnel came into Bitsy's room, she was wearing her pj's. "Which side do you want me to sleep on?"

"Take the right, if you don't mind." Bitsy pointed.

McConnel slid in and covered herself with the sheet and light quilt.

Bitsy opened the window, turned out the light, and then sat on the edge of the bed for a moment. "Are you sure you don't mind? I'm sorry to ask."

"Not at all."

Bitsy plugged in her cell, placed it on the nightstand, and swung into bed. She scooted toward McConnel, the nearness of her body comforting and reassuring, chasing out the fear, and worry, and stress. She shouldn't ask what she knew she was going to, but she couldn't help herself. "McConnel?"

"Yes?"

"Would you hold me?"

McConnel didn't speak but moved closer, slipping her arm over her waist. "It's all right," she whispered. "Sleep."

The last thing Bitsy was aware of was the song of the night creatures in the darkness and how McConnel's body molded to hers.

She sat up, soaked in sweat. The curtains swayed softly from the gentle breeze coming through the open window. The sunlight danced on the rug. She touched the empty bed beside her. Where was McConnel? She slid from the mattress and went directly to McConnel's room, but she wasn't there. Bitsy returned to her room and showered, the eerie sensation of déjà vu clinging to her as she dressed. She slowly descended the stairs, relieved when she heard Momma and McConnel laughing and the clamor of breakfast preparations. She entered the kitchen.

Momma held a spatula in her hand and watched her as she neared. McConnel turned toward her.

"Darlin, you're so pale," Momma said. "Sit before you fall."

McConnel scooted out the chair beside her and patted the seat. "Did you sleep well?"

Bitsy sat. "Well enough."

Momma brought a plate of eggs, bacon, and grits and set it in front of her. She then placed a cup of coffee next to it. "Eat. I'm not kidding. You haven't had more than a few bites since you got here."

"Where's Daddy?" Bitsy asked. She picked up her fork, which was unusually heavy and large. Why was it so big?

"He already ate and went to town to get something or other for the garden." Momma sat and continued her meal.

Both McConnel and Momma stopped eating and watched her intently.

"What?"

"Where have you been, young lady?" Momma abruptly stood.

McConnel moved next to her, resting her hand on her gun, clipped to her side.

Bitsy dropped her fork. It hit the china plate, bounced, and then in slow motion landed on the edge of the tablecloth, now covered in blood. She pushed herself away and staggered backward, trying to get her balance. "What's happening?"

"Why did you do it?" McConnel pleaded.

"Do what? I didn't do anything."

Momma pointed toward the kitchen door. "You killed Hallie Lynn. You didn't tell who he was, and now he'll come after all of us."

Confusion and fear twisted in her gut, clawing at her. She could see his shadow outside the kitchen door, lurking. He was coming for them, and no matter how much she begged him to leave them alone, he'd get to them. She lunged for McConnel's gun, pulling it from the holster, then turned and tried to squeeze the trigger.

He ripped the screen door off the hinges and came toward her.

The gun wouldn't fire. She kept pulling the trigger, but it wouldn't go off.

"The safety," McConnel yelled. "The safety's on."

Bitsy inspected the gun but couldn't find the latch to unlock it.

He grabbed at her.

She screamed as loud as she could.

He gripped her shoulders and shook her.

McConnel's voice came from somewhere above her. "Bitsy, wake up. You're having a nightmare." She was leaning over her, her hand on her shoulder.

Bitsy reached for her and pulled her toward her. "He's here. He's here."

McConnel hugged her, then sat on the bed next to her and stroked her arm. "It's all right. It's just a dream. You're safe."

A hint of daylight peeked in from the window.

Bitsy clasped McConnel's hand.

"It's just a dream," McConnel said. "Nothing more."

Bitsy let go of her and positioned the pillow against the headboard, then scooted against it, scrubbing her face. "What time is it?"

"Around five. I got up to go to the bathroom, and when I came back you were calling out." McConnel remained by her side. "Can I get you some water or something?"

"No. Just stay here for a minute."

"Are you all right?"

Bitsy didn't know. Was she still dreaming or finally awake? Her head was throbbing, her heartbeat pulsing through her temples.

McConnel watched her, not saying anything.

Bitsy massaged the sides of her head. "I hate dreams where you can't tell if you're awake or not."

"Those are the worst," McConnel said.

Bitsy yawned. "I don't want to get up this early."

McConnel went around the side of the bed and got in next to her. "You don't have to."

Bitsy slid down, repositioned her pillow and covered up, then took McConnel's hand. "Thanks for spending the night with me. It helped."

"I'm sorry you had a bad dream." McConnel stroked her hair. "Sometimes those demons are hard to chase away."

"Tell me about it."

"Close your eyes and go back to sleep," McConnel said.

Bitsy did as she was instructed and tried to ease into that gentle place where all the negative emotions slid away and faded into nothingness. "Your voice is very soothing. Talk to me."

"I don't think anyone has ever said that about me."

Bitsy relaxed in the comfort of McConnel's closeness.

"I probably shouldn't say this," McConnel said, her voice softer, "but I loved being next to you in the night."

Intrigued, Bitsy couldn't keep her eyes closed.

McConnel grinned. "The purpose of this is to help you relax."

Bitsy smiled and let her lids flutter closed again. "That thought may not help me get back to sleep."

"Oops. Sorry. I like your family, even Louise."

Bitsy grinned. "That's because you don't know her. Just wait." She began to relax. *Wait.* Would McConnel have a place in her future?

"Your mother plays with her poker chips when she has a good hand."

"Um." Bitsy began to drift off.

She woke, but before she opened her eyes, she reached out for McConnel, relieved when she felt her next to her. She rolled and looked at the clock on the nightstand. Seven fifteen.

McConnel stirred, then repositioned, facing her.

She had a softness about her, a gentle presence, yet she was strong and capable. Why wasn't she attached to someone? "Have you ever been in love?"

McConnel placed her hands under her chin. "That's a deep question for first thing in the morning." She said it softly, then smiled, looking charming and full of comfort.

McConnel didn't answer right away. "I thought I was once." She cleared her throat. "But I'm afraid I've always been too selfish to really love, at least the way I think I should. How about you? Did you love your wife?"

Bitsy hadn't expected her to ask about her marriage. "I think I did at the time. At least as much as I was capable of. I look back now and can see the mistakes I made. Love can be elusive…And fragile. At least that's been my experience."

"How long did you know her before you got married?"

"Evidently not long enough."

McConnel laughed. "I find it fascinating that we spend so much time with those we care about, and we think we know them, but we don't."

Bitsy was sure there was deeper meaning in McConnel's words. "Anything you want to talk about?"

McConnel pursed her lips. "Not really."

She'd withdrawn. It was sudden, like a door being shut. Bitsy watched her, seeing sadness. What memories had brought it on? What had caused this change? "Was it painful?"

"What?"

"I see it in your eyes."

"Maybe someday we can talk about it, but not today. I need to get a shower."

McConnel left the bed and went to her room.

Bitsy was suddenly alone. It was a hollow, empty feeling, and she felt it to her core. Had she gone too far? Had she penetrated some shroud of protection McConnel had wrapped around herself? Why was it there? She simply wanted to know her, not on the surface, but inside. She was sure it would be worth the price, but did they have the time?

CHAPTER TWENTY-TWO

It was difficult for McConnel to have to stand by and watch Bitsy struggle with increasing fear and nightmares. Her anxiety seemed to grow with each passing day.

In hopes of helping her, she set up a time on Monday for Bitsy to meet her security team at a hotel in downtown Savannah. If the killer was following Bitsy, it was important he didn't discover their identity. Kathrine was already exposed because she'd been to the house, but they needed to keep the others off the grid as much as possible.

McConnel and Bitsy arrived at the hotel and took the elevator to the third floor.

Kathrine answered the door and motioned for them to come in, then introduced Bitsy to her assigned team. Bitsy seemed more relaxed after they explained the process of guarding her, their qualifications, and experience. Would this make a difference? Would Bitsy be able to get through the rest of the investigation without more trauma? It was important to McConnel that she help her as much as she could, yet stay focused on what she had to do.

The conversation was moving along until Bitsy brought up something not totally unexpected.

"I know McConnel can't stay with me all the time. I want one of you at the house with me when she can't be."

Kathrine glanced at McConnel as if she'd prepared for Bitsy's question. "That can be arranged. As a matter of fact, it's much easier for us if at least one team member is near you."

Bitsy uncrossed her legs, relaxed her shoulders, and stopped gripping her hands. "I was worried it might be a problem."

"Not at all," Kathrine said.

This could be a good thing for Bitsy, and it would free up more of McConnel's time. Each team member was capable, but Kathrine would be the best choice, given that Bitsy was more familiar with her.

"I can stay with you," Kathrine said.

The details were worked out, and then McConnel took Bitsy home. She'd tried to get her to ride with Kathrine, but Bitsy refused, insisting McConnel not leave her.

"If you want security with you, you should let her drive you," McConnel said. "That way you can get to know her, and you'd feel better about being with her."

"She'll be there at the house. We can visit then, and she'll go with me to work."

"How are you going to explain her?"

"She's my second cousin."

McConnel laughed. "I'm glad you decided to have her stay with you."

"I don't see how I have much of a choice. I'm hoping I'll feel better."

When they arrived home, McConnel moved into the murder room and gave Kathrine her bedroom. It didn't matter now where she slept, since she spent most of her time in there poring over the information anyway, searching, trying to figure out what she'd missed or studying the pieces to connect them. The answers were there, somewhere.

A message from Jenkins was waiting when she opened her email, containing an overwhelmingly long list of people who owned trucks and another of bull bars ordered in the area. She could spend weeks sorting through it and needed help to narrow it down. Was it time to call in more agents? The killer knew she was here. Did it matter now? Maybe more agents would flush him out, but then again, the increased number could backfire and spook him. He could take off. Disappear. She was only one investigator. How much of a threat was she? She wanted him to have confidence, and overconfidence was even better.

She picked up her cell and called Bitsy's daddy. "AC, I need your help."

They discussed types of trucks and which ones would be more likely to have a steel front push bar and why.

"It'd be a heavy-duty utility truck or a wrecker," he said. "Don't worry about them getting the bull bar online. Start with the dealerships. No respecting truck owner would get it anywhere but from there. They last a long time, so go back at least ten years. In the South, they're almost as common as gun racks in the cabs. You need me to come help you?"

She hesitated. He might get too much information and go off on his own. She'd gotten to know him over the weekend, and one thing was very clear. He'd do anything for his daughter. "I appreciate the offer, but I think I can get what I need. You've been a great help. Thank you."

"I hate to say it, but you'll get better results if you let me and some of the boys assist you. We'll be discreet."

He was being honest, and as much as she didn't want to believe it, it was true. The South was a different culture, and it was his way of saying, *You're a woman and you're an outsider. Don't go where you aren't wanted.*

"We have our own way of dealing with things down here," he said.

Was this something better left to *the boys*? No. Screw that. It was her job and she had to do it, no matter what the cultural differences were. Sometimes she felt like she was stepping back in time. He couldn't legally get what she needed no matter how much he wanted to help her.

"You do know you're grasping at straws," he said.

There was a deafening silence. She could hear him breathing. "Every little thing will help."

Was he trying to get more information from her so he could go off on his own?

"Thanks, AC."

She ended the call after briefly updating him about Bitsy and then immediately contacted Jenkins. She reported what she was doing. "I need a list of all truck dealerships in the designated radius and steel front bumpers—bull bars—installed. I know I have your list of bull bars ordered, but I need to narrow it down."

"Are you serious?"

"I've already had someone tell me I'm grasping at straws. Don't you say it, and don't tell me how long it's going to take. I need it as fast as you can get it."

"I'll do what I can, but I have to ask. What if he bought a used truck from someone else and didn't go through a dealership? And for that matter, what if it's not even his truck?"

McConnel stopped and took a breath. "I know it's a desperate move, but please. I'm closing in. I just need a break."

"I'm not trying to squash your ideas, but who ever told you you're grasping at straws was mistaken. It's not straws. It's shadows. Your theory has so many holes it's a sieve."

"I know. Humor me."

"You still dealing with culture shock?" There was teasing in his voice.

It eased the tension at the back of her neck. "I'm trying to adjust."

"I'll jump on it and get back to you as soon as possible. The vacation schedules will take time. How are things going?"

"I think my witness is falling apart. I need to wrap this up."

"Are you sure you don't want more agents?" He now asked that question every time he talked with her.

"It'll only cause more trouble than it's worth. The last thing I need is to draw attention to myself and the case. If things change, I'll let you know."

When she ended the call she flopped across the bed, looking up at the ceiling. Yes, she was grasping. Discouragement was a big deterrent in her line of work, especially cold cases. It was constantly banging at her door. She had to ignore it. She just needed something that could put this case over the finish line.

Two frustrating days later she read Jenkin's text. *Good news. Check your email.*

She hurriedly opened it, then printed out the attachments. The area dealerships, names and addresses of truck purchases with the license numbers, and the bull bars ordered. Two thousand three hundred and thirty-two bull bars had been purchased within the criteria area she'd requested. She compared their names to the list of suspects she'd compiled. None of them matched. Of course not. Why would it be easy? It took her a day to set up the database into the program Kathrine had given her.

The next morning, she entered the parameters, hoping the probabilities would give her what she needed. It came back with forty-two possible names.

Kathrine knocked lightly and then entered. "Bitsy's going shopping. She wanted me to ask if you need anything."

McConnel wasn't aware she'd come into her room until she spoke. Focused on entering the owners' names into her travel app, she didn't look at her. "No. I'm good." She kept entering the names. "Where to start?" she mumbled to herself.

"What?"

McConnel looked at her, bringing her back into the conversation. "I'll most likely be out the rest of the day."

"Need any help?" Kathrine asked.

"No, thanks."

Kathrine left.

McConnel chose the nearest address and pulled out of the driveway.

Nine hours later, she'd eliminated five trucks and interviewed ten owners. None of them were who she was looking for, although she was positive a few had committed some type of crime.

She drove to number eleven's address—a small, one-story house, set back from the road. An older gray Ford F-250 was parked in front of the single garage. The vehicle was mud-caked and had a deep dent on the front quarter panel. She matched the license plate and then inspected the front steel bull bar. It looked well used, banged up, with several specks of embedded silver and red paint. Chief Gibson's daughter's car was silver, the most common color for its make and model.

She reviewed his name from the list. Everett Bigalow.

Her heartbeat quickened as she approached the front door and then knocked several times. No answer. She moved to the window, spying past the broken screen and peering into the cluttered living room. No lights. No sign of anyone. Perhaps he had another vehicle. She circled the house, stepping around the discarded trash and piles of scrap metal and not seeing any other outbuildings or structures on the property. She approached her car, observing her surroundings for a few moments. Nothing out of the ordinary. It was almost dark, too dark to continue her search for other trucks, but this vehicle was promising. She'd run a more thorough search on him and return in the morning.

❖

When she got back to the house, Bitsy met her at the front door. "Where have you been all day?"

McConnel entered. "Out following up on leads."

"I tried to call you, but you didn't answer."

"I'm sorry. I had my phone on mute. I figured if it was important, you'd leave a message."

"What's the point of having a cell phone if you don't answer it?"

She reeked of alcohol.

McConnel looked past her at Kathrine, who shrugged and left them alone.

"How was your day?" McConnel couldn't think of anything else to say. Bitsy's now-frequent outbursts were beginning to be worrisome and distracting, and she was drinking more. Kathrine had reported that when Bitsy wasn't at work she was constantly in her studio—not painting, just staring at the canvas. Each time McConnel had checked on her, Bitsy had a glass of alcohol in one hand and a paintbrush in the other. Conversations were limited to telling McConnel to be careful and how Bitsy wanted this all to be over. It seemed as if each hour she became more fragile.

McConnel took Bitsy by the hand and led her to the sofa, sitting her down beside her. "Bitsy, this has to stop."

"What?"

McConnel pointed to her. "This. Have you looked in the mirror lately?"

"What's that supposed to mean?"

"When's the last time you slept? I hear you up at all hours of the night."

"I'm doing the best I can."

"I'm worried about you, and so are your mom and dad and everyone else who cares about you."

"You care about me? That's news. You haven't said two words to me in days."

"I've been busy, trying to solve this case."

"How would I know what you're doing? I never see you, and when you're here, you're hiding in *that* room."

"Bitsy, you know why I'm in there, and you know why I don't want *you* in there."

Bitsy stood. "I can't take this anymore." She began to pace.

It was heartbreaking to have to stand by and watch her deteriorate. "I think you should see your psychiatrist. It'd be good to talk about how you're feeling."

"She'd just tell me to quit drinking and take those damn pills."

"Maybe you should."

Bitsy stopped and glared at her. "You too? I swear it's a conspiracy. Momma, Daddy, Dr. Take These Pills and Get Some Rest, and now you."

McConnel moved toward her, grasping her shoulders so she couldn't turn away. "Bitsy, listen to me. We all care about you. For me, more than I want to admit. You need rest. A good night's sleep can do wonders, and the pills the doctor ordered can help with that. There's nothing wrong with using them, but you can't take them with alcohol."

Bitsy didn't respond, her stare penetrating.

McConnel knew what Bitsy needed, what she wanted, but should she do it? It was only a temporary measure. In the long run was it the best thing for Bitsy? She ignored the internal caution. "If you like, I'll stay the night in your room with you."

Bitsy flung her arms around her neck and pulled her close. She was trembling. "Please."

"I have conditions."

Bitsy let go of her, and her eyes narrowed. "What?"

"You stop drinking, take the pills as prescribed, and see your psychiatrist as soon as she can work you in."

"Are you serious?"

"Yes, very."

Bitsy arched an eyebrow. "Wow! That's quite a list."

"How much do you want me in bed next to you?"

"You must think you're pretty special."

"No, Bitsy. I think you're the one who's *special*."

Bitsy eyes flooded with tears. "I know it'll be hard for you, but

I need you with me. It's the only time I can get a sound sleep. I tell myself Kathrine and the others are here, watching over me, but unless you're right next to me, I can't relax enough. I'm sorry."

McConnel heard the truth in her words. It would be difficult, but she wanted to do it for Bitsy. Could she hold off the thoughts of loving her, wanting her? She had to put them aside.

Chapter Twenty-three

B itsy gripped the bathroom sink and stared at her reflection in the mirror. "You're pathetic." But the thought of McConnel next to her all night brought nothing but relief. She no longer cared about anything but feeling safe and being with her. She'd do whatever she had to do to get through this.

She switched off the bathroom light and went to the bed where McConnel was already waiting. She crawled in beside her, reached over, and turned off the lamp.

McConnel wiggled slightly away. "Do you have enough room?"

"Yes." Bitsy scooted closer. "I'm not apologizing for wanting you in my bed."

McConnel laughed. "I hope not." She slid her arm around Bitsy's waist.

Bitsy took a deep breath and closed her eyes as relief flowed through her. "Thank you."

"You're welcome. Believe me, it's my pleasure."

Bitsy smiled as she drifted off to sleep.

She woke a little before daylight, grateful she'd slept through most of the night. She eased out of bed, trying not to wake McConnel. By the time she dressed and came out of the bathroom, McConnel was sitting up, propped against a pillow.

"Good morning. Feel better?" McConnel asked.

Bitsy wanted to kiss her but didn't. "I do. Thanks to you. I'm going in to work."

"You sure you want to do that? Might be best if you stayed home a few days."

McConnel had the most beautiful morning face. Bitsy sat beside her on the bed. "I think that's a good idea, but I need to take care of a few things. You do your job, and I'll do mine."

"That sounds like a good plan." McConnel drew her knees up and wrapped her arms around them. "I'll be out most of the day today."

"Something new?"

McConnel slowly shook her head. "No. Just follow-up and investigating truck owners."

"Can I fix you breakfast?" Bitsy asked. She wanted to repay her, do something to show her how much she appreciated all she was doing for her. Daylight slipped through the window, and her fear and anxiety ebbed. McConnel was right. It was time to see her psychiatrist. "Promise me you'll sleep in here again tonight."

McConnel reached for her hand. "I will if you need me to."

"Plan on it." Bitsy stood. "See you later."

She left McConnel and knocked softly on Kathrine's door.

"Come in."

Bitsy poked her head in. "I want to leave for work around seven. Is that okay?"

"I'll be ready."

Bitsy went to the kitchen and made coffee.

After breakfast, Kathrine insisted she drive Bitsy to work. It didn't matter to Bitsy who drove. Kathrine remained in the lobby while Bitsy went into her office.

Lilly came in, shut the door, and pointed backward. "Is *she* going to be here the entire day, every day? I feel like I'm being watched."

"She's going to be with me until this is all over."

Lilly placed her hands on her hips. "When will that be?"

Bitsy shrugged. "Not sure."

"Are you staying today or just here for a while?"

"I'm wrapping up some paperwork, and then I'm leaving."

Lilly slid into one of the chairs in front of the desk.

Bitsy leaned back. How much more would Lilly grill her? She didn't want to deal with it. "I'm not coming back in for a while. I don't know how long that's going to be. No, there's nothing new about the case, and if there was, I doubt McConnel would tell me."

"You look like shit."

Bitsy shrugged. "I look better than I did last night."

Lilly gave her a closed-lipped smile. "What can I do to help?"

"Nothing. Just keep things going the best you can." The anxiety began to build. She massaged her temple and noticed her hand was shaking. "If something critical comes up, call me. Otherwise, everything's on hold for now. Tell Bo to phone me with an update every couple of days. I don't want him or you coming to the house."

"I can't bring you anything? What if you need to sign something?"

"Send it by courier."

"No stop-bys?"

"No."

"I don't understand."

"You don't need to. Just wrap things up here. Forward office calls to your phone, and stay home starting tomorrow. I'll pay your normal salary."

Lilly's eyes widened. "You will?"

Bitsy couldn't help but laugh. "Yes. Come in only when you feel you need to until I tell you otherwise."

"I'll be glad when this whole damn thing is over," Lilly said.

"So will I."

Lilly left the room.

Bitsy called her psychiatrist and scheduled an emergency appointment, as per her agreement with McConnel.

Kathrine drove her there and waited in the lobby.

When she was summoned, Bitsy entered the office and sat on the small couch, as she'd done since she was eleven. She clutched her handkerchief.

Dr. Crenshaw, sitting directly opposite her in her overstuffed chair, crossed her legs and greeted her, then gazed at her without speaking.

Bitsy half smiled but didn't respond. It was odd that she'd made the appointment to talk with her, and now suddenly she didn't want to say anything. But then again, it was only the agreement with McConnel that had gotten her here in the first place. She stared at the lovely soft, muted lavender carpet. The idea that she could or couldn't talk about anything she wanted was comforting. She had a choice. If she wanted to spend the time looking at the floor or out the window, it would be all right with Dr. Crenshaw.

She was safe. Kathrine and her big gun were in the next room, the others were outside somewhere in a car, and McConnel was a phone call away, even if she didn't answer it, but she knew McConnel would return her call if Bitsy left a message. She cleared her throat. "You know about the FBI agent here to investigate Hallie Lynn's murder?"

Dr. Crenshaw nodded.

Bitsy tried not to wring her hands. She wanted to stand and pace. The nervous energy was building again, demanding she deal with it in some way. McConnel, the killer, and Hallie Lynn were enmeshed, connected, inseparable. Maybe that's what bothered her so much—the fact that she couldn't deal with one without the others. McConnel was bound to them, but Bitsy didn't want her to be.

A drink to calm her would be good. No. Not good. Pills? McConnel in bed next to her? She wasn't coping with what was happening. Well, she was coping, just not in a healthy way. She knew it, and so did everyone around her. It was easier to reach for a drink than muster the energy to work through the situation. She didn't have the strength. She was exhausted. Worn out. "I'm sick and tired of trying to cope."

"Are you taking the medication?"

"Do I look like I'm taking it?" It was a sharp retort, void of any feelings of courtesy. She reminded herself Dr. Crenshaw was not her personal punching bag. "Sorry."

She cleared her throat again. She must have been more nervous than she'd thought. It'd been three years since she was last here. The office hadn't changed. Same paintings. Same furniture. Same colors on the walls. Same carpet. "I have a bodyguard and security."

Dr. Crenshaw continued to watch her. "Did you arrange for it, or did the FBI agent?"

Bitsy couldn't recall whose idea it'd been, but then she remembered. "McConnel did." She leaned back in the chair, gripping the arms. Why was she so nervous about talking? Dr. Crenshaw had gone through her life with her, knew everything about her—the good, bad, and very ugly. The room was wallpapered with Bitsy's pain and anguish. Dr. Crenshaw probably knew her better by now than Bitsy knew herself.

Bitsy studied her. Her face had aged. The wrinkle lines around her mouth and eyes were more pronounced, her hair had thinned, and her brown eyes were softer now. When would she retire? It was a disturbing thought. This might be the last time she'd get to talk with her. The realization sank deep, bringing a sadness Bitsy hadn't expected. "Will you be retiring soon?"

Dr. Crenshaw smiled. "Oh, Lord, Bitsy. I'll be around until the Man in the Moon comes down."

Bitsy laughed. "You've been such a comfort to me over the years."

"You know you're my favorite, always have been since you were little, and now you're coming to the end of your journey with Hallie Lynn."

It was a curious statement. Why would she say it? "Am I?"

"Why do you think you're having such a hard time with it?"

Was that all it was? An ending?

"You've carried this with you all your life. Sometimes letting go can be the most difficult task."

Dr. Crenshaw had a way of helping Bitsy work through her confusion. One question could open a doorway Bitsy could walk through and find her way out. She placed her hands in her lap and took in a deep breath. "I'm afraid."

"Of what?"

Did Dr. Crenshaw not know her situation?

"I have bodyguards. McConnel is going to find him. I'm not coping well with the uncertainty. Chief Gibson is dead. McConnel thinks *he* killed him. Someone's been following me. McConnel thinks it's the killer. He thinks I know something, and now he's after me. I've told McConnel everything I can remember. I don't know anything else."

Dr. Crenshaw wrote something in her notebook, then looked at her.

Bitsy always wondered what she'd written about her over the years. A part of her wanted to read her record, but then a part didn't ever want to look at it.

"It's hard when we don't feel we have control of our lives."

Bitsy scoffed. "Tell me about it."

Dr. Crenshaw smiled. "At some point everything ends, Bitsy."

"I never thought this would. I honestly never thought I'd be able to put what happened down and go on."

"Yet you've worked toward it all your life."

Bitsy looked out the window. "I just want to feel safe."

They discussed what Bitsy could do and how to cope. Dr.

Crenshaw encouraged her to take the anti-anxiety medication and the sleeping pills. They set another appointment to meet in a week.

Bitsy left feeling a little better but still anxious. She had a lot to work through and couldn't do it in a one-hour session with Dr. Crenshaw. But at least now she had hope, and that would be enough to get her through the next few days.

Chapter Twenty-four

McConnel pulled into Bigalow's driveway, the morning sun already beating down on her. No truck. A rusty riding lawn mower, its tires flat, sat abandoned near the far side of the house, encased in a tomb of high weeds and grass. She banged on the door as she identified herself. No response. She knocked again and waited several more minutes, then left, satisfied no one was home.

She drove to the address of his last listed employment, a car repair shop nine miles north. She parked in one of the empty spaces near the main entrance. A loud, irritating buzzer went off when she entered the office.

An older man, in his late fifties, wiping his grimy hands with a green rag, sauntered in from the back area. He was wearing a blue-and-white-striped soiled shirt with the name Ray on the right side of his chest.

"Can I hep ya?" He tossed the rag onto the filthy glass counter.

McConnel flashed her badge and introduced herself.

His face tensed.

"Good morning. Are you the owner?"

"Yeah."

"What's your full name?"

He straightened and looked into her eyes. "Raymond Zigmond."

"Do you have an employee named Everett Bigalow?"

Ray's shoulders drooped, and he frowned. "I do, but that jackass never showed up for work this morning. Never called. Never said nothing. Just didn't show, and he knew we had that damn engine to rebuild."

"Is it like him to not come in?"

"Well, he's not the most dependable worker I have, but he's never left me hanging like this before. I swear when he finally gets here, I'm going to rip him a new one."

"How long has he worked for you?"

"About six years."

"Can you tell me anything about him?"

"Is he in some kind of trouble?"

"I just need to talk with him. Do you have a phone number for him?"

"Yeah, but he's not answering. It goes right to voice mail. I've called three times already this morning." He gave her the number.

"Can you tell me who he hangs out with?"

"Well, he likes the ladies." He grinned, revealing a missing tooth on the right side of his mouth. "He hangs out at the local watering hole about two miles south of here, County Line Tavern. He's buddies with some of the other guys who work here. Do you want to talk with them?"

She found out he also drove one of the cars from the shop on occasion but didn't own any vehicles other than his truck. She talked with the other employees but didn't get any new information. She instructed Ray to call her if Bigalow showed up, gave him a business card, and then left.

At ten fifteen she stopped for gas and coffee, then drove to the County Line Tavern. Two cars were in the parking lot when she knocked on the front entrance.

A gruff male voice responded. "We're closed."

"FBI. Open up."

After a pause, the handle moved, a latch released, and the door swung open.

"What can I do ya for?" A man in his late forties or early fifties, tall, with large muscular arms, stood in the doorway, grinning. He was wearing a stained white full apron and had a rope tattoo on his right wrist. He'd probably been a sailor of some sort.

"I'd like to talk to you about a man named Everett Bigalow."

"Can't help ya. I'm just the cook and part-time handyman. You need to come back and talk to the owner or bartender. They'll be in," he checked his watch, "around eleven."

"You by yourself?"

"Yes, ma'am."

"Whose vehicles are those?" She pointed to the parking lot.

"The green Chevy is mine. The black Ford is the owner's wife's. She was here but left with one of her friends. Don't know where she went or when she'll be back."

McConnel was satisfied he wasn't trying to hide anything. "Okay, thanks. I'll return later."

He nodded, then closed the door.

She drove to number twelve, thirteen, and fourteen on her list, which resulted in dead ends. It was after three by the time she revisited the tavern, where a dozen or so cars occupied the front end of the lot. She removed her sunglasses when she entered and made her way to the woman behind the bar.

She was slim, with harsh features. Her dyed blond hair and tan gave her a leathery look, like she'd spent her life lying on a blanket at the beach. Her name tag read *Cheryl*.

McConnel showed her badge and identified herself.

"Hiya," Cheryl said. "Would you like something cold to drink?"

It was hot and McConnel was thirsty, but she hesitated. She didn't usually drink or eat anything offered once she revealed who she was. You never knew what people would do. She didn't know anything about the bartender or the establishment.

Cheryl opened a can of ginger ale and poured it into a glass of ice, then slid it toward McConnel. "On the house."

McConnel had seen her open the can and pour it directly into the glass. She appreciated the gesture but still hesitated.

"I was told you'd be back," Cheryl said.

"Thank you. It is hot out."

"Just wait till August. Everett comes in here every few days. He and his girlfriend, Erlene Simpson, and a couple of their friends. Haven't seen him yet this week. Or her."

"Do you know where Ms. Simpson lives?" McConnel asked.

"Not sure. Savannah somewhere, I think."

"When's the last time you saw Everett?"

"Last Friday night. He and Erlene closed the place."

"Are you the only bartender?" McConnel licked her lips, avoiding the soda.

"We have one other. Jake. He won't be here till tomorrow."

Cheryl took a glass and poured a small amount of McConnel's soda into it, drank it, then slid McConnel's back to her. "We're a good establishment." She smiled.

McConnel nodded, then drank the cold liquid. "Just one of you work at a time?"

"Yep. Except weekends. Then we work together. We got two waitresses and me or Jake. The owner fills in when we're off or get too busy."

"Is the owner in?"

"He's upstairs. He said to tell you to come see him when you're ready." She motioned to her right.

McConnel thanked her and started up the steps, her hand on her gun, just in case. She knocked on the open door.

An older, partially bald man with a triple chin sat behind the desk writing something in a ledger. He motioned her in.

She introduced herself.

"Have a seat." His Southern accent was thick. "We don't get FBI agents in here. It's nice to meet ya. How can I help?"

He must have been running a clean business, or he wouldn't have been so open and quick to invite her in.

"Did you get what you needed?" he asked.

"Do you know Everett Bigalow?"

"Not really. I know of him. He's been comin' here a few years. He usually hangs out with his buddies from the body shop. He and Erlene have been an item for a while. She's a hot commodity around here. Real friendly, if you know what I mean."

McConnel did.

"Sorry I can't be of more help." He closed the ledger.

"I appreciate your time. Would you let me know if he shows up in the next few days?" She stood and handed him her card.

"Is he in some kind of trouble?"

"I just need to ask him a few questions."

"We'll let you know." He pushed himself up from his chair. "We'd be happy to fix you something to eat if you're hungry."

McConnel thanked him, refused the offer, and then left. She wanted to investigate a few more names before she called it a day.

She finally finished a little after seven and returned to Bitsy's, too tired to stop and get a meal. The scent of something delicious caught her attention when she walked through the door. Cookies or cake? Bitsy was in the kitchen, a table setting on the counter.

"What smells so good?" McConnel asked.

"I hope you're hungry. I saved you some roasted chicken we had for supper, and I made chocolate chip cookies."

"I'm starved. Thank you."

Bitsy poured tea over a glass full of ice and set it in front of McConnel. "Sit. I'll get your food."

She seemed in a better mood and more relaxed than she'd been in days. McConnel was glad. Had Kathrine being in the house with her made a difference?

Bitsy plated her food.

McConnel's mouth watered. She hadn't realized how empty she was until she saw the meal in front of her. She thanked Bitsy again and began to eat.

Bitsy sat beside her. "How was your day? Anything new?"

"Unfortunately, no. How about you?"

"I wrapped up some things at work. Went to see my doctor."

McConnel stopped eating and looked at her. "You went to your doctor?"

Bitsy nodded. "Yes. It was part of our agreement. I'm glad I did. I feel better. Thank you for encouraging me and not judging. I started on the medicine again." She hesitated. "I want to try it alone tonight."

"That's great." McConnel's mood lightened, although a part of her was disappointed. Any excuse to be in bed with Bitsy was now fine with her, and although she was glad Bitsy had taken steps to help herself, she'd miss being next to her, hearing her breathe, listening to her night sighs. She took another bite of the delicious chicken.

That night, as she lay alone in her bed, thinking of Bitsy and how she occupied her mind more and more, she forced herself to focus on Bigalow. Where was he? From what she'd found out about him, he seemed stable enough. He worked regularly, had friends, and was in some type of a relationship. So why had he disappeared? He must be hiding something, but what, and was it related to the cold case?

CHAPTER TWENTY-FIVE

Bitsy pulled the cool sheet around her, then grabbed the blanket and draped it over the bed. The night was unusually dark without McConnel next to her. She wanted her here, but she had to start making it on her own and might as well begin now. It was a depressing thought. She stared at the shadows from the curtain fluttering in the moonlight. Was he out there somewhere in the night? Did her security see him and not know who he was? A passing stranger? A man in a car? A supposed neighbor walking past her house on his evening sabbatical?

She shivered and closed her eyes, forcing the thoughts out. She lay there, unable to find that place where she would drift off to oblivion and have the relief she so desperately needed. She tossed and turned, then gave up an hour later and dragged herself out of bed. She paced, then finally reached into her purse and pulled out the bottle of sleeping pills. The prescription was for one per night, but two would be better. Surely doubling the dose would help her more than just one. Maybe three? She rolled the bottle in her palm, reread the directions, then sat on the bed, holding the container in her hand. When would she have a normal life? What was normal? What did it look like? Feel like? If someone were to ask her what normal was, she'd have to honestly say she had no idea. She reviewed her life, as many years as she could remember after Hallie Lynn's disappearance. Was she ever content? No. Had she ever felt completely at peace? No. Had she ever been able to let go of her childhood and just be who she was, without expectations, demands, regret, guilt? No! Never!

She ran her fingers through her hair. She wanted McConnel next to her, in her bed, beside her. She brought the peace she needed. She gave her the comfort and contentment she craved, but was she just a crutch, something to lean on to help her get through the long, desperate days and nights since Hallie Lynn had been found?

She opened the bottle and spilled several pills into her palm. She reached for the glass of water on the stand.

"Bitsy? I heard you up. Are you all right?" McConnel crossed to her from the doorway and knelt in front of her.

How had she gotten into the room? Bitsy never heard the door open. "Where did you come from?"

McConnel slipped her hand onto Bitsy's knee. "I heard you pacing and was concerned." She eyed the pills Bitsy held. "Just one would probably be enough. Why don't you put the rest back?"

The heat of embarrassment flushed in Bitsy's cheeks as she returned all but a single tablet. She popped it into her mouth and washed it down with a swallow of water. "I don't think I would have taken all of them."

"I know. Why don't you go back to bed?" She gently took the glass and pills from Bitsy and placed them on the nightstand.

Bitsy remained still, not speaking, watching her. Did McConnel believe her? Bitsy eased onto the mattress and laid her head on the pillow.

McConnel pulled the sheet and blanket over Bitsy's shoulders, then sat beside her. "If you don't mind, I'll stay a little while."

Bitsy took McConnel's hand and cupped it between hers. "I've been thinking about the shiny dark. I think it was metal or something."

"Could it be like a badge a law enforcement officer would wear?"

Bitsy stared at her. "Maybe. Do you think he was disguised as a police officer? It makes sense." She closed her eyes. There was so much she wanted to say to McConnel. Did she know how beautiful she was? How her eyes sparkled in the sunlight? How her touch had the most extraordinary, calming effect? How she looked forward to being with her? "You're so precious to me…Dear, dear, McConnel."

The room quieted, and she drifted into sleep.

When she opened her eyes again, the birds were chirping, but the sun hadn't peeked through the window yet. It couldn't have been later than five or a little after. She'd slept a few hours without waking. McConnel? She turned, surveying the room, but found herself alone, the prescription bottle still on the nightstand next to the water. She had an impulse to open it and check the contents, just to reassure herself she hadn't taken more than one. She knew she hadn't, but still there was a slight possibility she had and that she'd imagined McConnel had been there with her. She couldn't resist the urge. She reached for it, opened the lid, and spied the pills. It was full. A confirming relief entered as she returned it to the stand and stretched out, looking at the ceiling. How did McConnel know? She shouldn't worry about being safe. McConnel was with her. Kathrine was there. The others were outside. Yes, the killer was out there too, but he would definitely have to go through McConnel to get to her.

Kathrine seemed capable. Bitsy liked her. She'd been there only a few days, but Bitsy could tell immediately that she was highly intelligent, confident, and good at her job. She'd watched her from the living room as she cleaned her gun at the kitchen counter. Bitsy wasn't sure if Kathrine meant for her to see her doing it. Either way, it was clear that Kathrine knew how to handle a weapon. How she took it apart, then put it back together again was almost an art form.

She closed her eyes, more relaxed, at ease. It wasn't a buzz, but a feeling that things weren't as bad as she'd thought last night. Was it the anti-anxiety medication combined with the sleeping pills? Or was it finally being able to get a good night's sleep? Things weren't as dark as they'd seemed yesterday. She inhaled deeply. She'd always loved the mornings, the freshness in the air, the birds welcoming the dawn. She drifted off, and when she woke it was full daylight. After lying in the bed a few more minutes, she dressed and went to the kitchen. She sat at the bar and scanned her phone for local news while she waited for the coffee to finish.

Kathrine came in, already dressed. "Good morning. How'd you sleep?"

Had McConnel told her what had happened? "Surprisingly well, thank you. Anything going on outside?"

"No. Not at all. Do you have any plans to leave the house this morning?"

"No. I'm going to paint."

Kathrine nodded.

"What can I get you for breakfast?" Bitsy asked. She felt obligated to prepare Kathrine's meals.

"That's not necessary. Go about your day. I can get my own food and clean up. Happy to do it."

"Are you sure? It's no trouble."

"I'm good."

McConnel came into the room, still in her pj's. "You two are up awfully early."

"Look who's calling the kettle black," Bitsy said.

McConnel laughed. Then her cell rang, and she left the room as she answered it.

Bitsy wanted to know who was calling her this early. Was it news about the case? Had something happened? She walked to the Ninja coffeemaker and poured herself a cup, then added cream. "She's off to an early start this morning."

Kathrine didn't respond.

Bitsy reached for another cup from the stand and poured Kathrine some coffee, set it on the counter, then placed the creamer beside it. She drank hers the way Bitsy did.

"Many thanks."

"Kathrine, have you ever had to shoot someone?"

Kathrine took a sip as she looked at her and grimaced. "Unfortunately, yes."

Bitsy sat next to her at the bar. "Was it hard to do it?"

"Not as hard as you'd think, especially in a life-threatening situation."

"Did you have a choice?"

"You mean did I have a choice to shoot or not shoot?"

"Yes."

"Weapon use is a last resort," Kathrine said. "I've had extensive hand-to-hand combat training. I don't pull my gun unless I intend to use it. If I can resolve the situation any other way, I will, but I won't hesitate to use my firearm if the situation warrants it. Every law enforcement officer is taught the same thing. Hesitation can cost you your life or someone else's."

It was comforting to know Kathrine had the training she needed to protect herself and others. "I hope you don't have to use your gun while you're guarding me."

Kathrine took another drink. "So do I, but I will if I have to. I don't want you worrying about it. You pick up your paintbrush when you do your job. I pick up my gun when I do mine. It's the field I've chosen."

"Do you like your job?"

"Most of the time. I don't have second thoughts about it. Each case I work is different in its own way, and I get to travel a lot."

"Are you married? Do you have someone?"

"My companion is a singer. She works in Las Vegas and also travels back and forth to Cleveland and Chicago."

Kathrine was a lesbian. Bitsy had suspected but wasn't sure. "Wow! That sounds like she has an exciting job." She wanted to ask more questions, but the conversation was getting too personal. She wanted to know Kathrine, but she didn't have the emotional reserve to invest in any other new relationships.

"Our schedules conflict, and we don't see each other as often as we'd like, but we make it work."

Would a long-distance relationship with McConnel be difficult? She dismissed the thought. Kathrine didn't volunteer any other information, and Bitsy didn't ask any more questions. They sat at the bar in silence.

Bitsy finished her coffee and stood. "I know I told you this before, but I mean it. Make yourself at home. Fix whatever you want to eat. I'm going upstairs and change into my painting clothes and go to the studio. You'll be in the house with me, right?"

Kathrine nodded. "Of course. If you want to go somewhere, just let me know."

Bitsy started to leave. McConnel was still on the phone. Who was she talking to for this long and so early in the morning? Did it have to do with the case? Would she be gone all day? She needed her here with her. If McConnel left, would she be safe?

She checked the stove clock. It was time for an anti-anxiety pill.

CHAPTER TWENTY-SIX

McConnel talked to Jenkins in depth about what she'd found out and what she wanted to do next. "How's my list of law enforcement personnel and their leaves of absence or schedules coming along? Remember, a fifty-mile radius of the grave site, both active and retired."

"Staff's still working on it," Jenkins said.

"Whoever committed the crimes had to have taken time off to scout his victims and learn the area. He didn't live in three different states." She realized this was another long shot, but her instincts told her to keep digging and not give up. Somewhere in the information could be the clue she needed to connect the killer to Hallie Lynn.

She ended the call, visited a few minutes with Kathrine, and then went to her room to change and review her notes. After she dressed, she sat at the desk and browsed the murder book. Whether Bitsy realized it or not, last night she'd given McConnel a critical detail that could take her a giant leap forward. She entered the date and made a note.

Focusing on law enforcement. Or a wannabe???
Skilled. Informed??? How? Does he know what I'm doing?
How close is he? How can I rattle his chain?

A rap on the door stopped her. She laid the pen on the desk and stood.

Bitsy entered cautiously, immediately looking at the murder board. The entire wall was covered with pictures or notes. Her eyes widened.

McConnel quickly moved in front of her and blocked her view.

"Hey. What's up? You know you shouldn't be in here." She eased her into the hallway and closed the door behind them.

"That's a lot of stuff," Bitsy said. "What time will you be leaving this morning?"

"About nine. Why? You look a little frazzled."

Bitsy glanced at the closed door. "I'm okay. I was wondering if you'd like to go out this evening, maybe for supper?"

"I'm sorry. I have no idea when I'll be done today. I've got quite a few stops to make."

Bitsy seemed preoccupied, probably still in shock from the crime scene pictures on the wall.

"I'm sorry about the room."

Bitsy took a deep breath. "I understand. It's just…"

"I know it's disturbing." McConnel wanted to convey how important it was that Bitsy not go in the room, even if McConnel was in there. "Promise me you won't go in again, under any circumstances."

"Is it that bad?"

"You were only in there a few seconds, and look at your reaction. Yes. It's graphic. Please don't enter. Do I need to put up a sign?" She smiled, hoping her tease would ease Bitsy's mind.

"I feel like I'm twelve years old again."

"I don't mean to make you feel like that. It's just the information in there will upset you, and I don't want you to see it."

Bitsy nodded. "I'll try not to let my curiosity get the best of me."

McConnel reached for her hand and held it a moment, then let it slip from her grasp. "Trust me, no good will come from you going in there. Hey. You've got your painting shirt on."

Bitsy smiled. "Yep. I'm giving it a go."

"That's great."

"About last night," Bitsy said. "I…I wasn't going to take those pills."

"I know you weren't, but I understand how upset you were and thought you just needed a little help to get through the night."

Bitsy stepped forward and looped her arms around McConnel's neck. "I loved that you came in when you did, and that you stayed. It was the best thing you could have done for me." She moved closer and whispered in her ear. "Thank you. You're amazing."

Her breath and words sent a thrill through McConnel that lingered in her breasts and then drifted deeper, penetrating every part of her. She tried to resist the urge to return the embrace, and it worked for about a second, but then any will power disintegrated. She enveloped Bitsy in her arms, not wanting to let her go.

They held on to each other.

Did Bitsy feel it? The intensity? The pure emotion? The whole of her feelings for her? If McConnel spoke, she was sure her words would break the tenuous bond between them, and she wanted it to last as long as possible.

McConnel's phone rang, shattering the moment. *Damn.*

They stepped apart.

"I need to get downstairs and start painting. See you when you get home. Be safe."

"I will. Have a good day in the studio."

Bitsy descended the steps and was gone, leaving the hallway cold and empty, and McConnel yearning for more of her. She returned to her room and answered the call. "Special Agent McConnel."

"This is Sheriff Gordon in Bulloch County, northwest of Springfield. A buddy of mine owns County Line Tavern, and he said you've been looking for Everett Bigalow. I found something I think you'd be interested in."

A jolt ripped through her. Was this the break she'd been waiting for? "What's it regarding?"

"I don't want to say over the phone, ma'am. Could you come here right away?"

"Where are you?"

"Just follow the directions to Statesboro, then turn north on County Road 23 in Stillmore. Go four more miles. I'll have my flashers on." He sounded confident.

"I'm leaving now." McConnel disconnected and grabbed her badge and gun.

It took her almost forty-five minutes. The moment she came over the rise, she saw his flashing lights. No other police vehicles were nearby. He was leaning on the driver's side door, arms folded across his chest, but he straightened when she slowed and stopped in front of him. She lowered the window, immediately smelling smoke, not from wood, but more like a tire fire.

He moved to her car and tipped his hat. "Special Agent McConnel?"

She showed her badge and nodded.

"Follow me down this road here. We're going about a mile in." He pointed to his right. "This is all part of the state forest reserve."

A chained gate had been opened, leading to a dirt road.

He got into his vehicle and led the way.

About three-quarters of a mile in, she saw the fire truck and county coroner's van. What had happened that they would want her there? An edginess overshadowed her thoughts.

He pulled to the side, and she parked behind him, then got out, adjusted her gun, and quickly walked toward him. He led her past the fire truck and onto another side road, deeper into the woods. "We got the call about three o'clock this morning. Willard, at County Line Tavern, told me about your visit yesterday. I think we've found who you're looking for."

They went about five hundred yards farther and stopped in a clearing. In front of them was what was left of a burnt-out vehicle. A truck, the frame still smoldering. The stench was acidic and rancid—tires, mixed with metal, gasoline or some type of accelerant, and human flesh.

Two charred bodies still occupied the cab.

"We have no official identification yet on the remains, but we've ID'd the truck. Whoever did this removed the license plate, but we got a match from what was left of the VIN number."

McConnel moved closer. "Everett Bigalow and Erlene Simpson, I assume."

The sheriff rested his hands on his utility belt. "That's my guess as well."

"Damn," she breathed out. How could the killer have known what she was up to so fast? AC's caution, *Everyone knows everyone else's business,* came to mind.

"Coroner said one bullet to the side of the head for each of them. That's all he's got right now. There's nothing left in the truck to help us. I wish I could give you more, but that's all I've got."

McConnel toed the reddish dirt beneath her feet.

The sheriff pointed. "See how the area burned around the truck? Whoever did it had a fire extinguisher with them and was careful."

McConnel noted that none of the nearby trees had been burned or charred.

"Whoever chose this spot knew the area," he said. He motioned around him. "Any other place in this part of the park would have caught fire and gone up in a hell of a blaze, but not here."

McConnel took in the entire scene. She walked the area, the sheriff following close behind.

"I don't see any other vehicle tracks or tire marks," she said.

"Nope."

She scoured another one hundred yards. "Here." She bent and inspected two boot prints in the soft ground. "He hiked out, which meant he drove the vehicle to where you found it, set it on fire, and then left on foot." She turned to the sheriff, who was now watching her intently. "How far to the nearest place of business or home?"

The sheriff removed his hat, rubbed his head, then replaced it, adjusting it low. "The state lodge and campsites are about two miles north of here. It's a mile out, so he'd had to have walked at least three miles to there. Everything else is farther away."

"Any videos or other cameras in the area?"

"I wish. Nothing. No cause for them, and an extra cost to the state."

McConnel looked away, hiding her disappointment.

They returned to the burn site.

She stood quiet, still trying to process the information. The killer had found out what she knew and who she wanted to question, and had eliminated them because they could have given her information about him. "Talk to me."

"What?"

She looked over at the sheriff. "Sorry. I'm just thinking out loud."

"This guy's not stupid," he said.

"No. He's organized, methodical, prepared, skilled, but he's over-confident, even arrogant. I've got his number, and I'm going to find him."

"I hate to be territorial, but this is our case, not the FBI's. It's state property, not federal. You're looking for a kidnapper-child killer. I'm looking for an outright murderer. I doubt they're the same person."

"Sheriff, you called me, remember?"

"I contacted you because I knew you were looking for Bigalow. My obligation to you stops with that."

He was getting blustery, like all law enforcement who felt their jurisdiction was challenged.

"I appreciate your call and letting me come into the scene, and I'll note it in my report. The importance of your gesture can't be overstated. You didn't have to do it, and I thank you for it." She needed to smooth things over. She couldn't afford to destroy any bridges.

"We're keeping this confidential," he said.

She didn't tell him she suspected the killer was a law enforcement employee. No matter how confidential the sheriff kept it, the killer would find out, and probably as fast as it could be entered into the system, maybe even faster. He was connected and had sources of information. Another reason to think he was local.

She was even more alone than she'd thought. The moment she filed any reports, documented in any system, he'd know. More than likely he'd tapped phones and had video and ears everywhere. That's how he'd remained elusive all these years. And *that's* why he was such a threat to Bitsy. She needed to call Kathrine as soon as she got back to the car to tell her to restrict Bitsy's travel.

There was no point in looking any further for the truck that had rammed Chief Gibson's vehicle. She'd found it. But who'd driven it? Bigalow? Had he killed the chief and his daughter? She was certain he was involved somehow.

Chapter Twenty-seven

B itsy placed her paintbrush in the turpentine can and wiggled her stiff fingers. Hunger called. A doughnut and coffee lasted only so long, and it had to be way past suppertime. She hung her paint shirt over the chair, then stretched. He was out there somewhere. Who was he? She went to the window and peered out, weary of asking the questions. All this time he'd been alive, walking on the ground, knowing Hallie Lynn was rotting beneath it. Her stomach roiled. How could he have done it? Why? Her faint reflection in the glass caught her eye, reminding her of his shadowy figure long ago.

"McConnel will get you," she whispered. "I hope you try to run, you bastard. I hope she hunts you down like the vermin you are." The thoughts were vivid and vengeful, and they lingered as she returned to the canvas. She crossed her arms and inspected her work. Not quite the right color in the eyes, and the lighting in the background wasn't lucid enough.

Kathrine walked through the open studio door, then paused.

Bitsy waved her in. "It's okay. I'm through for now."

"Making any progress?" Kathrine asked.

Bitsy shrugged, not sure if *progress* was what she'd call it.

"Do you mind if I look at your pieces over there against the wall?" Kathrine pointed to the far side of the room.

"Go ahead. Just not this one." She always positioned a canvas she was working on so anyone entering the room couldn't immediately see it. She didn't like opinions while she painted. They influenced her too much. Good or bad, they disrupted her focus.

Kathrine perused the art.

What did she think? Bitsy began to clean another brush, deliberately distracting herself from watching Kathrine's reactions. She'd gotten better over the years, but it still made her nervous when others viewed her work.

"Bitsy, these are nice. My mother paints."

"What medium?"

"Acrylics. Dad makes all her frames. They have an art studio back home." Kathrine continued to browse.

"In Las Vegas?"

Kathrine stopped and turned toward her.

Bitsy tidied the table.

"No. Denver. That's my hometown. Have you lived in this area all your life?"

"Mostly," Bitsy said, then had a thought. "Would you like to go on the *Georgia Queen*? It's a riverboat. I can get us VIP passes."

Kathrine sauntered toward her. "Probably be better if we stayed closer to home."

Bitsy repositioned to block Kathrine's view of the canvas. "Am I a prisoner in my own house?"

Kathrine stopped. "No."

Bitsy had been on the *Queen* at least a dozen times, but her desire to go again swelled. Was it to test Kathrine's resolve? "We should do it."

"Maybe not."

"Then I'm a prisoner. I can't go where I want, and I'm followed everywhere. Sounds like jail to me. *He* goes wherever he wants. *He* does whatever he wants. And I'm behind bars."

"No, you're not. You just need to be careful for the time being."

Bitsy resented the restrictions, yet she didn't feel safe without McConnel or Kathrine near. She couldn't have it both ways. Confused, disheartened, and sick of it all, she tossed the rag onto the bench and approached Kathrine. "Call it what you want, but it comes down to the same thing." Her emotional highs and lows were exhausting. She left Kathrine standing in the middle of the studio and went upstairs to her room. She took a flying leap onto her mattress and landed facedown, arms out, and yelled into the bedspread, muffling the sound of her colorful expletives.

The doorbell chimed.

She gasped and sat upright, listening.

It chimed again.

She hurried downstairs but stopped a few feet from the door.

Kathrine was there, her hand resting on the gun in her holster. "Male," she mouthed. "Do you know him?"

Bitsy peeked out, then shook her head.

"Move away," Kathrine ordered. She gestured for her to get behind her as she drew her weapon.

"Oh, God!" Bitsy almost collapsed on the spot. She covered her mouth to keep from saying anything more. She crouched behind Kathrine. Was it *him?* Why would he come to the house? And ring the doorbell? That was stupid. He wouldn't do that. Would he? She tried to stop herself from trembling but couldn't. He looked younger. Too young. It couldn't be him. An accomplice?

Kathrine slipped her gun behind her as she cautiously opened the door. "Hi. May I help you?"

"Ms. Hanover?"

"No. She's not in just now."

"Oh. I'm Carter, Chief Gibson's grandson."

Bitsy moved closer so she could see him.

"I have some pictures here that my dad said Grandpa wanted the FBI agent to have." He offered a brown envelope to Kathrine.

She reached for it. "Thanks. I'll make sure she gets it."

"Okay then. See ya." He turned and left.

Kathrine watched until he backed his car out of the driveway, then shut the door. She holstered her weapon and looked inside the envelope. "Pictures, like he said." She handed it to Bitsy. "I imagine McConnel will want to go through them."

Bitsy placed the envelope against the lamp base on the stand beside the chair and sat. She'd stopped trembling, but her heart still hammered. She patted her chest. "I hate this feeling."

"I know."

"You're calm."

"I'm used to it. I made coffee. Would you like some?"

Bitsy nodded. She was tempted to go through the pictures just to see what they were but then decided against it. The envelope was for McConnel, not her. Her stomach rumbled. "On second thought, I don't want coffee. I need to eat." She went to the kitchen.

Kathrine sat at the counter, sipping from her cup. "I know this is hard for you, but attitude is everything in this type of situation."

"I don't like being confined."

Kathrine straightened. "We're just trying to keep you safe."

Bitsy opened the fridge and stared. Nothing looked good. She spied the leftover veggies and reached for them. Kathrine could get her own food.

"I think you need a distraction," Kathrine said. "A movie, maybe, or a game of cards. I hear you like to play poker."

What was the point? She'd still be caged. "No, thanks."

"Are you going back to the studio?"

"I don't know." Bitsy slipped the container of veggies into the microwave, set the timer, and stood silently, not wanting to talk. She checked the clock on the microwave. Time for medication. She appreciated Kathrine's efforts to distract her, but they didn't help. Where was McConnel, and what was she doing? It would be better if she were here. Maybe she'd be home sooner than she'd thought.

Bitsy pulled her cell from her pocket and called her. It immediately went to voice mail. Disappointed, she disconnected without leaving a message.

Kathrine left the kitchen.

Bitsy ate alone at the bar.

How much longer? It was a question she asked herself three or four times a day now. Would it end? Could McConnel find him? The thoughts buzzed around her like mosquitoes in the stillness after a summer rain. She took a pill when she finished eating, then climbed the stairs. Alone again. Her cell phone rang. McConnel? When she saw who it was, her disappointment oozed over the screen. "Hey, Momma."

"What you doin', darlin'?"

"Just finished in the studio." Bitsy continued to her room and sat on the bed, waiting for a response, knowing what the next question would be.

"Any news?"

"Not a thing, and quite honestly, I doubt McConnel would share if she had any."

"I see. Sounds like you're having a tough day. Why don't you come home?"

Bitsy rolled her eyes. Momma's solution to any problem was to come home. Maybe she should. She could leave McConnel alone here to do her job. She never saw her anyway. Would it help to put some distance between them? The idea of deliberately separating herself from McConnel stung, but Kathrine could protect her just as well there. Even better. Kathrine was always here, and McConnel had made it clear she didn't have time to be with her.

The room darkened suddenly. Bitsy went to the window and moved the curtain aside. Thick, gray clouds pushed in from the west. "A big storm's coming." She continued to watch as the sky grew more ominous. "Really big. Batten it down, Momma." A flash of lightning struck in the distance. The thunder shook the glass.

"Good Lord! I better go and get ready. You'll be all right?" Momma asked.

"I'm fine. You and Daddy be safe."

"We will. Love you, sweetheart." Momma ended the call.

Bitsy tapped the phone against her chin. Unless McConnel came home soon, she'd be out in it. She returned to the bed and sat, staring out the window as the clouds in the west grew darker and more threatening. She wished all of this was over and McConnel was here, but then if it was, McConnel would probably be back in Ohio. She sighed deeply, overwhelmed at the thought.

CHAPTER TWENTY-EIGHT

By seven McConnel was hungry and exhausted. She wanted to stop and get soup and a sandwich, then drive to Bitsy's, but it was just a matter of minutes before the downpour would hit. She'd never seen such thick, heavy, dark clouds. A bolt of lightning hit low about a half mile in front of her, followed by a roll of thunder so intense she felt it in her teeth. Jimmy B's was up ahead on the right. She could eat there and wait for the storm to pass. She turned in and parked, but the deluge hit as she dashed toward the entrance, soaking her blouse before she got through the doorway.

There must have been sixty or so patrons with the same idea. She went to the bar, not wanting to take a table. There, she ordered a ginger ale, Ruben sandwich, and a cup of French onion soup. The bartender poured her drink and told her the food would be ready in about ten minutes. She swiveled and eyed the crowd as a clap of thunder echoed through the room. Cheers erupted, many people raising their drinks in appreciation.

McConnel longed to share their carefree attitude. Her phone dinged. A text message from Jenkins informed her he'd sent an email with vacation schedules and notes. More to go over when she got to Bitsy's. She sighed, turned back toward the bar, and sipped the soda, savoring its cool refreshing taste.

"Come here often?"

McConnel followed the voice. Annabelle Sutter, Savannah's ADA, stood next to the empty seat beside her, a wide smile on her face. Her teeth and makeup were perfect. Her suit hugged her body in all the right places, and not a hair on her head was out of place.

McConnel had been tramping around in the woods all day, smelled like burning tires or worse, and hadn't bothered to check *her* hair, which had probably started to frizz and looked like someone had tried to jump-start her with battery cables. Nothing like feeling at a disadvantage.

"Mind if I sit?" Annabelle asked.

"I'm afraid I'm not the best company this evening. I've been literally out in the field all day."

Annabelle's smile widened. "You look great." She slid into the seat in one smooth action, then motioned to the bartender, who nodded. She'd done this before. A professional at work. How would Annabelle come on to her?

The food arrived. McConnel grasped half the sandwich and took a healthy bite. The rye bread had been perfectly fried with a generous portion of butter, and the cheese dripped in between the edges. It was crisp and delicious. McConnel wished she was alone so she could enjoy the pleasure of it even more.

"What brings you here?" Anabelle asked after the bartender brought her a Manhattan. She took a sip, set it back on the bar, then slowly ran her fingertip around the rim of the glass.

The gesture was seductive. McConnel could see why she was good at what she did. "Just trying to get out of the storm. How about you?"

"After-court celebration with some friends." She took another sip.

Traces of her lipstick smeared the glass. How might she kiss? Annabelle was probably good at everything she did.

McConnel readjusted in her seat and kept eating. It was best that she get out of there as soon as possible. She was tempted. Maybe it was because she needed distraction and relief, maybe because she was lonely or just plain needed sex. Whatever it was, Annabelle Sutter wasn't the solution. How long would it be before she and Bitsy could be together? Hopefully soon.

"What case are you celebrating?" McConnel asked, diverting her thoughts.

Annabelle went on about it as McConnel focused on her meal. When she finished her summation, she leaned in toward McConnel. "I have a great bottle of cognac back at the apartment, and I'd love to share it with you."

McConnel wiped her mouth with her napkin, then stood. "Thanks for the invitation. I'm sure it'd be lovely, but the timing's not right. Have a good night." She left, grateful the storm was over.

When she arrived at Bitsy's, she removed her shoes and went upstairs.

Bitsy's door was open. She lay on her bed in a peach-colored silk nightgown that clung to the curve of her hip. Her long legs were exposed, her arm tucked under a pillow.

She was there, hers for the taking if McConnel wanted it. And she did. She took a deep breath. She couldn't spend time with her, not in *that* room, and definitely not tonight.

"Hey, you're back." Bitsy leapt from the bed.

McConnel swallowed.

Bitsy came toward her, as if in slow motion. Her expression and the sway of her body were alluring and seductive.

All McConnel had to do was open her arms, and Bitsy would come to her. She could hold her, kiss her, and take her to bed and undress her. They'd caress and touch. McConnel ached to be with her, feel the subtle curves of her body, the softness of her lips. She swallowed again and sucked in a deep breath.

"I bet you're tired. Did you get caught in the storm? I missed you."

McConnel didn't want her to say that. It only made it harder to resist. "It was a downpour. I stopped for a bite to eat when it hit. Did you have a good day?"

Bitsy stood in front of her, close. When she was near, all McConnel wanted was more of her.

Bitsy scrunched her nose and sniffed "Were you at a fire?"

McConnel laughed. "As a matter of fact, I was. I need to take a shower."

"Long day?"

"Yes. I better bathe before I stink up the entire house." She started to leave.

"Can you come watch a movie with me when you're done? I'll make popcorn."

It would turn into more than that. McConnel knew it, and she was too far spent to resist. "I'm sorry. I have some emails to go through."

Bitsy's face filled with disappointment.

Didn't she know McConnel wanted to be with her? Wanted to

make love to her? How long could this continue? Moving in was not the solution now that Kathrine was here. Bitsy was protected. McConnel didn't need to be here any longer. It just made everything twice as hard. "Bitsy?"

"Yes?" She brightened.

"I'm sorry. It's best if I don't."

Bitsy sighed loudly. "I suppose."

McConnel reluctantly left her, then stripped in her bedroom and soaked in the shower, letting the water run over her. She struggled to clear her mind of all thoughts of Bitsy. Was it time to move back to the hotel? If the case couldn't be solved soon, she'd have to consider it.

She dried and put on her pajamas, then sat at the desk, turned on the computer, found Jenkins's email, and printed the attachments. His team had already arranged the suspects with their vacation schedules and coordinated the dates of the linked disappearances. Five names appeared consistently, each with extensive notes. Her gaze landed on the third one. A chill went through her. *Sheriff Gerald Atwater*.

Was it him? He was the right age, a deputy at the time of Hallie Lynn's disappearance, and lived in the area. As a county sheriff he certainly had access to what was going on in the surrounding states. He could get his hands on any information about investigations of other disappearances. She stared at the murder board. He was in almost every picture of the crime scene.

She reviewed his vacation schedule but became frustrated at what she saw. Only forty percent of the connected cases matched with his time off. Everyone knew him. He was recognized wherever he went. Maybe he wasn't such a great suspect after all. She scrutinized the other four names. Two were retired, one had been injured in the leg in a shootout and was on disability, and one had moved four times to different areas in Georgia and North Carolina.

How could she narrow the search? She reached for the flash drive. Would Rachel's program help? Probably not. All the men were too similar. She needed another perspective to help work through the information. She placed the papers on the desk and went to bed. She'd rest for a little while, then get back to it.

Someone shook her. She startled awake.

Kathrine was standing over her. "Your light was on. It's three in the morning."

McConnel rubbed her eyes. "I must have been more tired than I thought. I wanted to get a report from you but got into an email I received, then lay down for a minute. How's everything?"

Kathrine sat on the side of the bed. "Nothing out of the ordinary. Bitsy took it pretty hard when I told her that her movements had to be restricted. I don't think we're friends anymore." She grinned. "The rest can wait until later. Want me to turn out the light?"

McConnel waved her away. "Thanks. See you in the morning." She put her head on the pillow and was out again.

She woke at six, her mouth so dry she could hardly swallow. She coughed, stumbled out of bed, went to the bathroom, and gagged down a cup of water. She brushed her teeth, washed her face, and then went straight to the desk. Was it Atwater? She had just enough information to think it was, but not enough evidence to prove it. She smelled fresh coffee, dressed, and went to the kitchen.

Kathrine was pouring herself a cup. She offered it to McConnel and got herself another one, then sat at the bar next to her. "Rough night? You look spent."

McConnel took a sip of the brew, then cleared her throat. "I've got a suspect."

Kathrine set her cup on the counter and turned toward her. "Who?"

McConnel glanced around her but knew Bitsy wasn't up yet. Her door was closed when she'd come downstairs. "Atwater."

Kathrine's mouth dropped open. "The sheriff?"

McConnel nodded. "I want him under surveillance immediately. Pull your team off everyone but Bitsy and focus on him."

Kathrine stood and took out her phone. "I'll do it now."

"I don't want Bitsy knowing about it. She's having a hard enough time as it is."

Kathrine nodded. "Understood." She punched in a number and began talking as she opened the kitchen door and walked outside.

McConnel drained the cup. "I need something solid."

"What are you mumbling about?" Bitsy came around the counter and poured herself some coffee.

McConnel pressed her hands together. "You're up. I didn't hear you come down." Had Bitsy listened to any of her and Kathrine's conversation? She didn't act like she knew anything.

"I heard your voices and couldn't go back to sleep."

"I'm sorry."

"Oh, that's fine. I've had enough rest. I kept hoping you'd change your mind last night. I saw your light was on a long time."

"I fell asleep. Kathrine woke me about three and turned it off."

"Are you going out this morning?" Bitsy sat beside her. "I haven't seen much of you in days."

"I'll be here for a while."

"Oh, crap! That reminds me. Something came for you." Bitsy went to the living room and came back carrying a brown envelope. "Chief Gibson's grandson stopped by yesterday and dropped this off. He scared me to death. You should have seen Kathrine."

McConnel read her name on the front and immediately opened the flap. She pulled out a handful of photos and studied the first one, then began a more cursory examination of the rest. "These must be the ones Chief Gibson said he took."

Bitsy leaned on the counter and sipped her coffee. "Are they like the others?"

McConnel nodded. Nothing she hadn't already seen. Then she stopped. One was different. She stared at it.

"What's wrong?" Bitsy eased beside her.

McConnel's heart pounded. Adrenaline surged. "Do you know when this was taken?"

Bitsy hesitated.

"Bitsy, please."

"You know I hate looking at those things."

McConnel took a breath. She needed to be patient. "I understand, but this could be really important."

Reluctantly Bitsy took the photo and inspected it. "Obviously around the time Hallie Lynn was kidnapped." She handed it back.

"Do you know the exact date?"

Bitsy shook her head. "I can't be sure."

McConnel gripped it tightly. "Do you think your mom or dad would know?"

"Maybe. Why? What's so important about it? It's just the deputies standing around talking to some other cops."

Yes, it was, but there was one big difference. Atwater. Not that he was in the picture, but that he had a large bandage on the side of his face. She shot up from the stool. "We need to go to your mom and dad's right away."

McConnel couldn't get up the stairs fast enough. If this was what she thought, this could be the evidence she needed to connect him to Hallie Lynn's murder.

Chapter Twenty-nine

B itsy didn't see what all the fuss was about. Another photo of the crime scene. Big deal. It wasn't like McConnel didn't have sixty or seventy of them. She'd refused to talk about it when McConnel had brought it up again, and she was like a stone on the way to Momma and Daddy's. Now the three of them were in the kitchen having a covert conversation. The last straw was when McConnel had asked Bitsy to leave the room.

She had complied, but it was under protest. She paced in the game room, then sat and played solitaire. She kept glancing at the doorway, hoping they'd get done so she could spend time with McConnel. Something was up. McConnel seemed nervous, on edge, but also excited. What was so important about *that* picture? McConnel had ordered Kathrine to stay at Bitsy's house. If she were here, the two of them could at least go for a walk while the others plotted. Even though Bitsy didn't want to look at the damned photos anyway, it galled her that McConnel had kicked her out of the kitchen. What had McConnel seen that Bitsy couldn't? She slapped the cards on the table, stood, and began to pace again.

McConnel finally came into the room, an odd expression on her face. It wasn't sad or pleasant, more like the look of someone who'd misplaced something and couldn't remember where it was.

"Did you find out what you wanted?" Bitsy asked.

McConnel nodded. "I need to get back to your house."

"We haven't been here that long. Momma made pecan pie, and we're having chicken and dumplings for supper. You can't walk away from that."

McConnel didn't smile but should have. Instead, she stood there with that perplexing expression. "I need to go."

It irritated Bitsy. "Then do it. I'm staying here."

"No! You should come with me."

"I'll do what I damn well please."

Daddy came into the room and stood beside her. "She can stay. I'm armed."

"Armed? What the hell is going on?" Bitsy stepped away from him and put her hands on her hips, trying to figure out what McConnel was hiding. She'd had enough secrecy to last a lifetime.

Momma entered and looked at McConnel. "Did you tell her?"

"Tell me what?"

McConnel stiffened.

Bitsy eyed Daddy, who looked down and studied the floor.

Silence swept through the room like a stiff breeze in the pines.

Bitsy glowered at McConnel. "Tell me *what*?"

McConnel shook her head.

"She has a right to know," Momma said.

McConnel crossed her arms against her chest. "I can't."

"Well, I can," Momma said. "Darlin', McConnel knows who killed Hallie Lynn."

Bitsy's knees buckled. She couldn't catch her breath.

Daddy grabbed her and guided her to one of the chairs.

She raised a trembling hand to her temple and pressed. She couldn't believe what she'd just heard. She fisted her hand and slammed it against the table.

Momma startled.

McConnel took a step toward Bitsy.

She glared at McConnel, confusion and anger building. "You knew and wouldn't tell me?"

"I don't know. I suspect. There's a big difference. I can't talk about it."

"Oh, the hell with your ethics. I'm sick of them. You tell me right now." Bitsy pounded the table again, the release exhilarating. She was free to say whatever she wanted. "You can't withhold it from me. It's my life you're screwing with. Damn you, McConnel."

McConnel just stood there, stoic, her jaw muscles flexing.

"Who is it?" Bitsy screamed. The sound reverberated off the walls and back into her ears.

Daddy leaned down beside her and grasped her shoulder. "Atwater. It's Sheriff Atwater."

McConnel took another step toward Bitsy. "He's a suspect. I need to investigate more. You have to let me do my job."

Daddy straightened. "You won't have to. I'll kill him myself."

McConnel raised her hands. "Everybody just calm down. No one is going to kill anyone. AC, you need to stop. If you force me, I'll arrest you."

"That's horseshit," he yelled.

"No, it's not. I'll put you in handcuffs and take you right now. I can't allow you to interfere in my investigation. I never told you it was Atwater."

"You didn't have to," he said. "It was written all over your face when I gave you the date that photo was taken." He went to brush past her.

"AC, don't," McConnel shouted.

"You think you can stop me? I'm twice as big as you are. Get out of my way. That bastard has it coming. No one will blame me or even hold me accountable. Everyone in the area will want to kill him once they find out it's him. It'll be a lynch mob with everyone singing and dancing, and I'll be in the lead cheering them on."

"Not another step," McConnel ordered.

He ignored her.

Bitsy stood. Maybe he shouldn't be so bold.

McConnel moved to her right, tripped him, then pushed him facedown. He hit hard with a thud. Blood from his nose dripped all over Momma's recently polished wooden floor.

Momma screamed.

Before he could turn over, McConnel had his hands cuffed behind him and was holding him down. "Take it easy, AC."

Momma lunged toward them. "My God, McConnel. That's my husband. Look what you've done. He's injured."

McConnel raised her hand toward her. "Stop. Don't come another step."

Momma backed away. "I've never had such a thing happen in all my life. This is outrageous, and in my own house."

Bitsy didn't know what to do. What was happening? Daddy's face was beet red. Blood from his nose was smeared on his chin. "If you don't let him up, he's going to have a heart attack."

McConnel repositioned and knelt beside him. "AC. Can I trust you to behave?"

No response.

"He's dying," Momma yelled. "Call 9-1-1."

"Mattie, he's fine," McConnel said. "AC. What's it going to be? Calm down or go to jail."

"I'm all right. Help me up."

"The handcuffs stay on until I know I can trust you."

Bitsy couldn't move, still stunned by what she'd witnessed. McConnel had put him down like a side of beef, and it was kind of hot. Bitsy didn't know whether to admire her or cuss her out. The whole situation was a confusing fiasco.

McConnel maneuvered him to a standing position, then led him to a chair next to the game table and sat him down, the handcuffs still on as she watched him intently. "What am I going to do with you?" She got a tissue from the stand next to the sofa and gently wiped his nose and chin. "You're a mess. Mattie, can you get him a warm, wet cloth?"

"I've never seen such a thing. Good Lord!" Mattie hurried from the room.

Daddy looked up at McConnel with a sheepish grin. "You're in her shit-house for sure. I 'spect you won't get any pecan pie." He laughed. "Damn, McConnel." He shook his head. "Hell of a thing."

Was the crisis over? Bitsy sat in her chair and watched them.

McConnel placed her hand on his shoulder. "You have to give me your word you won't go after him. You could ruin the entire case I'm building against him. If you can't restrain yourself, I'll have to lock you up until this is over."

Daddy nodded. "I understand. I give my word I won't do anything more than protect my family."

McConnel shook her head. "That's not good enough, AC. I have to know you won't pursue him, that you won't even leave your property until this is over, or call anyone, or invite your friends over and have a meeting about it. Nothing. If you do anything, it could put me or other agents in danger."

He frowned. "How long do you think it'll take?"

"I'm hoping no more than a few days."

Mattie came into the room and started to wipe his face.

He resisted and pulled away from her. "Wait a minute, darlin'."
He looked up at McConnel. "I give you my word, Special Agent of the
FBI McConnel. I won't go after him, but if that asshole comes on my
property, I'll shoot him dead."

"Fair enough," McConnel said. She reached behind him and
removed his cuffs.

Bitsy sighed in relief.

Momma handed him the washcloth and a bag of ice.

He wiped his face and asked for a drink of tea, then pressed the
ice pack to his nose.

Momma kissed his forehead and gave McConnel the stink eye as
she went by.

McConnel glanced at Bitsy. "I think it's time for me to leave.
Bitsy, you can stay here or come on back to your house. Either way,
your security team and Kathrine will remain with you twenty-four
hours a day."

Now she was giving her a choice? She wasn't sure what to do.
"What do you think, Daddy?"

"I think if you go with McConnel, you're in very capable hands,
but I'd like you here with us."

She watched McConnel's expression. She looked focused and
determined. She had a job to do. She'd be occupied with closing the
case. She'd be leaving soon. Bitsy's heart sank. "I want to talk it over
with McConnel." She walked to her. "Let's go out on the veranda."

"Why don't we go up to your room instead. I'd rather not have
you outside in the open."

The comment reminded Bitsy just how serious the situation was.
"All right, if you prefer."

They climbed the stairs to her bedroom.

Bitsy closed the door and sat on the bed.

McConnel sat in the overstuffed chair across from her.

"Are you going after him?" Bitsy asked.

McConnel nodded. "I need to do some things first, but yes, that's
the plan."

The emotion swelled. Bitsy tried to control her breathing. "You'll
be leaving then?" She pressed her hands together in her lap, straining.

"I don't know what to feel." She tried to clarify her thoughts, but everything was pressed together in a massive mountain of sadness, anger, resentment, and heartbreak. It was too much.

"I know we need to talk, but I have to focus on the case," McConnel said. "I understand you have questions, but I can't answer them. I have to leave. I need to get back to your house and work through some things. It's a critical time in the investigation." McConnel stood. "It's better you stay here. I'll call Kathrine. As soon as she gets here, I have to go."

McConnel didn't wait for any kind of response. She pulled her cell from her pocket and punched in a number, then left the bedroom. "Kathrine." She closed the door behind her.

Bitsy was alone. Had McConnel found the killer? Was it Atwater? That sneaky, foul son of a bitch. All this time. No wonder Daddy wanted to kill him. She did too. She breathed a cleansing breath—deep, long, satisfying. He'd pay for all of it. All the pain. All the heartbreak. But it wouldn't bring Hallie Lynn back. It wouldn't help Bitsy regain all those years of emotional trauma. She scrubbed her face. *Atwater*.

Chapter Thirty

Once Kathrine arrived, McConnel left Mattie and AC's. She drove as fast as she dared, trying to get back to Bitsy's to review her notes and make sure she was on the right track. Unfortunately, she ended up behind some type of tour bus that seemed to slow at every house or moss-covered tree. It finally turned right, but everything was taking too long. She pulled off the road and parked, went secure on her phone, and called Jenkins. "I've narrowed down my suspects and think I know who the killer is." She could hardly catch her breath to get the words out. "I'm almost positive it's Atwater."

"Congratulations. Do you need backup?" Jenkins asked.

"Send at least four agents."

"It's going to take a few hours to fly them in."

"I'll be at Bitsy's house." She gave him the address.

"Will you arrest him or bring him in for questioning?"

"Questioning. I don't have concrete evidence yet. Since there's nothing from the other cases, I'm going to have to go for a confession."

Jenkins let out a low whistle. "He's pretty slippery. How are you going to get him to talk?"

"I have no idea yet. There must be evidence somewhere. I just need to find it."

"Okay. I'll line up the additional agents and head them your way. Let me know if you need anything else."

"Will do."

She watched the vehicles pass. It was almost over. She raised her fists in triumph.

Just as she started to pull out onto the road her phone chimed. *Kathrine.*

McConnel touched the button on the steering wheel. "What's up?"

"He's gone."

McConnel pulled back onto the shoulder and slammed on the brakes. "What do you mean, he's gone?"

"The team reported he slipped surveillance. He stopped for gas about forty minutes ago, went in, and never came out. He must have had another car nearby."

"This can't be happening." McConnel made a fast, illegal U-turn and headed back to Mattie and AC's. "I'm about twelve minutes out. Redirect all security to where they lost Atwater and start the search from there. Do not call local police. He's tapped into all of it. I'll see you in a few." She disconnected and immediately redialed Jenkins.

"We've lost Atwater," she said, as soon as he answered. Discouraged and disappointed, she reviewed the details of everything that had happened.

A few minutes later Bitsy's number appeared on the screen.

"I'll get back to you. I need to answer this." She ended his call and pressed the button. "Bitsy?"

Bitsy screamed into the phone, crying. "You have to come back here. He took her."

McConnel could barely understand what she was saying. "Who took who?"

"Atwater. He took her. He took our Mary Ruth. McConnel, help us. Oh, God! He took her. McConnel, help."

Mattie and another woman were shrieking in the background. Where was Kathrine?

"I'm almost there. Hang on. I'm just a few minutes away. What happened?"

"What are we going to do?"

Bitsy was hysterical. All McConnel could hear was crying and shouting. She turned into the long driveway, then skidded sideways when she came to a stop. She jumped out and ran toward the house.

Bitsy raced out the front door and leapt from the veranda, followed by AC, Mattie, and Tilly, all converging on McConnel, yelling and screaming.

Kathrine stepped from the doorway, her cell to her ear.

McConnel grasped Bitsy by the shoulders. "Calm down. What happened?"

Bitsy was pale, her eyes wild. "He took her from the dance studio."

"It's your fault, Bitsy," Tilly shouted. "You caused this."

Mattie was yelling at AC to do something.

AC stalked toward McConnel. "I'm going to kill him."

"How do you know it was Atwater?" she asked.

Bitsy tried to speak in between sobs. "He called me."

"Atwater called *you*?"

"Yes." Bitsy trembled. "He told me if I didn't come to where he said, he'd kill Mary Ruth."

McConnel's phone rang. *Unknown caller.* She answered.

"By now you know what I did."

McConnel couldn't hear with all the yelling, crying, and blaming. She stepped away and put her hand over her ear. "Atwater?"

"Bring Bitsy. No one else, or I'll kill the girl. I've got nothing to lose, so you know I'll do what I say. You've got forty-two minutes to get here. Leave now. Stay on the phone. I'll tell you where to go. No other calls."

McConnel met Kathrine's eyes and motioned for something to write with. She tried to slow her heartbeat as her thoughts raced. He wasn't giving her any opportunity to work through the situation. No time to plan or develop a response, or to call for backup. "Just don't hurt her. I've got to calm Bitsy, and we'll leave. She's upset, as you can well imagine."

"Don't think I can't hear everything you say. You talk to anyone else, and I'll kill the girl and Bitsy."

Kathrine jogged to her and handed her a pen, holding up a notepad for her to write on.

"I understand," McConnel said into the phone as she printed, *Atwater. Tracking phones? Follow me.*

Kathrine read it, then showed it to Bitsy.

"Where do you want us to go?" McConnel asked him, stalling for time.

Bitsy's eyes widened as she looked at McConnel questioningly.

McConnel drew a line through the original message, then wrote *Follow my lead.* She gestured for Bitsy to get in the car, then scribbled down Jenkins's name and number and pointed to Kathrine.

Kathrine nodded.

"Leave now," Atwater said.

"I'm getting Bitsy in. Just give me a few more seconds."

"Hurry up, and don't try anything."

His voice was gruff and full of emotion. He was on edge and hopefully not thinking rationally. It was something that could work in her favor. Had he had time to thoroughly plan this out? "We're leaving now. Bitsy, slide into the passenger side. Put your seat belt on."

Bitsy did as she was told.

Mattie screamed. "No. Not Bitsy."

McConnel put her finger to her mouth to signal Mattie to be quiet. AC started toward his car.

Before McConnel could react, Kathrine grabbed AC and put him in a hold, whispering to him. He nodded, and she relaxed her grip, then got in her vehicle.

All Kathrine had to do was let Jenkins know what was going on, and he would take care of the rest.

McConnel climbed behind the wheel. "We're leaving now." She spoke as calmly as she could. "I'm pulling out of her driveway."

"I'm tracking all your cell phones. Turn left. If you don't, I'll know. Go four-point-two miles and then pull off to the side of the road, get out, and get the cell phone in the mailbox marked *Zimmerman 4381.*"

McConnel continued to drive. He was more organized than she had originally thought.

Jenkins could still track her rental car. She looked in the rearview mirror, couldn't see Kathrine, but knew she was there.

Bitsy watched her closely. She'd stopped crying.

McConnel motioned for the pad and pen. She positioned it on her thigh and wrote, *Everything's okay. Do what I say,* then handed it to her.

Bitsy flipped the bird toward the windshield.

McConnel grinned and nodded.

At the mileage Atwater had instructed, she pulled to the side of the road. "I'm at the mailbox."

"Get the phone."

She did as she was told. It was a burner, as she suspected. Untraceable. It rang.

"Throw your and Bitsy's cells into the ditch, not on the road. Turn right at the next intersection. Go fourteen-point-four miles and stop."

"In the middle of the road?"

"Don't be stupid. Do what I say."

McConnel did as he ordered and drove away. At any point he might be watching. If he was, unless Kathrine stayed back, he'd know she was following them. Most likely he was holed up in a secluded area somewhere. It would take forty-two minutes. McConnel guessed it was somewhere in the state or national forest, probably close to where he'd taken Bigalow's truck. It also had to be somewhere that had technical support capabilities.

Was Jenkins tracking her? She glanced in the review mirror. *Was* Kathrine really behind her? She couldn't count on either one. She reached across the console and took the notepad from Bitsy's lap, then held her hand out for the pen. She wrote, *If he ties you, clench your fists, flex your wrists. Wiggle hands free when can.* She turned the pad so Bitsy could read it.

Bitsy stared at the words for a long moment, then nodded.

How was McConnel going to keep Bitsy safe and free Mary Ruth?

They arrived at the mile indicated, and McConnel's heart skipped a beat. Another car. A silver Ford Focus. Kathrine would never know what vehicle they'd changed to. She stopped. "Now what?"

"Both of you get out. Put your weapons under the driver's seat. If I find any on either one of you, I'll use them on Bitsy. Is that clear enough for you, Special Agent McConnel?"

The rustling of wind through trees and multiple birdsong sounded in the background, as did the clumping of footsteps on what seemed to be a wooden floor. A forested area? But was he inside a building or on a deck?

"Get into the Ford," he said. "You have seventeen minutes. Don't deviate. Don't slow down. For every minute you're late, the girl gets punished. Clear?"

"Perfectly," McConnel said. She knew he meant it.

She and Bitsy got into the Fusion, where the key fob lay on the console. McConnel started the engine and drove forward.

"Go the speed limit. Continue north. Pass the state forest marker. Turn right onto the access road. At the dead end, get out and follow the footpath to the building."

"Do you think he'll kill Mary Ruth?" Bitsy's voice was low, desperate, and strained.

McConnel scanned the passenger side of the roof to the edge of the sun visor. A small camera was wedged near the swivel. Audio *and* video. "I have no doubt he'll do what he says he will."

"That's right, bitch," Atwater hissed into her ear. "I'll do exactly what I say I will."

She tightened her grip on the phone. She couldn't let Bitsy hear him. She moved her eyes again, back and forth to the camera, hoping Bitsy would track them.

She did.

"Try not to worry."

"I will, but I'm shaking so hard I can hardly think or move." Bitsy held out her hand.

When they got to the end of the access road, a marked trail led into the woods. They got out and started down the path.

"If we lose the signal," Atwater said, "keep moving. If you're not here in six minutes, I'll kill the girl."

As if on cue, the call dropped.

McConnel slipped the phone into her pocket. If they got out of this alive, it'd be evidence.

Bitsy grabbed McConnel's arm and leaned in. "What are we going to do?" she whispered.

"Your job is to get Mary Ruth and get out, period," McConnel said quickly. "No matter what happens. He's wired everything. I'm sure he has video and probably audio on us right now."

"Will they find us?" Bitsy whispered.

"I hope so. They're going to do all they can. I'll need to stall him for time."

Bitsy slowed.

McConnel grabbed her elbow and moved her along. "Remember what I told you."

"I do. I know this place," Bitsy said. "It used to be a girls' camp. We're headed for the dining hall."

"What do you remember about the building?" McConnel asked.

"It's big, kitchen in the back, typical gathering place at a camp."

McConnel hurried their pace and checked her watch. Four minutes. "What are the windows like. Glass? Open?"

"No glass, just shutters." Bitsy tripped on a root and almost went down.

McConnel steadied her. "Come on. We have to pick up the pace."

They were now almost at a half run and came to a clearing. The rustic structure was larger than McConnel had expected, with an open porch along the entire length of the front. The heavy wooden door was open, all the windows boarded. No chance for a shooter to take him out.

"Get in front of me," McConnel whispered.

Bitsy moved into position.

McConnel stayed directly behind her as they began to maneuver around a large fire pit. She reached down and grabbed a handful of ash and stuffed it into her pocket, then brushed the residue on her pant leg.

"Stop." Atwater called from far enough inside that she couldn't see him. More than likely he had a gun aimed at them. "Come in one at a time. You first, Bitsy. Hands up."

Bitsy glanced at McConnel with terror on her face and pleading eyes.

McConnel wanted to grab her and stop her, but she knew that for now they'd have to do as he instructed. She nodded.

Bitsy hesitantly climbed the steep stairs, then approached the doorway.

All McConnel saw was the flash of his arm as he reached from the dark interior and yanked Bitsy inside. It took every ounce of restraint she had to not charge in after her.

A muffled sound, then Bitsy called out, "Mary Ruth!"

"Shut up. Hands behind your back."

Shuffling. "You bastard."

The sound of a slap, then stillness.

A few minutes went by.

"Come in, Agent McConnel."

She put her hands behind her head, interlocked her fingers, and began to move forward.

"No. Hold 'em high."

She repositioned. He wasn't falling for it. She could have used her elbows to attack. Holding her hands in the air kept her at a disadvantage. She reached the doorway. The contrast between the bright sunlight and the shadows inside made it hard to see.

He pulled her in and slammed the door shut. "Hands behind you."

Her wrists were zip-tied before her eyes adjusted to the faint light seeping in between the boards covering the windows. She squinted.

Atwater slid a long plank over the door frame and dropped it into place.

No one was busting through that entrance anytime soon. She could understand why he'd chosen this place. It was built like a fortress. It probably hadn't been officially used in a decade or so, but signs of local teens looking for a party spot were everywhere. A central fireplace was full of charred logs, an iron poker resting on the hearth. The room smelled of stale beer and pot. Several frayed, worn-out blankets lay on the floor beside a broom, and stacks of old wooden chairs were piled against the far wall, many broken. A hunting knife and a backpack, presumably Atwater's, lay on the end of the only dining table left.

Bitsy sat in a chair several feet from the table, her lower lip swollen, her ankles bound to the wooden legs, her hands zip-tied to the outer spindles of the back. McConnel's hope deflated. Unfortunately, he'd used thick white plastic ties, the hardest to get out of. It wasn't impossible, if Bitsy had done what she'd written, but McConnel would need some space to get out of hers.

Mary Ruth was tied the same as Bitsy, but a gag covered her mouth. Tears streaked her cheeks. Had he hurt her? She doubted it. Mary Ruth was his bait. He was really after McConnel and Bitsy. The girl's facial features were similar to Bitsy's, same hair color and eyes. They both looked so much like Mattie, anyone could see the three of them were related.

Atwater grabbed McConnel by the crook of her arm and pulled her in front of him. She didn't resist. Let him think she was an amateur. Let him feel superior in every way. He slapped her across the face. It stung and knocked her off balance. He jerked her to him, then raked his fingers over her breasts, under her arms, and down her stomach.

He grinned as he groped her crotch. "You like that, don't you?" He tossed the cell from her pocket.

All the while she tried to get a read on him.

He sweated, the stench of alcohol on his breath. He spun her around and ran his hand over her shoulders and back. He squeezed her buttocks.

She tried not to flinch.

He leaned in, close to her ear, as he rubbed himself against her. "You're tight. I bet I could slip into you and get off in just a few strokes. That little bitch over there is a fine piece of ass, just like Hallie Lynn, my first. You know we always remember our first." He sneered. "I think I'll let you watch."

McConnel clinched her jaw with rage. "How many?"

"Twenty-seven, and then there'll be you three."

"Which states?"

"Let's see. Georgia, North Carolina, Tennessee, and Alabama. I had my pick. You people couldn't have found me if I'd given you a map."

"Any souvenirs?"

"From every one of them."

There was her confession. A jury would never hear it because she knew in that moment she'd kill him. The hell with a trial.

CHAPTER THIRTY-ONE

Bitsy continued to tug against the zip ties. She'd followed McConnel's instructions to the letter, and they'd worked, giving her the possibility of escape. She jerked her right arm upward. If she could just get the base of her thumb beneath the hard strip of plastic. She was almost there, thanks to the slickness of the blood from the sharp edge of the restraint cutting into her wrist.

Every time she met Mary Ruth's terrified eyes, her heart sank. She kept trying to look reassuring, but how would they ever get out of this situation? She couldn't hear what Atwater was saying to McConnel, but whatever it was, McConnel's face contorted. Nor could she reach over and comfort Mary Ruth. Words would have to do. "Don't you worry, sweetheart. We're going to get out of here." She whispered as softly as she could.

Atwater glared at her. "Shut up." He shoved McConnel to the floor and stomped over to Bitsy, replacing the gun in his hand with a hunting knife from the table as he walked by. Running the side of the blade over her cheek, he said, "One more word and I'll cut you into pieces. Nod if you understand."

Bitsy did. Bile rose in her throat, and she swallowed to keep it down. He was every bit as terrifying as he'd been thirty years ago.

He was in uniform. That's how he'd lured Mary Ruth and Hallie Lynn.

Mary Ruth struggled against her restraints.

One step and he was in front of her. "You."

Mary Ruth stilled. "If you don't stop, I'll slice *her*." He pointed the knife at Bitsy.

Mary Ruth looked at her with a pleading expression and burst into tears.

Bitsy shook her head. *He won't. McConnel won't let him.*

McConnel curled in a fetal position, rolled, and then managed to get her hands over her feet. She jumped as she raised her arms, fisted her hands, and broke the ties over her thigh as she came down.

Atwater pivoted, then went for the gun on the table.

McConnel grabbed the broom, knocked the knife out of his hand, and then swept the revolver to the floor. She broke the handle against the table, then stabbed the jagged edge at him.

He backed away.

Bitsy saw her chance. She threw her weight sideways and slammed to the floor. With all her strength, through gritted teeth, she wrenched her right hand free, the flesh of her knuckle ripping. She cried out as she groped for the knife, bucking her body to get to it. She gripped the handle, severed the zip tie on her left wrist, then quickly freed her ankles.

"Go," McConnel yelled.

Atwater kicked at McConnel, then grabbed the metal poker from the fireplace. "Two can play at this game. Now what are you going to do?" He thrust the point toward her.

Neither moved. Both eyed the gun.

As fast as she could, Bitsy freed Mary Ruth.

Mary Ruth clung to her.

"No time." Bitsy dropped the knife and clutched Mary Ruth's hand, practically dragging her to the entrance. They both lifted the heavy board away from the door and swung it open.

When Bitsy turned, Atwater had McConnel around the neck from behind. McConnel spun and did something with her hands, but it happened so fast Bitsy wasn't sure what she'd done. McConnel kicked him in the groin, and when he doubled over, she kneed him in the face. He went down. They both made a move for the gun at the same time, Atwater crawling toward it, McConnel lunging.

Bitsy pushed Mary Ruth outside, then raced for the nearest weapon—the broom handle.

Atwater got hold of the gun first and aimed it toward McConnel.

She grabbed his wrist and shoved it away from her face.

Atwater fired. The bullet hit the side window frame. He struggled to break free of McConnel's grasp. With his other hand he clutched her throat.

Her face flushed as she choked and gasped for air. She reached into her pocket and threw something powdery into his face.

"You bitch," he yelled. He released her neck and wiped at his eyes.

It only took a millisecond for Bitsy to decide. She went to him, raised the broken handle, then brought it down hard between his shoulder blades.

He screamed and whipped his arm around, knocking her to the floor.

She hit hard, seeing flashes of light, pain exploding in her head. The percussion of a gunshot reverberated in her ears. She sucked in a breath. "No! No! No! Please, not McConnel."

He moaned.

"This is for Hallie Lynn," McConnel yelled.

Another shot went off.

Atwater slumped, exhaling loudly, then stilled.

"Is he dead?" Bitsy shouted, lifting herself to a sitting position.

"If he's not, I'll shoot the bastard again." McConnel pried the gun from his hand and then checked the artery in his neck. "He's dead."

Bitsy stood, staggered backward, then finally got her balance. His blood was everywhere, splattered across the floor, on the front of her pant leg, her hands.

McConnel slowly got up, her blouse soaked in blood.

Bitsy gasped. "Are you shot?"

McConnel looked at her shirt. "No. It's his."

"Thank God!" Bitsy struggled to catch her breath. "We're a mess." Her right hand ached. Blood dripped from her knuckle and wrist.

"Yeah, but we're alive."

The thrum of an approaching helicopter sounded from somewhere above the cabin.

"Mary Ruth?" Bitsy ran to the doorway and shouted for her. Every second she didn't answer, Bitsy grew more frantic. "Mary Ruth?"

"I'm here, Aunt Bitsy." She emerged from the woods.

Bitsy raced to her and cradled her in her arms, kissing her hair and holding on. "Did he hurt you? Are you all right?"

Mary Ruth buried her face into Bitsy's chest. "He tied me up and scared the hell out of me."

Bitsy laughed. "My brave, brave, girl. I'm so proud of you."

The helicopter circled, then hovered. "FBI," a male voice echoed from a speaker. "Where's Special Agent McConnel?"

Bitsy gave a thumbs-up and pointed toward the building.

"Help is on the way," the speaker blasted.

Sirens blared in the distance.

"Now they get here." Bitsy kissed Mary Ruth's cheek, then guided her toward the benches near the fire pit.

McConnel was standing in the doorway, watching.

They were safe. *He* was dead and couldn't hurt them anymore. Had McConnel guessed who Mary Ruth was or why Atwater had taken her? Did it matter?

CHAPTER THIRTY-TWO

McConnel descended the steps. Bitsy and Mary Ruth stood locked in each other's arms. In spite of the sound of sirens and the circling helicopter and the chaos, McConnel enjoyed the scene before her. The bond of love between Bitsy and Mary Ruth was beautiful to witness.

McConnel settled on the bottom step and took a deep, purifying breath. She'd done it. They'd done it. Thoughts rushed in about what would happen later, but she pushed them back, savoring this moment. The consequences of the secret she'd kept would come soon enough.

Bitsy led Mary Ruth to her. "McConnel, I'd like to introduce you to my niece, Mary Ruth. Darlin', this is FBI Special Agent Cecelia McConnel."

Mary Ruth eyed McConnel's blood-soaked shirt, then offered her hand. McConnel was happy to shake it. "You're a brave young woman. Are you all right?"

Mary Ruth nodded. "Thanks to you and Aunt Bitsy. Are you hurt, ma'am?"

McConnel looked down at her shirt and pulled it away from her stomach, inspecting it. "No. It's not my blood."

Mary Ruth grimaced. "I'm glad."

Bitsy's left temple had a dark red mark, her cheek was swollen and beginning to turn purple, and she was already getting a black eye.

"You'll need to have your face and hand looked at," McConnel said. "You both need to go to the hospital."

"I'm sure I'll be fine," Bitsy said.

"Me too," Mary Ruth chimed in.

"Maybe so, but I'll have to go there too, so we'll all go together." McConnel smiled inwardly. Bitsy and Mary Ruth were so much alike. Tough and feisty.

Mary Ruth frowned.

Several sheriff's deputies and state police in patrol cars sped into the clearing from access roads. AC jumped out of the first car and ran toward them, holding out his arms.

Mary Ruth darted toward him. "Pa-paw."

He picked her up and twirled her, kissing her cheek and stroking her hair. "You're all right. You're all right." He settled her onto the ground and then grabbed Bitsy and wrapped her in an embrace, the way Bitsy had done with Mary Ruth. Tears streamed down his face. "Bitsy, darlin'. Oh, my darlin' girl."

"Daddy. It's okay. I'm safe. McConnel saved us."

He held her in his arms for a long time, then stepped away, his gaze sweeping over McConnel. "Are you hurt?"

"No, sir. It's all his blood."

"Is he dead?"

McConnel nodded.

Park rangers on four-wheeled vehicles and other emergency personnel arrived and swarmed the area.

McConnel identified herself to law enforcement and told them where the cars were parked and where her gun was but refused to let them do anything but guard the structure until her fellow agents arrived.

Kathrine drove in and parked behind the police vehicles. McConnel motioned for her to come to her side. "Stay with Bitsy and Mary Ruth. I'll need to give my report."

"I've got it," Kathrine said. "I'll take good care of them."

The four FBI Agents arrived. McConnel knew one, Kennedy, from another case. She reviewed what had happened.

"I see you took care of business," Kennedy said.

She nodded. "No need for a trial."

"Let's get you out of that shirt." He slipped off his jacket and handed it to her.

She thanked him, put it on, then pulled the bloody shirt off underneath and tossed it onto the ground. "Bitsy's going to need something for her hand."

"I'll tend to it," one of the park rangers said as he passed them.

He approached Bitsy and then led her toward one of the emergency vehicles.

"Walk us through it," Kennedy said.

He and the other agents started toward the building with McConnel.

Her body ached and her knee was strained, but she tried not to limp as she went up the stairs and into the entrance.

AC started to follow.

Kennedy stopped, motioning for him to not enter. "Sorry, sir. FBI only."

He scowled, and then nodded and returned to Bitsy.

Kennedy immediately went to Atwater and inspected his body. "Looks like you put up one hell of a fight. How'd you do all this?" He circled Atwater and looked at the broom handle in his back.

"Bitsy did that. I shot him."

"How many times?"

"Two. Three shots fired in all. One went into the window frame over there." She pointed to the side wall. "I managed to gain control of the gun while he was still holding it and fired the other two shots into him."

"Your witness out there did *this*?" he asked, pointing to Atwater's back.

"Yes. She saved my life. If she hadn't stabbed him, he would have overpowered me."

Kennedy leaned in and pointed to Atwater's face. "What's that?"

"Ash. I threw it in his eyes."

"State law enforcement and the coroner can do forensics," Kennedy said. "Looks like a clean kill. We'll get the search warrants and start things rolling."

"He said he had souvenirs from each one." McConnel spoke softly, not wanting to make it real. His words haunted her. She felt sick to her stomach. "He admitted to twenty-seven."

Kennedy shook his head and stabbed his finger at Atwater. "He deserved everything he got. Why do they always want to keep trophies to relive what they did?"

McConnel glared at Atwater. How could he have gotten away with it for so many years? All those victims. Sweet, young, innocent girls. *Hallie Lynn.* She wanted to scream at him. Kick him. Shoot him again.

"We'll need statements from your witnesses. Do you want me to handle it?" Kennedy asked.

McConnel nodded. "Ms. Hanover and her niece, Mary Ruth."

"Go get checked at the hospital, write your report, and email it to Jenkins," Kennedy said. "He instructed me to tell you to take it easy and that he'll see you in the Toledo office on Wednesday. That means get some rest. You look like you could use it. Hell of a job, McConnel. Glad you're all right."

The others congratulated her.

She stepped outside, into the light. Law enforcement continued to gather in the clearing, and then the media—TV, radio, local, national— started to swarm. McConnel wanted no part of it. It was Kennedy's show now.

Bitsy was surrounded by her dad, niece, Kathrine, and others.

McConnel hobbled to her. "You, me, and Mary Ruth need to go. My colleagues will contact you to get your statements."

They were transported to the hospital in separate ambulances.

McConnel looked out the window when they shut the ambulance door. So many lives. So many families shattered by what *he* did. Reporters were wrangling anyone for an interview to get the story. The scoop. No wonder Bitsy felt the way she had.

Mattie, Tilly, and Bitsy's other sisters and their presumed husbands were waiting for them when they arrived at the hospital, along with more media and reporters shoving microphones in their faces, jockeying to see who could get closest and shout the loudest to snare a comment. Someone must have made a few calls and tipped them off. Hospital security guards were everywhere.

McConnel thought back to the computer probabilities and the data. All the victims entered into the program came from lower-income families. Maybe if more money had been involved, the media would have taken a bigger interest in their cases, and maybe Atwater could have been found sooner. It was a cynical thought, but McConnel didn't care.

She was transported into a cubicle, assisted onto a hospital bed, and the curtain was drawn.

The sounds of relief and joy from Bitsy's family as they greeted her and Mary Ruth funneled into McConnel's area. She was envious.

She scanned the cold, white walls of her cubicle as she waited alone for someone to examine her.

The curtain was abruptly pulled back.

McConnel startled. AC, Mattie, and Tilly stood there, smiling. They surrounded her bed, kissing her forehead, patting her arms, thanking her. She laughed. "Does this mean I get some pecan pie?"

"All you want, darlin'," Mattie said, stroking McConnel's hair. "For the rest of your life."

McConnel, Bitsy, and Mary Ruth were released from the hospital a few hours later, but Bitsy was on concussion protocol. Bed rest for twenty-four hours, then only light activity for a couple of days. AC and Mattie insisted McConnel stay with Bitsy at their house.

"One night," McConnel said. "Then I need to get back to Bitsy's and wrap up the case."

She stripped in the bathroom and inspected the bruises on her arms, wrists, and thighs. The mirror revealed deep bruising and Atwater's fingerprints where he'd grabbed her throat. Her knees hurt, her back ached, and even her nose was sore. She stepped into the shower, letting the hot water run over her. She washed and shampooed twice, then dried and slipped on a blouse and slacks Mattie had given her. She went to Bitsy's bedroom.

Mattie sat in the overstuffed chair next to the bed, her tatting now making a familiar, almost comforting sound.

Bitsy lay on her side, facing the door, apparently asleep, her black eye more evident now. Her wrists were bruised like McConnel's, and she had a large white bandage wrapped around her right wrist and hand.

McConnel entered.

Mattie rose and slipped her arm around McConnel's waist. "Would you like to sit with her awhile?" she whispered.

"Yes, thank you." McConnel lowered herself into the chair Mattie had vacated.

"Can I get you something to drink?" Mattie asked.

"Ice water would be great."

Mattie smiled. "I'll be right back." She left.

Bitsy's breathing was even and rhythmic. McConnel couldn't take her eyes off her, enjoying the peaceful expression on her face as she slept. Birds chirped. A slight breeze blew in from the open window, the evening shadows softening the room, intensifying McConnel's feelings. Things needed to be said. Secrets needed to be revealed. But not tonight.

McConnel whispered Bitsy's name. She didn't want to wake her, just hear the sound and feel it as it moved over her lips. She breathed it out once again, then leaned her head back and closed her eyes.

She startled awake, gripping the sides of the chair. The lamp beside the bed was on. She rubbed her eyes, then looked at Bitsy.

She was watching her, a hint of a smile on her lips.

McConnel wanted to be next to her, to hold her. "How are you feeling?"

"A little better. You look tired. Why don't you go to bed?"

"I will. I just wanted to sit with you a while."

"Momma brought you some water, but I'm afraid the ice melted."

McConnel cleared her throat. She reached for the glass on the stand and drank half of the cool liquid.

Bitsy rolled on to her back and gingerly touched the side of her face. "It hurts."

"It looks painful," McConnel said.

"It'll heal." Her eyes moistened. She gently rested her bandaged hand on McConnel's knee. "McConnel." Tears ran down the corners of her eyes. "You saved us all."

McConnel leaned forward and tenderly linked their fingers. "*You* saved *me*. He had the advantage. If you hadn't intervened, he would have probably killed all three of us."

"We saved each other?" Bitsy swiped at her tears.

"Yes, we did."

"You won't leave town until I can get back home, will you?" Her face tensed.

"I'm going to your house in the morning, but I'll be there a few more days. I have a lot to follow up on."

Bitsy grinned. "*I* have some things I want to follow up on too." She closed her eyes.

McConnel stood. She bent and whispered into Bitsy's ear, "Looking forward to it." She stroked her arm. "Do you want me to turn out the light?"

"Yes, please."

"Sleep well, Bitsy."

"You too. McConnel?" Bitsy's voice trailed off.

"Yes?"

"Nothing. I just wanted to say your name. Good night."

McConnel switched off the lamp and left her room. AC and Mattie were talking in the living room. She was hungry but didn't want to go downstairs. AC would want all the details, and she still couldn't discuss them until the case was officially closed. She went to her room and stretched out on the bed, finding comfort in the darkness.

Now she'd be able to put some of the pieces together. Atwater had admitted he'd collected tokens from his victims. Once they were found, they could connect them to the missing girls. They might never find where he buried them, but at least they could put their names with the items and give the families some measure of peace. And Hallie Lynn? She'd discuss her burial with Bitsy. They'd work it out, somehow. And Bitsy? McConnel closed her eyes. Worry and apprehension flooded her, pulling her into a current of uncertainty. How would Bitsy take the truth? Was what they felt for each other strong enough to survive McConnel's secret?

Chapter Thirty-three

Momma pulled into Bitsy's driveway and parked. Bitsy unbuckled her seat belt, disappointment washing over her when she saw McConnel's car wasn't there. It'd only been two days. They'd talked several times on the phone, but Bitsy couldn't wait to see her, be alone with her. She grabbed the tote Momma had given her, stuffed full of bandages and supplies, and opened the door.

"Do you need me to carry that in for you?" Momma asked.

Bitsy kissed her cheek. "No. I've got it. I'm fine. I promise I'll call you in a few days."

"Do you need me to take you to your follow-up visit with the doctor?"

Bitsy climbed out of the car. "I'm good."

"How long will McConnel be here?"

"I don't know, Momma. I'll find out."

"You sure you don't want to come on back to the house and stay a few more days?"

"I'm perfectly capable of taking care of my own needs. Quit hovering. Thank you, more than I can ever say, for all you've done. I love you. Now go home."

Bitsy shut the door and made her way up the steps to the porch. She waved as she inserted the key into the lock.

Momma backed out, slammed on the brakes when a car went by, and blew her horn.

Bitsy tossed the bag onto the floor by the sofa and walked into the kitchen, then snatched up a note that lay on the counter.

Welcome home. See you about six.
McConnel

She checked the stove clock. Five twenty. It was good to be back. She wandered through the house, touching, looking, not sure why. Maybe to remind herself she was home and that she was safe.

Suddenly overwhelmed, she went into the living room and plopped into a chair. She'd carried the sorrow, guilt, and sadness of Hallie Lynn's murder for so long, it was odd to not feel it. It wasn't all quite gone yet, but the burden was lighter, more bearable. She had room for hope to fill the empty spaces that change had left, and that hope brought a freedom, lifting her as she thought about her future. What about McConnel? How would she fit into all of it? Would she? Bitsy wanted her to be a part of her life. She was a deep part of it now, even if neither of them acknowledged it.

She inspected her wrists. A hint of yellow was forming around the purple bruising, but she needed to keep the bandage on her right hand for a few more days. Her black eye had darkened, but she was improving each day. The headache was gone, and she no longer felt dizzy.

She glanced at the stairway. Should she go to her bedroom and put on some makeup? Would it make a difference? She touched her temple. Probably not. Was she ready to go to the murder room? Open the door and look inside? Would it be better to wait for McConnel? The thoughts drifted away, like dandelion puffs on a spring day.

She walked to the kitchen and got a glass of tea, then went to her studio. There she tapped the worktable, picked up a brush, returned it, then trailed her finger over the collar of her paint shirt hanging on the back of the stool. She stood in front of the canvas, sipping her drink. Then, tilting her head, she inspected the unfinished painting. She'd captured the lighting. Why had she been so critical of it before? And she'd gotten the color of McConnel's eyes correct. She laughed. Well, one, at least. Just a hint of gold. She leaned closer, considering the beginning brushstrokes of what would be her face. She stepped back a few paces, changing her perspective. It was a good start.

She was ready to paint, but McConnel was due home in a few minutes. She'd wait until morning. She needed to go back to work. Was she ready? Would she be able to deal with all the questions? What about Hallie Lynn's funeral? When could it happen? Would she be able to obtain her remains? She wanted so desperately to properly put her to rest. She took another drink, then wiped her mouth with her fingers. Freedom. Hope. What wonderful words.

She heard the front door open and practically ran to the kitchen, set the glass on the counter, and anxiously waited.

McConnel came through the living room, holding a bouquet of red roses. "There you are. Welcome home." She offered the flowers.

Bitsy thanked her and placed them in a vase of water. Then she sidled up to McConnel. "The case is closed," she whispered.

It only took a moment to see the answer in McConnel's eyes.

Bitsy slid her arms around her neck, bringing her closer, slowly, deliberately.

McConnel moaned and stiffened.

Bitsy let go and backed away. "What's wrong?"

McConnel took a deep breath. "I'm just a little sore."

Bitsy undid the top button of McConnel's shirt and slowly spread her collar. She was bruised from one side of her throat to the other with deep purple prints where Atwater had dug his fingers into her flesh.

"I'm so sorry. I didn't realize how bad it was."

"It's okay." She smiled. "It only hurts when I swallow."

"Not when you kiss?" Bitsy grinned.

"I don't know. I haven't kissed anyone yet."

"Let's find out, shall we?"

McConnel smiled and nodded.

Bitsy moved toward her again, but this time she slipped her arms under McConnel's and pulled her close. Her lips were full and inviting. Bitsy didn't usually take the lead in sexual matters, but it was different with McConnel. It had been from the very beginning. Everything was different with her. She wanted to initiate their joining. She'd had to wait so long.

She moved against her, hesitating only a moment before she brushed her lips over hers, then pressed. McConnel's lips parted. Their kiss was full of warmth and softness, igniting pleasure that swirled through Bitsy's breasts and then downward. She turned McConnel slightly, guiding her backward, slipping her thigh between her legs as she pinned her against the refrigerator. She deepened the kiss.

McConnel responded, opening, inviting her in.

Finally, this was happening. Bitsy wanted more. So much more. She couldn't get close enough, wanting the feel of McConnel next to her, desperate to have her body against hers.

A loud clunk shattered the moment.

Bitsy startled and withdrew. "What was that?"

McConnel chuckled. "My gun. I probably should take it off."

"Can I watch?"

McConnel blushed but laughed. "I'm a little nervous."

Bitsy stepped away from her. "So am I."

McConnel reached to her side, slightly behind her, snapped something loose from her belt, then pulled the gun and holster free. She placed them on the counter by the roses, then caressed Bitsy's bruised face as gently as butterfly wings brushing against her.

"It doesn't hurt," Bitsy said.

"It looks a little better."

"Are we making small talk?" Bitsy asked. "There's no need."

"Let's go in the other room," McConnel said.

"Let's go upstairs to my bedroom."

"I need to talk to you about something. Can we wait?"

"Why? I don't know about you, but I've waited long enough." Bitsy led her to the stairs.

McConnel hesitated at the bottom step. "Bitsy, I don't want to be someone you'll regret."

Bitsy took her hand again and looked into her eyes. "Nothing could ever make me regret you." She claimed McConnel's mouth with a hard, desperate kiss.

McConnel moaned and pulled her into a tight embrace, her own kiss hungry and wanting.

Bitsy eased away, and McConnel followed her up the stairs.

When Bitsy reached the bedroom, she clasped McConnel's hands, walking backward, leading her in. Then she guided McConnel toward the bed. "I've waited a long time. I want to spend every second I can with you. We can talk logistics later. Right now, I need to be with you, more than I've ever needed anything" She untucked the tail of McConnel's shirt from her pants.

"I haven't stopped thinking about making love to you since I left you at your mom and dad's." McConnel began to unbutton Bitsy's blouse, then slid it from her shoulders and peeled it off.

Bitsy's breasts swelled at the thought of what McConnel was going to do. Her knees weakened. She sat on the bed.

McConnel knelt in front of her. "Are you all right?"

"Very."

McConnel slipped Bitsy's bra off and began to caress and fondle her breasts.

Bitsy's nipples hardened with each touch of McConnel's fingers and lips. She fumbled to unbutton McConnel's shirt, then threw it onto the floor, undid her bra, and gazed at her firm, erect nipples. She brought her to her, taking a breast into her mouth, moaning with delight at the taste and feel.

McConnel whispered her name, then stood.

Bitsy unbuckled McConnel's belt and slid her slacks and panties over the curve of her hips and down her legs, then helped her step out of them. She stood naked before her.

"You're even more beautiful than I imagined," Bitsy whispered.

McConnel got onto the bed and guided Bitsy next to her. She kissed her, devouring her mouth, then her neck, her breasts, stomach. Bitsy lifted her hips, and McConnel removed the rest of her clothing, then mounted her, kissing, demanding.

Bitsy had never kissed anyone so deeply or fully. Each movement, each touch consumed all her thought and focus. She had no room for anyone but McConnel.

McConnel repositioned and offered her breast.

Bitsy gladly touched, caressed, and then slid McConnel's hard nipple into her mouth. She wanted more. She tried to position McConnel to get on top of her, but McConnel resisted and slid down, kissing, licking.

Waves of need and pleasure shot through Bitsy as McConnel slid her fingers into her.

Bitsy moved to the rhythm McConnel set with her thrusts. She started to enter McConnel, but she stopped her. "I want you, Bitsy. I need all of you."

Bitsy kissed her, willing to wait to please her if that's what she wanted.

McConnel continued to thrust. She kissed her, then her face, neck, and downward.

Bitsy lifted herself to offer her breasts, and then need and pure lust

SUZIE CLARKE

engulfed her as McConnel released her nipple and trailed her lips down her stomach. She kissed Bitsy's thighs, then spread her. McConnel's hot breath against her sent rivulets of anticipation and desire so powerful Bitsy opened her legs wide and cried out for her. And when McConnel took her into her mouth, Bitsy cupped McConnel's head and began to glide with pleasure. Her lover's warm mouth and skilled tongue sent Bitsy over the edge. She imploded into fulfillment, writhing in ecstasy as wave after wave of elation swept through her, like she'd been holding back for only McConnel for a thousand years. McConnel continued to titillate her.

Bitsy forced her to release and pulled her to her, pressing her thigh against her hot, slick center as she guided her upward, slipping her fingers into her. McConnel lowered and kissed her as she rocked her hips gently against Bitsy's thrusts. Bitsy kneaded and fondled her firm, full breasts, McConnel's nipples hardening with each caress. She withdrew from McConnel, then guided her to her mouth, spread her, and consumed her. McConnel opened, accepting her, submitting. She gripped Bitsy's shoulders, thrusting. Bitsy went deeper, stronger, feeling the release of McConnel's satisfaction as she took her to fulfillment.

McConnel repositioned and collapsed into Bitsy's arms.

They didn't speak for a long time, the silence comforting, reassuring. Bitsy didn't have words to express how she felt. Of course she'd been satisfied by other women, but this was different, a total union. They'd taken all of each other. Bitsy couldn't discern if she was completely empty or completely full. The feeling was impossible to describe.

McConnel slid half off Bitsy and licked her nipple, then revealed the gentlest, sweetest smile Bitsy had ever seen.

Bitsy pulled the sheet over them and tucked it beneath McConnel.

"Bitsy, I don't know what that was, but...I—"

Bitsy put her finger to McConnel's lips and stopped her. "I don't want to talk about it. I just want to enjoy it."

McConnel kissed her, full and consuming.

They made love again, seeking each other's needs and desires, sharing their fulfillment.

Bitsy nestled next to her. "This is all so overwhelming."

McConnel held her. "I know, but given what we've been through, why wouldn't it be?"

Would it lead anywhere, or was it nothing more than a conquest, Bitsy finally getting what she wanted? Her feelings for McConnel were strong and deep. She was sure of it. She didn't want her to leave, especially now, but McConnel had to return to her job, to her life, and long-distance relationships rarely worked out.

CHAPTER THIRTY-FOUR

McConnel woke early, guilt summoning her from sleep. She had to tell Bitsy who she was, but how would she take it? She should have done it last night. If only she'd been stronger, but she'd been just as desperate for them to be together as Bitsy had. The longer she put it off, the harder it would be, and the more damaging. Bitsy had been so open and accepting. McConnel couldn't bear the thought of anything less than what they had at this moment, but their foundation was on sandy footing until she told her the truth.

Bitsy stirred, then opened her eyes. "It's early." She scooted toward McConnel and draped her arm over her waist.

Her closeness stirred McConnel's desire, still smoldering from last night's lovemaking.

"Did you get any rest?" Bitsy asked.

"Some. How about you?"

"I slept like a baby." Bitsy tracked her fingertips along McConnel's stomach, toward her breasts. "I don't think I've ever been so fulfilled."

McConnel touched the side of Bitsy's face. "I feel the same way." She closed her eyes and surrendered to Bitsy's caress. "That's so wonderful. I've never responded to a touch the way I do to yours."

"Mm. Do you want to explore that some more?" She closed the space between them and moved against McConnel.

McConnel couldn't resist the softness of her body, her warm lips against her skin, the way she caressed her. To surrender and fulfill were full of joy and excitement, a completeness she'd never known. How could she resist or give it up? She wanted nothing more than to be with Bitsy.

They made love.

When they were once more satisfied and entwined, McConnel lay beside her, studying her, capturing her beauty and everything she was at that moment. Bitsy looked so relaxed, content. But why did McConnel feel like she'd just stolen something priceless from her? Each time they made love and the passion ebbed, the weight of the guilt and shame of withholding the truth from Bitsy grew harder to bear.

She deserved this time with Bitsy. Why couldn't she wait to tell her? They both had a right to enjoy these moments. The acidic ache in McConnel's stomach grew more intense with each thought. She alone was responsible for the mess she'd made, and she had no one else to blame but herself. She threw the covers off and slid out of bed. "Damn it."

Bitsy reached for her. "What's wrong?"

McConnel couldn't face her with the truth. Not yet. "I have to wrap some more things up about the case, and I'm not sure what time I'll be back."

"Don't go. Stay with me. You've got all day."

Why not? This might be the last time she'd ever be in bed with Bitsy, the last time she'd share her body and give herself to her. She was so easy to love. All McConnel had to do was put the lie out of her mind. But she couldn't. It was eroding her peace, standing like a stone wall between them, destroying any chance she'd ever have for a full, deep relationship with Bitsy. McConnel had learned the hard way long ago that intimacy wasn't built on sex. Intimacy and strength in a relationship came from honesty and trust, and until she told Bitsy who she was, they didn't stand a chance of having what she needed and wanted with her. She couldn't continue to build what they had on a lie. Sooner or later it would come crashing down. She had to tell Bitsy, but Jenkins needed to know first.

She couldn't remain with her. Bitsy would insist they stay in bed, and McConnel would want to. They'd make love and lie in each other's arms and talk of their life and the future they had together, and each moment they did, the secret McConnel kept from her would chip away at what they were trying to build. She had to leave now, not tomorrow. "I have to go, Bitsy."

"I wish you didn't."

"I know, but I've got to meet with my team, review the case, and write my report." The words soured in her mouth. They were all true, but she didn't have to do it now. The job could wait, but this couldn't. She leaned over and kissed Bitsy, maybe for the last time. The possibility ripped at her heart.

"Call me when you can."

"I will." McConnel dressed and left as quickly as she could before she changed her mind. She spent the better part of the morning at Atwater's house with the other FBI agents, combing for any remaining threads of evidence. Was the pair of glasses they found among the items Hallie Lynn's? She wanted to snatch them up and hide them, but they were evidence. After they finished, she booked her flight back to Toledo, Ohio.

She bought a drink and sandwich at the local Quick Stop, then drove to the park where they'd found Hallie Lynn. She texted Bitsy, too much of a coward to call her.

I'm so sorry. I must go back to Toledo later this evening to talk with my boss in the morning about a critical issue that's come up. Be back at your house around six to pack.

It wasn't a lie, but it wasn't the entire truth. It wounded McConnel, as surely as if she'd stuck a knife into her own chest.

Bitsy texted back a few minutes later. *It breaks my heart, but I understand.*

Bitsy had only a piece of the truth. How would she respond when she heard all of it?

McConnel made the ten-minute walk to Hallie Lynn's burial site, then sat beneath the junipers, eating her lunch. Since this was where it had all begun, it seemed a fitting place to spend some time here on her last day of this chapter in her life. She thought of Hallie Lynn, remembered the first day she'd learned she had a sister who had gone missing, recalled the gut-wrenching pain of the news that the remains of her ten-year-old body had finally been found. Then the lie began. She'd hidden from her superiors that she was related to the victim when she asked to be assigned to the case, and then later from Bitsy. Would she do it differently if she had the opportunity to do it over? She didn't know.

Back on a shaded park bench near her car, she spent several hours finishing and fine-tuning her case report. When she could stall no longer, she glanced at her watch. Five o'clock. She gathered the paperwork, got into her car, and drove to Bitsy's to say good-bye, the dread and apprehension overwhelming. She glanced in the rearview mirror. "It's your own fault," she reminded herself.

Bitsy met her at the door. "How much time do you have?"

"Not long. I have to pack, drop off the rental car, then catch my flight. I'll be back as soon as I can."

"When do you think that will be?"

"Hopefully, just a couple of days."

"How long will you be able to stay?"

"I'm not sure."

Bitsy slid her arm around McConnel's waist. "Don't worry. We'll figure it out."

"I'm counting on it."

McConnel's heart was so heavy she could barely climb the stairs. She packed as Bitsy watched from the side of the bed.

"I won't think about you leaving, just returning soon," Bitsy said. "That way I can bear this separation. Otherwise, I'd be falling apart. We need to talk about Hallie Lynn's funeral arrangements when you come back."

"Of course. I'm sure everything will be wrapped up soon so they can release her remains."

"McConnel, are you all right?" Bitsy clasped her hand. "I know this has been a strain, but you should be so proud of yourself for what you did for Hallie Lynn, and for me." She kissed her knuckles.

McConnel traced the line of her jaw with her finger. "I'll miss seeing your beautiful face, even if you still have a black eye."

Bitsy laughed. "I'll be wearing makeup the next time you see me."

"Will you be going back to work soon?" McConnel asked.

"I planned to return Thursday, but since you're leaving a day early, I'll go tomorrow," Bitsy said. "Lilly and Bo are having major anxiety about the workload."

McConnel closed her suitcase. The murder room was in its proper order. She'd cleaned it out before Bitsy had gotten back from her mom and dad's. No trace or any sign of why she'd been there remained. She'd even emptied the wastepaper basket. The only things left were a few telltale tape marks above the desk. She'd offered to pay to have the room repainted, but Bitsy refused, arguing that they would remind her of her.

"All set?" Bitsy asked.

McConnel scanned her area, looking for anything she'd forgotten. Bitsy had her heart. She'd never be able to take that back. "Ready." She lugged her suitcase down to the living room.

They stood in front of the door, and Bitsy embraced her. "Promise me you'll get back here as soon as you can."

"I will."

Bitsy studied her face. Did she see the lie? "Then we can talk about whatever's bothering you so much."

McConnel kissed her as she held back her tears. No one had or ever would kiss her like Bitsy did. She grasped the handle of her suitcase and walked out the door.

Bitsy stood on the porch, never taking her eyes off her. McConnel couldn't bear the pain. She looked away, then left.

❖

Toledo's cool air brought a chill. McConnel missed the warmth of Georgia and Bitsy's touch. Ohio didn't feel like home anymore.

Jenkins, the coordinator, placed his cup of coffee on his desk when McConnel entered and motioned for her to sit. When she did, he came around and settled into one of the cushioned chairs next to her.

"I know we told you yesterday what a fantastic job you did, but I wanted to express again how much I appreciate all your hard work. Because of your investigation into the Peeples case, we closed twenty-one others, and an additional five we hadn't yet tied to Atwater. Twenty-seven lives accounted for. Twenty-seven little girls. That's amazing. Truly amazing."

McConnel placed the envelope she was holding on his desk. "Sir, I want you to know I'm grateful for all the help, praise, and the confidence you've had in me, especially in this case, but I need to tell you something."

His smile disappeared "Concerning what?"

"I don't know how to say this, except to just get it out. I held something back I should have revealed when I asked to be assigned to the Peeples case."

His jaw muscles flinched, and he crossed his legs. "What exactly?"

McConnel had reviewed the ramifications of what she was about to say and tried to prepare the best she could for the outcome, no matter what it was. She deserved whatever she got. "As you know from my records, I was adopted as a baby. What you don't know is that my biological mother's best friend was my adoptive mother."

"Okay. I don't see any problem here."

"My biological mother was Lou Anne Peeples, Hallie Lynn's mother. Not only that, but Hallie Lynn was my fraternal twin sister."

Jenkins's eyes glazed over, and then he stared at her for what seemed like minutes. Finally, he waved his hand. "Wait a minute. You're telling me you're related to the victim, Hallie Lynn Peeples?"

"Yes. I'm her twin sister."

"Her *twin*? You? Her *twin sister*?"

"Yes. Fraternal."

He slumped in his chair. "Holy shit!" He uncrossed his legs and then scooted his chair to look more directly at her. "When did you find this out?"

"That's the bad part. I knew when I requested to be assigned to the cold case. I've unofficially investigated her disappearance since I found out who she was to me when I was eighteen."

He postured. "That's not just bad—that's unethical. It's a break in policy, and a huge conflict of interest." He stood. "Do you realize what you're telling me? You could lose your job for this. You're lucky Atwater is dead, or it could jeopardize all the other cases connected to this one." He began to pace, clasping his hands. "Holy shit! You killed him!" He stopped and wrapped his arms around his chest, then squared his jaw. "McConnel, what were you thinking?" He kicked the trash basket so hard it flew across the room. "That gives you motive. You could be up for murder charges in Atwater's death."

McConnel felt the blood drain from her face. There was a slim chance, but she knew it was true. Hearing it out loud from Jenkins made it so much more real. She swallowed hard and pointed to the envelope she'd placed on his desk. "That's a copy of my adoption papers. The records are sealed, but I'm sure you could get the information with an official order if you needed it."

"Damn it." He rubbed his head. "I'm going to have to put you on administrative leave until I can figure out what in the hell to do about this. Turn in your badge and gun and get out of here. Not one word to anyone about this. Do you understand? Not one damn word."

McConnel stood. "Yes, sir." She removed her weapon and badge, eyeing them one last time before she laid them on the desk. She left, the weight of all of it almost unbearable.

She went back to her apartment and got drunk, trying to still the thoughts swirling in her head.

Bitsy called that evening, but McConnel couldn't face her. She let it go to voice mail.

Bitsy said in her message that she missed her and hoped she was all right.

McConnel wasn't all right. Her world had started to collapse around her. A firestorm was growing, and the winds of regret and consequences were beginning to gust.

Bitsy called again at ten p.m. and repeated herself, and the next morning at nine.

McConnel dragged herself out of bed at ten and nursed her hangover.

Jenkins called at eleven. She let it go to voice mail. "Be in my office at four this afternoon. He paused. "Damn you, McConnel." The call ended.

He wanted the least number of staff in the offices when he dealt with her. Her job was toast.

She entered the Toledo building promptly at three fifty-seven and stopped on the main floor to look at the official seal. She'd taken an oath and had broken it. She'd probably be lucky if she didn't go to jail. She got off the elevator on the seventh floor and walked to Jenkins's office, where two other people were seated at the conference table with him. An older man and a middle-aged woman.

"Have a seat," Jenkins said, motioning to the chair at the end of the table, closest to the door.

That was appropriate. She sat.

He introduced the others. "This is Administrative Assistant Special Agent Jerome Allen, and this is Human Resources Director Lynette Colby."

They nodded.

"Hello," McConnel said.

"Special Agent McConnel, you have an outstanding record," Allen said. "And until this incident, you have been exemplary, both in conduct and job performance. However, due to the serious nature of your deception about the Hallie Lynn Peeples case, we must approach your actions with caution and appropriate resolution."

Couldn't they just get on with it?

Director Colby adjusted her glasses. "I have two forms here." She held them up. "After careful consideration of your admission without coercion or any persuasion on the part of your supervisor, FBI Toledo offers you the following options. Resign with your full benefits or face an administrative hearing." She slid the papers toward McConnel. "Whichever you choose is up to you. I'm sorry your service in the FBI has to end this way."

They'd already decided her fate. McConnel glanced from one to the other, her stomach roiling. She met Colby's gaze. "If I choose an administrative hearing, what could be the outcome?"

Colby leaned forward, folding her hands on the table. "After a thorough investigation, which will include a deeper look into the shooting and possible murder charges, although that is a very, very slim possibility, you could receive termination of service without benefits. Suspension without pay for a specified period of time. Written reprimand. Or no action." Director Colby leaned back in her chair.

McConnel reviewed the forms, reading each twice. She hesitated. She had a right to appeal whatever happened in an administrative hearing. She could fight it, but in the end, she had been wrong. She'd deliberately withheld pertinent information.

No one spoke.

She looked around the room at all of them. What choice did she really have? She signed her resignation, then placed the pen beside it.

Jenkins handed her an envelope. "It's an open letter of reference. You're leaving in good standing."

McConnel stood. "I know I was wrong in not declaring my genetic connection to Hallie Lynn, but legally, I have to say I'm not a relative. I never knew her or my biological mother. I wonder if her case would have ever been solved, or the other twenty-six for that matter, if I hadn't been an FBI Special Agent. As far as Atwater's death goes, it was kill or be killed, along with two other lives. I doubt any jury would find otherwise. I was operating within the scope of my duties, and yes, I did have a personal interest in this case. Thank you for the training and expertise. I couldn't have found my sister's killer without it."

Jenkins stood. "I'm sorry, but it's best for the agency."

She clasped his offered hand, then placed her cell phone and FBI credit card on the table.

"Good luck, McConnel," he said.

She picked up the envelope, walked to the elevator, and never looked back.

Outside, she hailed a cab to her apartment, where she stared at herself in the mirror on the hall closet door. Being out of a job so suddenly caused an empty, hollow sensation that raked over her. No gun. No badge. Stripped of her identity. She fought back tears and reminded herself it was no one's fault but her own. But if anything had been different, Atwater would probably still be out there, and Bitsy would still be locked in a terrifying past. It was worth it to have had the privilege of helping her out of that miserable pit.

She straightened. Her wardrobe needed a change. She no longer looked or felt like an FBI Special Agent, just a dyke with bad taste in clothes. Something lacy and feminine would be nice. She'd have to do some shopping.

She used her personal cell to call Bitsy, but it went to voice mail. "Bitsy, this is McConnel. I have a different phone." She gave her the number, then stopped to gain control of her voice, fighting back emotion. She valued her job, and now it was gone because of a secret, but the worst was yet to come. She could still lose the one person who made her life worth living. "I'll be there tomorrow evening." She paused again. "Not sure of the time yet, but I'll let you know." She disconnected.

McConnel had money in her savings account, plus her 401(k), over twenty thousand in investments, six thousand in her checking account, and cash in the safe in her apartment. She'd manage. She'd just lost her job and part of her identity. Now she'd face the hardest task of all—telling Bitsy who she really was.

CHAPTER THIRTY-FIVE

Bitsy got home late from work, too tired and upset to eat. She'd called McConnel, but the phone message said her number was no longer in service. What had happened? She scrolled her calls again. Four from people in her phone list, and one unknown, probably a solicitor. Three voice mails. She reviewed two and was about to erase the unknown but changed her mind at the last second and decided to listen. She almost dropped the phone when she heard McConnel's voice but, instead, immediately called the number.

"Bitsy?"

"McConnel, where in the hell have you been? What's happened? I was worried sick about you. Why haven't you called me back before now?"

"I'm so sorry. I can't explain over the phone. I'll be there tomorrow night at your house around nine."

"I'll pick you up. What airport?"

"I'm renting a car. I'll drive to your house."

"That's not necessary. I can come get you."

"It's best I drive myself."

Bitsy gave up trying to talk her into letting her pick her up. Maybe she had some official business to wrap up. "I'm glad you're coming back. I've missed you."

"I've missed you too. More than you know. How are you doing? How are your mom and dad, and Mary Ruth, and your sisters, and Bo and Lilly?"

Bitsy burst out laughing. "I can't tell you how good it is to hear from you. They're all fine. Well, Louise is on a rampage because Mary

Ruth thinks she can cuss whenever she wants. After her ordeal, Tilly said she could do whatever she wanted for a while. Other than that, everyone's good. I'm sure missing you."

"I can't wait to see you, Bitsy. We have some things to discuss."

"Sounds serious. Good things?"

"Things." There was a deep sadness in her voice.

They talked about Bitsy's work, and then Bitsy questioned her. "How's it going for you? Did you get awarded any medals yet?"

McConnel was quiet.

The inquiry had probably offended her. Bitsy regretted it. "I'm sorry. I was teasing."

"I know. Don't worry about it. I need to go. I'll see you tomorrow. Rest well."

"You too. Good night."

Bitsy was relieved, although McConnel's serious tone concerned her. She showered and put on her silk pajamas and then opened a container of soup, doctored it, watched a movie, and fell into bed, exhausted and excited that McConnel was returning so soon. It was a good sign.

The next afternoon she began to count the hours until McConnel would arrive and then worked late to make the time go by faster. She arrived home at seven, showered, applied fresh makeup, redid her hair, and then put on the sexiest dress she owned. She went downstairs and lit every candle in the living room, turned on her romantic playlist, then sat in her favorite chair, laid her head back, and enjoyed the music. After the third song she realized she was overselling it. A couple of candles would have been enough, and no music. Well, at least not *that* music. She switched to a lighter fare.

She went into the studio and reviewed her progress on the canvas, careful not to get near the worktable. It was coming along nicely. She checked her watch. McConnel was late.

When the doorbell rang at nine thirty, Bitsy tried not to run to answer it. She swung the door open. McConnel looked pale and drawn.

"Get in here." Bitsy reached for her. "What'd they do? Work you until you begged them to let you leave?"

"I'm exhausted." McConnel almost fell into her arms.

Bitsy planted a kiss on her that would have aroused a sloth…but nothing from McConnel.

"What's wrong? What is it?" McConnel didn't have her badge on her waist or her gun at her side. "What'd you do...get yourself fired?" Bitsy laughed.

McConnel didn't.

"Oh, God, McConnel. What happened?"

McConnel motioned to the living room. "We better sit for this conversation."

Bitsy took the overstuffed chair, and McConnel slumped onto the sofa.

"Do you need something to drink?"

"A whiskey, neat."

Whatever McConnel wanted to discuss, it wasn't good. Bitsy hurried to the kitchen, poured the drinks, and brought them back. She handed one to McConnel, then set hers on the coffee table.

McConnel took more than a sip. The slight tremble of her hand gave away her state of mind. Whatever happened was traumatic. The bruising on her wrists and neck were not as purple, and the slight discoloration in other areas had faded to pale yellow, matching Bitsy's.

Bitsy didn't say anything, allowing McConnel to gather her thoughts. They sat for a long time, McConnel holding her glass, staring at the carpet. Bitsy watched her, trying to figure out what had happened. She became aware of the music in the background, picked up the remote, and turned it off.

McConnel set her empty glass on the table next to Bitsy's untouched drink. She clasped her hands together and met Bitsy's eyes. "I resigned yesterday."

Bitsy gasped. She didn't mean to. She just suddenly needed air. "Why? You're so good at your job."

"It was either that or face an administrative hearing."

"Oh my God. What happened?"

McConnel rubbed her thighs. "Bitsy, I haven't been honest with you."

"What are you talking about? What do you mean?"

McConnel stood and began to pace. "I had a personal interest in Hallie Lynn's case."

Bitsy eased back into the chair. That wasn't so bad. "So did I." She smiled. "We all did."

"Yes, but more than that." She stopped and slipped her hands into the pockets of her slacks. Her intense gaze was riveted on Bitsy. "I...I'm Hallie Lynn's twin sister."

A wave of confusion swept through Bitsy. "What do you mean? Hallie Lynn didn't have a sister."

McConnel crossed her arms and took a step back. "My biological mother was Lou Anne Peeples. I was adopted by her best friend when I was a baby. Hallie Lynn and I were twins. Fraternal twins. Her mother couldn't take care of both of us, so she let her best friend adopt me."

Bitsy listened, her mouth falling open incrementally as McConnel spoke. She massaged her forehead, above her brow. "Wait a minute. Slow down. This isn't making any sense."

McConnel stopped. "Okay."

Bitsy stared at her. How could this all be true? "Did Hallie Lynn know?"

McConnel seemed to consider her question. "I don't think so. We never met. I didn't find out about her until I was eighteen, long after she'd gone missing."

Bitsy struggled to make sense of it all. McConnel had been adopted. Hallie Lynn had disappeared when she was ten. McConnel had found out she had a sister when she was eighteen. And then what? She'd lied to her. "All this time you've known and didn't say anything? Why? Why would you do that? Why would you deceive me like that? How could you?" The more the information sank in, the more anger, and resentment, and indignation raged through Bitsy, boiling to the surface in a matter of seconds. "God! How could you do that to me? I don't understand. You knew how I felt about Hallie Lynn. You knew what I went through. To deceive me like that is...unthinkable. I let you into my home. And my bed. And into my heart." She wanted to lash out, hurt McConnel the way she'd just hurt *her*.

"I'm so sorry. I couldn't tell you."

"Yes, you could have. You could have told me. You could have said something."

"No. I couldn't. The FBI didn't know. My job was in jeopardy."

"Well, how's that working out for you now?" Bitsy felt vindicated. McConnel deserved it. And Bitsy was just getting started.

"Bitsy, from the bottom of my heart, I'm sorry. I wanted to tell you so many times."

"Why didn't you? Why lead me on like that? You not only lied to me but to Momma, and Daddy, and the rest of *my* family. Was it worth it, McConnel? Did you get what you wanted from it? Was that night in my bed worth it?"

"No. That doesn't have anything to do with me not telling you about my connection to Hallie Lynn. Remember that I was eighteen years old before I even knew I had a sister. She'd already been missing for years, and when I found out, I started looking for her. I joined the FBI so I could develop the skills to locate her. If I'd told you, they could have found out, and I could have been removed from her cold case. Everything I'd worked for my entire adult life would have been for nothing. I needed their resources. I needed what they could provide to find her."

Bitsy stepped toward her and stabbed her finger at her. "You used me, McConnel. You used me like another resource. That's all I was to you. A means to get what you wanted, with some extra benefits on the side."

"That's not true. I tried to contact you years ago, but you wouldn't have anything to do with me."

Bitsy folded her arms across her chest and squeezed. "What are you talking about? You never did that."

"Oh, yes, I did. I introduced myself, tried to get you to talk to me about Hallie Lynn."

"You even tried to use me back then. You didn't care about me. You were like everyone else. You wanted information from me. You didn't care that what happened to Hallie Lynn practically destroyed me."

"That's true. I didn't back then, but it all changed when I finally met you. I thought I knew you from what I'd read and studied about you all those years, but when I came into your office that day, I realized I didn't know you at all."

Her words were confusing, yet they tugged at Bitsy's heart. She didn't want to feel sympathy. It was easier to be enraged. "You need to leave."

"Bitsy, I'm sorry. I'm so sorry. Please forgive me. What can I do to make this right?" McConnel's eyes were pleading and filled with tears.

"You can go, right now."

"Is that what you really want?"

"It is." Bitsy stalked to the front door and opened it. "Get out."

McConnel swept past her and left without saying anything more.

Bitsy slammed the door shut and locked it as loud as she could. "Son of a bitch!"

She went to the coffee table and swilled down the whiskey, then gagged and almost threw it up. She wiped her mouth, kicked off her heels, chased them, and then tromped up the stairs. "I'll be damned if I ever let that woman into my life again."

She threw her shoes into the bedroom and then dropped onto the bed and sobbed for two hours. Finally, she got up and changed, throwing anything she could get ahold of around her. Slippers, handbags, pajamas from the drawer, pillows, her bottle of sleeping pills, box of tissue, and, last of all, the half glass of water on the nightstand. When it hit the wall and shattered, she came out of her rampage. "Oh, shit." She slipped on a pair of shoes and began to pick up the pieces of broken glass. When she'd collected as many as she could, she vacuumed the rug, though she couldn't do anything about the dent in the wall. She left the rest of the room as it was and took a shower, pressing her palms to the tile and letting the hot water run over her, soothing her stiff muscles. She was exhausted.

McConnel's words filled her mind. It must have been hard for her to tell her. No. She wasn't going to feel sorry for her. McConnel had been wrong to do that to her. It was horrible. Well, maybe not that horrible. Yes, it was. The entire time McConnel had been with her, she'd used and manipulated her, lied to her. It was disgusting. She leaned against the wall and sobbed.

Chapter Thirty-six

McConnel drove to the same Marriott in Savannah where she'd stayed before. After checking in and taking her suitcase to the room, she headed for the bar. There, she sat in a side booth and ordered a bourbon neat. People came and went without her paying any attention to them. All she could think about was the stricken look on Bitsy's face, which wasn't unexpected. McConnel had hurt her, but she'd hoped Bitsy could have understood. She tried not to beat herself up, but each time she reviewed the night's events, she came up short. Everything Bitsy had said was true. She had every right to react the way she did, and McConnel had zero chance of making it right with her. She had two more drinks, tried not to stagger on the way back to her room, and went to bed.

The morning came too quickly. She talked herself into staying in bed until ten. Why should she get up? What reason could she possibly have? She had no job, no plan for the future, and no Bitsy. The only thing she had to look forward to was wearing herself out enough to go back to sleep. She convinced herself to shower, knowing she couldn't stay in the hotel room all day. It only made things worse. She changed into some decent shorts and a sleeveless top. The hell with the sun. She didn't care if she got burned.

She grabbed the purse she never carried, slipped on her sunglasses, and took off to see the sights of the city everyone was always talking about. After three hours of looking at gardens, historic houses, and flowers, she sat on a bench under the live oak trees, taking her sunglasses off every so often and watching the people pass by. They had lives and were going to appointments, meetings, rendezvous, and home. She, on the other hand, had nothing to do but keep her butt on the bench and feel sorry for herself. Eventually, she bought a sandwich and cold drink from one of the nearby shops and strolled around downtown, ending up back on the bench in Chippewa Square. Was it too soon for whiskey? Probably. She went back to the hotel, stared at the TV until eight o'clock, then changed into slacks and a white lace top that scratched her burned neck, arms, and chest. Sunscreen might have been a good idea.

Restless, she drove to Jimmy B's. The parking lot was jammed with cars, the music loud, and the people were packed in so tight she had to practically shove her way to the bar. She shouted her order, the barman nodded, and her bourbon neat arrived a few minutes later. She downed it and immediately ordered another, settling into a cushioned leather chair and watching the reflection of the crowd in the mirror. She'd lost her desire to assess her surroundings. She spied a man in his forties, slicked hair, athletic build. For all she knew he could have been a dope smuggler or embezzler. Who cared? It didn't make any difference to her. She finished the last of her second drink, the alcohol starting to go to her head. Exactly what she wanted.

"Back so soon?"

McConnel looked up. "Annabelle. What a surprise."

"You seem a little lost." Annabelle grinned. "And I see you got some sun."

McConnel's face, neck, and arms were on fire. "I'm fine. What brings you out tonight?" She was looking hot in her tight skirt, clinging blouse, and with those long legs. McConnel must have ogled her too long.

Annabelle laughed and maneuvered her way next to her. "I'd say you had a bad day."

McConnel snickered and stared into her empty glass. "A couple of bad days. Can I buy you a drink?"

"Absolutely." Annabelle motioned toward the back. "I have a booth with some friends. Why don't you join us?"

"Absolutely." McConnel signaled the bartender for two more drinks.

"Got ya," the barman said.

"Freddy, have the waitress bring them back to my booth," Anabelle said, "and I'll have a Manhattan."

"Please do, Freddy," McConnel said, watching the sway of Annabelle's ass as she led her away. "To the web," McConnel shouted over the crowd.

Annabelle turned toward her with a smile. "You're in a mood tonight."

"Yes, I am. Absolutely!"

Three other women sat in the round booth. "Girls, I'd like you to meet McConnel. She's an FBI agent."

"Shh," McConnel said. "I'm incognito. I'm just a civilian now."

Anabelle tilted her head and eyed her. "Meet Peggy, Rosemary, and Sally."

"And what do you ladies do?" McConnel asked. "Are you all *in* law?"

"Two are, one is in finance. Can you guess which one?" Annabelle asked. She gestured for the others to give her and McConnel room, and they immediately moved to the right. Annabelle scooted in and patted the leather cushion beside her. "Why don't you settle here, McConnel?"

"Absolutely," McConnel said and slid in.

The drinks arrived. Then two more, then another. Not only didn't McConnel guess who was in finance, but she also couldn't remember their names. She was either drunk or just didn't give a damn.

Annabelle kept rubbing up against her. The more she did, the less McConnel wanted to be with her. But the drinks were good. She knew she'd need a ride back to the hotel because she couldn't drive in her condition. *Condition?* "Secrets will kill you. Remember that, ladies." McConnel raised her glass, then downed the golden liquid.

"You should go easy on that," Annabelle said.

McConnel shrugged. "Why?" By ten thirty, she was so drunk she couldn't remember where the bathroom was, none of the conversation made any sense, and her lips were numb.

"Oh, shit," maybe Peggy said. "Look who just came through the door."

Heads turned.

McConnel tried to focus on who they were looking at and suddenly saw Bitsy, who was headed straight for them.

McConnel emptied her glass and raised her hand to the waitress to bring her another.

Annabelle cleared her throat and inched away from McConnel.

Bitsy marched to the booth like a woman on a mission and stood in front of McConnel but didn't say a word.

Annabelle spoke first. "Evening, Bitsy. Have a seat."

"No, thanks. McConnel. You're drunk."

"Absolutely," McConnel said. It was funny. She laughed. "Sit yourself down and have a drink. Hell, have two. You aren't speaking to me. May as well drink with me."

Suddenly Lilly and a younger man stood beside Bitsy.

McConnel gave Lilly the once-over. "Where'd you come from?"

Lilly glanced at Bitsy and leaned on the table. "I told you."

"Oh, Lord. She's plastered," the man beside Lilly said.

"Bo, help us get her out of here." Bitsy wrapped her arm around McConnel and tried to move her to a standing position.

McConnel resented the intrusion. "Wait a minute. I'm not going anywhere with you. You were mean to me."

Bo directed Bitsy out of the way and moved in next to McConnel. "Come on, sweetie. Up you go." His hand went around McConnel's waist.

She scooted out and stood next to him. "Thank you, young man. That's very sporting of you."

He laughed.

McConnel tried not to weave, but her balance was off. Bo grasped her tighter with his reassuring grip and she walked beside him, making sure she put one foot deliberately in front of the other so she wouldn't stumble or trip.

"Where's your car, McConnel?" Bitsy asked.

"Why? Do you need a ride home?" She laughed. "It's in the parking lot. I'm too drunk to drive. I need to take a taxi. Bo, will you call me a cab?"

"Let's get you outside first," he said.

"My purse. Where's my purse?" McConnel stopped just as they got to the exit.

"I've got it," Lilly said. She held it up for McConnel to see.

"Don't steal that. It's got my credit cards and license in it. Don't have a badge anymore." McConnel lost her balance, but Bo tightened his grip and steadied her.

"Put her in my car," Bitsy said. "We'll get hers tomorrow."

The night air hit McConnel in the face, its coolness swirling around her. She took in a deep breath. "I love the smell of Georgia at night."

Bo made her keep walking, but she couldn't remember where they were going. "Are we there yet?"

"A few more steps," he said.

A car door opened. He lowered her in and fastened her seatbelt, then shut the door. It was quiet. A swish of air blew over her. The car started. McConnel looked over and saw Bitsy. "Hey. What are you doing here?"

"I'm driving you home."

"The Marriott, downtown Savannah. My keycard's in my purse. Do you know where my purse is?"

"It's in the seat behind you."

McConnel laid her head back. Everything was spinning. Streetlights were flashing by. People on the sidewalks were moving so fast. "Where's everybody going?"

A blinking sound. A rumbling noise. It was so dark. Then a light. The car door opened, and McConnel almost fell out.

Bitsy reached across her.

"You smell good." Something released around her waist.

"Come on." Bitsy had her arm around her, familiar and comforting.

McConnel got out of the car and went up some steps, then more. She was sitting on a bed. "Thanks for getting me home. I'll be okay."

"Sure you will."

McConnel became aware of trying to unbutton her blouse but couldn't get the button through the hole. She looked down, barely able to see it. "I don't know what's wrong with this damned thing. I'm not used to these girly shirts. I bought it today. Isn't it nice?" She tugged at it, then tried to slip it over her head. Nothing worked.

Bitsy stood in front of her and began to unbutton her blouse.

It was nice. McConnel let her. But she had to get rid of her shoes. She bent over to slip them off but kept on going, falling into a heap on the floor. "Ow. What happened? That hurts."

"Not as much as it will in the morning."

Someone was lifting her, telling her to stand. "I'm trying. Don't rush me."

She was back sitting on the bed. Warm long sleeves slipped over her arms. "Mmm. I'm cold."

Her legs were lifting. She wasn't doing that, was she? A cover went over her, warm and comfortable, and then darkness.

❖

McConnel rolled over. Her head throbbed. Her face, arms, and neck stung. Her back hurt. She opened her eyes slowly—one, then the other. She raised her hand to block the light, but it was all around her. "What the…?" She scanned her surroundings. She was in the murder room. How'd she get there? Then she remembered. "Oh, crap." She crawled out of bed and almost fell over. As she grabbed the edge of the nightstand, she saw a large glass of water and two pills that Bitsy must have left for her. *God, Bitsy.* She'd been so mad, but she had to still care about her, or she wouldn't have done something so kind. She took them, gulping down the cool liquid, which felt good on her throat.

She managed to get to the bathroom but had to lean against the door frame and hug it to steady herself. When she reached the sink, a new, wrapped toothbrush, tube of toothpaste, and sunburn cream were on the counter. Her skin flamed, and her mouth tasted like someone had tramped through it with muddy boots. She looked in the mirror. "Holy shit!" Her face was the color of the red raspberries she used to pick as a kid. She brushed her teeth and scrubbed her tongue. How many drinks had she had? As she stripped her top off, she winced. Her arms felt like someone had scraped them raw with sandpaper. She got into the warm shower and then immediately readjusted the water to cool. By the time she applied the sunburn cream and got back into the bedroom, she felt barely human. Every movement was filled with pain. On top of all that, she had to go downstairs and face Bitsy. It was bad enough she'd ordered her out of her house once already. Now McConnel would probably have to be humiliated again. She dressed, the lace of her blouse digging into her burnt skin. Then she grabbed her purse on the desk and trudged down the stairs, following the scent of coffee and dreading the moment she'd have to see Bitsy.

Bitsy was leaning on the counter in the kitchen, reading something on her cell, a steaming mug in front of her. She lifted her gaze to McConnel but didn't speak. Probably better to say nothing rather than kick her out of the house again.

McConnel remained silent too, placing her purse on the edge of the counter and sitting while watching Bitsy watch her. She glanced at the stove clock. Eight ten. "I better leave. I'm sure you need to get to work."

"I'm not going in today."

Silence.

Bitsy poured McConnel a cup of brew and slid it toward her, then placed the creamer and a spoon next to it.

"Thank you." Embarrassed, McConnel couldn't bring herself to make eye contact. She doctored her coffee and took a swallow, feeling Bitsy's gaze on her. What must she think of her? Wait a minute! Why should she care? Bitsy had thrown her out. McConnel had every right to get drunk if she wanted to. It was none of Bitsy's business. She'd apologized to her for what she'd done. If Bitsy couldn't forgive her, that was *her* problem. Revealing her secret to Jenkins and then Bitsy had cost McConnel everything. If Bitsy couldn't understand, the hell with her.

Bitsy still watched her, just drinking her coffee, not saying anything.

What did she want from her?

CHAPTER THIRTY-SEVEN

Bitsy set her cup on the kitchen counter. McConnel looked like hell. When she'd first seen her in the bar the night before, the sight of her sunburn had almost assuaged Bitsy's anger. Then, when she'd realized just how drunk she was, she'd softened even more.

It'd been two days since McConnel had admitted to Bitsy who she was. Bitsy had talked with Momma and Tilly, and they'd both said she'd been too hard on her. McConnel had come all the way down to Georgia and confessed something that had to be very hard for her and asked forgiveness. And all Bitsy had done was accuse her of using her and throw her out of her house. She'd never seen McConnel so vulnerable. She'd turned her back on her, and, worse than that, she'd shamed her when she was hurting and needing comfort.

Yes, it had been devastating to know McConnel had kept that secret all this time, and when she'd told her, Bitsy had thought it was cruel, but now she could see that McConnel had revealed it as soon as she felt she could. Neither one of them was to blame. If they had it to do over again, they would have both probably done it the same way. She'd hurt McConnel by being so callous. She sipped more of her coffee, watching her, remorseful and unsure how to start the necessary conversation.

McConnel set her half-empty cup on the counter. "How'd you know where to find me last night?"

Relieved, Bitsy straightened. "Lilly and Bo were at Jimmy B's. They called me when they saw who you were with and how drunk you were."

McConnel nodded. "Thanks for coming to get me. I'm embarrassed you had to see me like that. By the way, do you have any idea where my rental car is? I think it's still in the parking lot. I hope."

"It is. We can go get it in a little while. If it was your goal to get falling-down drunk, congratulations. You did a great job." Bitsy couldn't help but grin.

McConnel fiddled with her spoon. "I'm sorry, Bitsy. I'm truly sorry for not telling you earlier who I am. I know I hurt you."

Bitsy moved from around the counter and sat next to her. It was a risk. She wouldn't have blamed McConnel if she rejected her, but what if McConnel needed her? Wanted her? They both had been through hell and back. "McConnel, *I'm* sorry. I was self-centered, and rude, and an ass. You risked your life for me, and I'm ashamed of how I treated you the other night. I was wrong."

"Bitsy." McConnel clasped her hand.

Bitsy laced her fingers with hers. "I'm so overwhelmed to think you're Hallie Lynn's sister. Her twin. It's a miracle we found each other." Bitsy stood and stepped away from her, trying to see the resemblance, but it had been thirty years, and Hallie Lynn had been so young. "You're her sister. McConnel, it's…I can't believe it. Do you think you look like her?"

McConnel turned on the stool and dug into her purse. Then she swiveled back around with two photos and handed them to Bitsy. "Here's a picture of each of us when we were seven."

Bitsy stared at them, holding one up, then the other, then side by side. "I can see it. You can really tell." She handed them back to McConnel.

McConnel put them away, then stood, tears in her eyes. "If she'd grown to adulthood, she would have felt blessed to have you as her friend."

Bitsy couldn't hold back the flood of emotion, relief, sadness, connection. It was confusing to see their resemblance as children, to know they would have had similar features as adults. McConnel was Hallie Lynn's sister, and she was right in front of her. She studied her. "I'm so sorry. I'm sorry I couldn't remember—that I couldn't save her. Can you forgive me, McConnel?" She tried to hold back tears, but she began to sob.

McConnel wrapped her in her arms. "Bitsy, there's nothing to forgive. I think if Hallie Lynn were standing here right now, she'd tell you how grateful she is for what you did for her."

When Bitsy finally stopped crying, McConnel let her go. "Do you really think she'd still want me as her friend?"

McConnel handed her a paper napkin. "I do."

Bitsy wiped her tears and blew her nose. She took a steadying breath, then gently cupped McConnel's face in her hands. "I love you, McConnel. I love you for the wonderful human being you are, for the gentle and sweet spirit you have, for never giving up, for the way you protected me and Hallie Lynn. But most of all I love you because I can't help myself. I think I fell in love with you that first day in my office."

McConnel moved closer, taking her hands. She brought them to her lips and kissed her palms. "Bitsy, my love, my heart. I wanted to tell you who I was, but I was so scared you'd reject me. It ate away at me each time I was with you. It was a wedge between us that I couldn't stand. I don't want anything to separate us. I want to be free to love you with all of me, every part. You're everything that's good in my life. It was hard to lose my job, my career, but I couldn't carry the weight of losing you. I love you."

McConnel's tears trickled over Bitsy's fingers.

Bitsy kissed her and wrapped her arms around her waist.

"Can we go upstairs?" McConnel whispered.

Bitsy eased away and laughed. "Are you really up to bedroom activities with that sunburn?"

McConnel smiled sheepishly. "Well, maybe not, but I want to be close to you."

They lay on Bitsy's bed, and Bitsy stroked McConnel's hair, the one place she knew wouldn't hurt her.

They fell asleep.

By the time McConnel stirred, waking Bitsy, the room was cast in late-afternoon shadows.

Bitsy eased away. "Do you feel any better?"

McConnel gazed into her eyes. "I love waking up with you."

Bitsy smiled. "Is that a yes?"

"Definitely." McConnel traced along the hollow of Bitsy's throat with her finger. "Did you have a good rest?"

"Yes, but I dreamed about Hallie Lynn in the morgue." Bitsy moved closer. "I hate that she's still there."

"As Hallie Lynn's biological sister, I have the right to claim her remains," McConnel said. "I've thought a lot about it, and if it's okay with you, I'd like to have her cremated and buried in your family cemetery like you want. That way she'll be near."

Tears welled in Bitsy's eyes again. "How soon can we do it?"

"I'll call first thing in the morning and get the process started."

"I can't believe she's coming home." Bitsy grabbed McConnel and started to move on top of her.

McConnel cried out and went rigid, her face distorting in pain.

Bitsy jerked away. "Oh, my God! I'm so sorry! Are you okay? Please tell me you're okay."

McConnel gulped for air. "I'm okay," she said feebly. "Just give me a second."

Bitsy ran to the bathroom and retrieved the sunburn cream. When she returned, McConnel still lay in the exact position she'd left her, but she looked more relaxed.

"Can I put some of this on you? Will that help?"

McConnel held out her hand. "You can if you're gentle…And if it leads to something more." She smiled. "I get to be on top."

Desire swept through Bitsy. After throwing McConnel out, she hadn't known if they would ever be together again. She unbuttoned her blouse and mustered the most seductive look she could manage. "I can live with that. For a very long time."

EPILOGUE

In the small meeting room behind the sanctuary of the church, Bitsy and McConnel stood in front of the urn that she and McConnel had chosen for Hallie Lynn, purple trimmed with gold. Bitsy couldn't believe it was finally happening. It'd taken over a month to get through all the paperwork and DNA testing—never mind the typical bureaucratic muck—to allow McConnel to claim the remains.

McConnel placed Hallie Lynn's ashes in the urn and stood beside Bitsy.

"She's with us now," Bitsy said, gripping a white tatted handkerchief Momma had made. One for Bitsy, one for McConnel, and a white doily, edged in bright yellow, for Hallie Lynn. In preparation for the funeral, they'd already arranged Hallie Lynn's doily on the table in front of the altar in the sanctuary, situated between a picture of Hallie Lynn and a vase of daisies.

"There's one more thing," McConnel said. She reached behind her neck and unclasped the heart-shaped pendant her mother had given her, then retrieved Hallie Lynn's matching one from the pocket of her slacks and placed them together inside the urn. "For you, my beloved sister. Rest well."

Bitsy wrapped her arm around McConnel's waist as they stood side by side.

Almost the entire county and many others turned out for Hallie Lynn's funeral. Bitsy and McConnel sat together with Momma on one side and Daddy on the other. The entire family gathered around them. Bitsy had never felt such pure support and love, but more than all of that, McConnel was with her.

At the end of the service, after mourners passed Hallie Lynn's urn sitting regally on the white tatted doily, each of them went to Bitsy and McConnel to shake hands or offer their condolences and comfort. Many simply thanked them for what they'd done to bring justice for Hallie Lynn.

Family and close friends gathered at Momma and Daddy's home for food and fellowship after the burial. They assembled in the house, out on the veranda, and in chairs scattered on the front lawn. There were tears, laughter, and stories.

Bitsy mingled and tried to greet each one, never wandering very far from McConnel.

Momma, Tilly, and Mary Ruth sat on the porch swing, McConnel beside them in one of the wicker chairs, laughing and discussing something that had to do with Mary Ruth's new choice of words. Bitsy climbed the steps and caught the gist of the conversation.

"Well, hell, Momma. I need those shoes."

Tilly frowned, but McConnel burst out laughing. Momma wrapped her arm around Mary Ruth and hushed her.

Bitsy sat in the chair next to McConnel.

"I can't get over the resemblance of Mary Ruth to Bitsy and your mom," McConnel said.

Tilly smiled. "There are reasons for that."

Bitsy grinned.

"Aunt Bitsy carried me in her tummy," Mary Ruth said, beaming. "I'm a miracle."

"Oh, girls. No," Momma said.

"McConnel is almost part of the family, Momma," Tilly said. "Besides, I can't believe she hasn't heard it already."

Momma waved dismissively. "There's nothing wrong with being discreet." She took Mary Ruth by the hand and led her down the steps to a group of women gathered in a circle, laughing and talking.

Janie, Louise, and a few others gathered around Bitsy, McConnel, and Tilly.

"Clifford and I tried for years to have children," Tilly said, patting Bitsy's arm. "We never had the blessing. Bitsy decided she wanted to do something about it, so she offered to be artificially inseminated with Clifford's sperm. The result was Mary Ruth, named for Bitsy's first name and my middle name."

Bitsy clasped Tilly's hand and kissed it.

"We're a close family," Janie said, massaging Bitsy's shoulders.

Everyone laughed.

Bitsy watched McConnel for her reaction.

McConnel gave her a tender look. "That doesn't surprise me at all."

Kathrine and a man Bitsy didn't recognize walked toward them. They'd attended the funeral, but then left shortly after. He was Hollywood handsome—tall, well built, gray at the temples, and tan. He removed his sunglasses as he came onto the veranda.

Kathrine motioned toward him. "Bitsy, McConnel, I'd like to introduce my boss, Jack Ralston of Ralston Enterprises. Jack, this is Bitsy Hanover and Cecelia McConnel."

He gently shook hands with them and offered his condolences. They made small talk in the group for a few minutes.

"May we speak with you, McConnel?" Kathrine asked.

McConnel rose. "Let's walk."

They descended the steps.

McConnel turned. "Bitsy, would you like to come with us?"

Bitsy stood. "I'd love to."

The four of them strolled near the edge of the front lawn for a few minutes, then stopped.

"I've heard great things about you, McConnel," Jack said.

"Did you also hear I resigned rather than go through an administrative hearing?"

He smiled coyly and toed the grass. "I did." He glanced at Kathrine. "We'd like to offer you a position with my company. We're looking to expand into the South, and we like Georgia for our satellite office. Kathrine will be heading it up, and we want you to join her team. Of course, I can't guarantee you'd always work in this part of the country, but you'd spend at least half your time here."

"To work in security? I don't know. That sounds a little…quite frankly, boring."

Jack laughed. "That's only a small piece of what we do." He reached into the inside pocket of his linen coat and showed his badge and identification.

When he did, Bitsy noticed his weapon holstered at his shoulder.

"Many of our employees work for the American Defense Council," Jack said. "We do things the FBI and CIA can't because of restrictions."

McConnel perked up. "Now I'm interested."

Jack grinned. "Good. How about we fly you out to our main facility in Las Vegas. You can take a look around, meet the staff, and get to know us. Kathrine will call you with the specifics in a couple of days."

He shook McConnel's hand. "I think you ran an amazing investigation. I don't know anyone who could have done a better job than you did." He leaned toward her and lowered his voice. "And by the way, the FBI not standing by you was total bullshit." He looked at Bitsy. "And you have skills."

He and Kathrine said good-bye and went to their car.

Bitsy walked McConnel back toward the veranda. "I have skills."

"Oh, you most assuredly do." McConnel laughed.

Bitsy looped her arm around hers. "The job sounds promising."

McConnel nodded. "Very."

Bitsy and McConnel sat in the swing. The evening birds began their serenade, and family and friends moseyed past to say their good-byes.

"Darn it." McConnel slapped her thigh. "I keep forgetting. I have something that belongs to you, but I have to get it upstairs."

"Hurry back." Bitsy brushed McConnel's arm as she rushed away.

McConnel returned a few minutes later. "This is yours." She held out her hand.

Bitsy laughed. "Oh, my gosh! I looked all over for that." She took the black letter *A* from McConnel's palm.

"It fell off the Plexiglas the first time I was at your office. I didn't know what to do with it."

"Keep it. It's yours," Bitsy said.

Momma stepped out from the doorway. "McConnel, want some pecan pie?"

"You bet."

Momma went back into the house.

"She's never offered that to any of the other women I've dated, not even my ex-wife," Bitsy said.

McConnel sat beside her and slipped her hand into hers. "She likes me. We're buds. Ever since I put Daddy on the floor, she thinks I'll do it again if he gets out of control."

Bitsy smiled and rested her head on McConnel's shoulder, then looked out into the pines. "We did it, didn't we?"

McConnel breathed deeply. "We did."

Hallie Lynn was home, and so were Bitsy and McConnel.

About the Author

Suzie Clarke is a native of Northeast Ohio and has a medical and business background. Before her life as a writer, she specialized in public health, working with women in all aspects of their lives. When not writing, she can be found spending time with her family, backpacking, or out on the golf course.

Books Available From Bold Strokes Books

Brooke Takes Queen by Alaina Erdell. Brooke Staley faces personal and professional upheaval when Elizabeth Bettancourt, the emotionally scarred new owner of the resort she works for, considers selling. (978-1-63679-886-8)

Coda by Anna Gram. Parker is intriguing, magnetic, impossible to ignore—and completely wrong for Hannah. But sometimes love's melody refuses to end. (978-1-63679-926-1)

The Debutante Dilemma by Jane Walsh. Two debutantes are engaged to wealthy and titled brothers...but discover they only have eyes for each other. (978-1-63679-896-7)

The Love Book by Gun Brooke. When literary agent Rowan Cross receives an anonymous manuscript that deeply resonates with her, Verity realizes she has accidentally sent her own manuscript, complete with her very real feelings for her boss! (978-1-63679-850-9)

Secrets Under the Junipers by Suzie Clarke. Who killed Hallie Lynn Peeples? Cecilia McConnel needs to know. Bitsy Hanover holds the key. Can love uncover secrets? (978-1-63679-845-5)

Traveling Toward Forever by Erin Dutton. When almost-strangers take a road trip through America's national parks, love may be the final destination. (978-1-63679-894-3)

Beautiful Things by Emma L McGeown. A warmhearted romance of missed chances, undeniable chemistry, and a stubborn love that maybe, just maybe, can find its way back. (978-1-63679-934-6)

The Great Popcorn Romance by Georgia Beers. Opposites attract, and Riley Shaw stands no chance of resisting Hannah Kramer's magnetic pull. But opposites know just how to drive each other crazy... (978-1-63679-910-0)

Love Takes a Village by Karis Walsh. As Lena Preiss struggles to manage a busy restaurant in the Bavarian Christmas village of Leavenworth, Washington, chocolatier Devin Meyer brings an unexpected richness into her life, along with her delicious desserts. (978-1-63679-902-5)

Secrets of the Heart by Jenny Frame. When a beautiful stranger starts asking questions about Nikki Sharkey, head of an infamous crime syndicate, Nikki will stop at nothing to protect her daughter Isla. (978-1-63679-653-6)

Talon and the Songbird by Julia Underwood. In a world where survival depends on strategic alliances, Makayla and Talon must navigate not only complex politics but also the dangerous territory of their hearts. (978-1-63679-970-4)

Three Blissful Days by Dena Blake. Kendall Jackson attempts to make her ex regret dumping her by announcing she's dating beautiful park ranger Ivy Patterson. But there's nothing fake about how attracted Ivy is to Kendall. (978-1-63679-707-6)

Chasing Her Scent by MJ Williamz. When Sheridan Rousseau walks into Lisette Mouton's charming little bookstore in Quebec City, she unknowingly holds the key to a mysterious box hidden in a secret room. (978-1-63679-900-1)

Heart's Run by D. Jackson Leigh. Hoping to recover an escaped racing mare, stock transporter Tobie Mason locks horns with local wild horse advocate Maggie Wilkes. (978-1-63679-825-7)

Scandalous by Kris Bryant. When a Hollywood actress trades places with her twin sister, everyone's in an uproar about getting duped, but Lindsay's more concerned about finding out which twin she made out with. (978-1-63679-874-5)

The Art of Love by Ali Vali. When Mimi and Bianca both set their sights on Jolly, sparks fly, loyalties are tested, and hearts collide as they navigate the unpredictable nature of their hearts. (978-1-63679-719-9)

Iceberg by Gun Brooke. When Lady Arabella hires Zandra, she never expects to find love, especially not as a disaster looms on the horizon. (978-1-63679-908-7)

The Secrets of Rhydian Hill by Ronica Black. A doctor in need of a new start. A woman running from a killer. A love story that could end in tragedy. (978-1-63679-880-6)

www.ingramcontent.com/pod-product-compliance
Lightning Source LLC
Chambersburg PA
CBHW022007010726
47494CB00003B/923